CALEDONIA
A SONG OF SCOTLAND

William D. McEachern

authorHOUSE®

AuthorHouse™
1663 Liberty Drive
Bloomington, IN 47403
www.authorhouse.com
Phone: 1 (800) 839-8640

Published by AuthorHouse 09/02/2015

ISBN: 978-1-5049-2806-9 (sc)
ISBN: 978-1-5049-2807-6 (hc)
ISBN: 978-1-5049-2805-2 (e)

Library of Congress Control Number: 2015912747

Print information available on the last page.

KJV
Scripture quotations marked KJV are from the Holy Bible, King James Version (Authorized Version). First published in 1611. Quoted from the KJV Classic Reference Bible, Copyright © 1983 by The Zondervan Corporation.

For Kathleen, my wife, my muse, my
love and my best friend.

ACKNOWLEDGEMENTS

The author greatly appreciates the editing work done by Margaret L. McEachern. Any errors in this text are the author's and the author's alone.

Scotland

This is my country,
The land that begat me,
And those who toil here
Are flesh of my flesh

Sir Alexander Gray

Book I

Scotland Arises

LORD ULLIN'S DAUGHTER

A Chieftain to the Highlands bound,
Cries, 'Boatman, do not tarry;
And I'll give thee a silver pound
To row us o'er the ferry.'
'Now who be ye would cross Lochgyle,
This dark and stormy water?'
'Oh! I'm the chief of Ulva's isle,
And this Lord Ullin's daughter.
'And fast before her father's men
Three days we've fled together,
For should he find us in the glen,
My blood would stain the heather.
'His horsemen hard behind us ride;
Should they our steps discover,
Then who will cheer my bonny bride
When they have slain her lover?'
Outspoke the hardy Highland wight:
'I'll go, my chief - I'm ready:
It is not for your silver bright,
But for your winsome lady.
'And by my word, the bonny bird
In danger shall not tarry:
So, though the waves are raging white,
I'll row you o'er the ferry.'
By this the storm grew loud apace,
The water-wraith was shrieking;
And in the scowl of heaven each face
Grew dark as they were speaking.
But still, as wilder blew the wind,
And as the night grew drearer,
Adown the glen rode armed men-
Their trampling sounded nearer.

'Oh! Haste thee, haste!' the lady cries,
'Though tempests round us gather;
I'll meet the raging of the skies,
But not an angry father.'
The boat has left a stormy land,
A stormy sea before her-
When oh! Too strong for human hand,
The tempest gathered o'er her.
And still they rowed amidst the roar
Of waters fast prevailing;
Lord Ullin reach'd that fatal shore-
His wrath was chang'd to wailing.
For sore dismay'd, through storm and shade,
His child he did discover;
One lovely hand she stretch'd for aid,
And one was round her lover.
'Come back! Come back!' he cried in grief,
'Across this stormy water;
And I'll forgive your Highland chief,
My daughter!- oh, my daughter!'
'Twas vain: the loud waves lash'd the shore,
Return or aid preventing;
The waters wild went o'er his child,
And he was left lamenting.
-Thomas Campbell

Introduction

> "For what is the life of a man,
> if it is not interwoven with the life
> of former generations by a sense of
> history?" –**Cicero**

Scotland in the past, as it is still now, was and is a land of contrasts, a land of two minds, so to speak. Surely, everyone knows of the Highlands and the Lowlands. This seems to be the most evident of the contrasts that there could be. Still, even this most widely known of the contrasts of this nation is deceptive and misleading: the highest place in Scotland is in the lowlands and the flattest place in Scotland is in the Highlands. So what is high is not necessary the highest...

It could be that the land is one born of a confused geography, for the Shetland Islands are closer to the Arctic Circle, than they are to southern England. The Orkney Islands are above 60 degrees north-as far north as Alaska-but still sport palm trees, because these islands lie in the Gulfstream.

Still more inconsistent is the very geology of the place for it is riven with dichotomy: the Shetlands, scientists tell us was part of the pre-Ice Age Scottish/Scandinavian Continent, whereas, the rest of Scotland below the Highland Boundary Fault, was part of the Baltica Continent in the Aegir Sea.

The Highlands and Islands are largely comprised of ancient rocks, actually the most ancient that exist on earth-the Lewisian gneisses. These formed some three billion years ago. They formed as igneous rocks blasted molten from the bowels of the earth and mixed with rocks that were metamorphosed such as marble, mica schist, and quartz. The granite here is anorthosite, and is similar in composition to rocks found in the mountains of the Moon. So are the Highlands a neighbour of a celestial body?

During the ice age, the glacial ice under which the lands of the Shetland lay weighed it down so heavily, it sank into the ocean, until only the tips of the mountains remained and formed the Shetlands. The Highlands and the Islands geographically lie north of the Highland Boundary fault, a geological rift, which cuts across the land in a diagonal from the northeast to the southwest. South of this line are the Lowlands. But even this is fraught with contradictions. The highest villages in Scotland, Leadhills and Wanlockhead, are located in the Lowlands and much of the Highlands are actually flat lands.

Could it be because the people themselves are so divergent in origin? The people of the Islands and the Highlands claim Pict, Irish, and Norse or Viking descent, whereas the Lowlanders claim the Anglo-Saxons as their forebears. Then also, the Picts were there before the Norsemen, well before the Norsemen. The Picts have survived in memory long after their race disappeared from the face of the earth. Scotland would not be Scotland without the Picts. The memory of them casts a long shadow across the consciousness of every Scot. All Scots believe that there are fairies. Some say that the fairies are the diminutive children of the long-lost Picts. Others say that, at least, the fairies are the long distant memory of the Picts that touches the soul of every Scot alive today.

How is it that from these pagan beginnings come the most religious of peoples, the most Christian of Christian people? How is it that the Highlanders became Catholics-devout Catholics-devoted to their form of worship and ne'er bending to the Protestant English who had led astray their Lowland brothers, when the Highlanders began as the most pagan of pagans? How did the Scots become a cradle of civilization, boasting scientists, leading lights of literature, creating the banking system and life insurance, when their forebears were Picts, Celts, Druids, Norsemen, and rampaging tribes of Anglo-Saxons? How did civilization spring forth from a people who thought that reaving cattle from other Clans was an art form?

The culture of the Highlands would lead no one to believe that it was high or sophisticated. Nightly, bawdy songs were sung extolling the virtues of great sexual prowess. How can this place be a cradle of civilization? They quaffed much whiskey-a mind numbing drink-which many cannot tolerate. Again, how can this place be a cradle of civilization?

The Highlands system of governance could only be described as feudal in nature. A clan chief held life and death over his vassals, the so-called pit and gallows power. His vassals, for they were vassals, though they did not call themselves that, had to pay the chief rents to farm his land and owed him military service whenever he called them forth to fight his battles.

Yet the Chiefs, their sons and others, often spoke Latin and Greek, French and English, as well as their native Gaelic. Many went to University, whether in Aberdeen or Edinburgh or Paris. They traveled aboard and drank in the culture of Amsterdam, Paris and Rome, among other European capitals. They knew the latest continental dances and often had clothes of the latest European fashion.

It is simple: Scotland is land of contradictions. When Bonnie Prince Charles landed and began the Rising of '45, he was trying to re-establish the Stuart dynasty on the throne of Scotland. He was a Catholic Prince, and yet many of his followers were Protestant, because they believed the Stuarts were the rightful family to rule Scotland. Many Highlanders, though who were Catholic, remained loyal to King George II. At the same time, the English king, George (who was really German) was able to attract many Scots to fight for him; Charles, a Scot who spoke no Gaelic, still attracted many Englishmen to fight for him, as well as Irishmen and Frenchmen. The Rising caused Scots' brother to fight brother, Protestant to fight Catholic, as well as Catholic to fight Catholic, and Protestant to fight Protestant. Some say that the Rising, as romantic as it might have been, was a cause struggling against the tide of time, against the inevitable.

Was the Rising, however, more a protest against the Union of Scotland and England than an attempt to restore the Stuarts? The history of the Stuarts was one that had not brought Scotland much joy. James I had engaged in a massive campaign of trickery and intrigue to gain the English throne and once he became king, he turned his back on Scotland and outlawed its then greatest clan: the MacGregors. His son, Charles I tried to destroy the independence of the Scots kirk which led to a national uprising and ultimately his beheading. Charles II led Scotland to war against England with simply calamitous results. After that, he never visited Scotland again. His agents in Scotland went on a pogrom against Protestant sects known as the Covenanters. They were so ruthless; it was called the 'Killing Times'. James II of England and VII of Scotland was summarily deposed because he had tried to carry the concept of the "Divine Right of Kings' further than anyone before him. The Scots Estates, that is the Scottish Parliament, held this was against the Scottish Constitution-the king serves at the will of the people.

So what would drive a Scot to fight to restore this dynasty, which spent so little time in Scotland, which had brought so many unhappy times to Scotland, and which had been so religiously divisive? Is the answer that under the Stuarts Scotland was an independent country? Were the Stuarts the way whereby Scotland could undo the Act of Union of 1707, which created the United Kingdom?

While some Scots benefitted greatly from the Union, such as the merchants of Glasgow, who then could trade with the colonies in America and the Caribbean, for others, such as the Highlanders, the Act of Union was the ring of the death knell of their way of life. Scotland is a land of many complications and complexities. Nothing is ever simple in Scotland; no matter how much a Scot may protest that it is.

Scotland is a marvelous land with beautiful landscape and bucolic scenes. One can scan the hillsides and see sheep grazing up the heights. Small waterfalls seem to be everywhere and the sounds of rushing brooks and streams fill the air. The air is clear and cool even in summer on the hottest day. The sea water intrudes in the land creating stunning vistas of color, where shimmering water sparkles with sunlight, white clouds float above the bens, that is the Scottish mountains, and the heather spreads its purple mantle across the velvet green of the grass. A Highland cow, in all its reddish-brown shaggy fur glory, with a horn span as large as a Texas longhorn, lows as it grazes. And maybe across the glen, the lilting sound of the bagpipe of a lone piper is heard playing Amazing Grace. The music tugs at your heart-strings and calls you back to Scotland.

Chapter 1

A Clan Chief Is Executed

> "For my part, I die a martyr for my country!"-**Simon Fraser**, the 11th Lord Lovat and leader of the Clan Fraser, April 9th, 1747

Lord Lovat, MacShimidh Mor, in Gaelic, stood upon the scaffold. He pondered his fate. His ancestor, who was William Wallace's compatriot against England in the Scottish Wars of Independence, once captured by the English, was hung, drawn, and quartered. Today, he would join his ancestor and he, too, would die for Scotland. So also, would die his dream of an independent Scotland; a dream of his nation adhering to the ways of the Highlands with the Highland chief the leader of the Clan who reigned as a feudal lord; a dream of Scotland under at Jacobite King with order, law, and hierarchy reestablished.

Simon Fraser was many things. His life had been full; it had been filled with drama; he'd been a fugitive; he been accused of raping his wife; he had been heralded as a charitable man; he'd been accused of being a spy; he had been lauded for lowering rents on his tenants during the economic crisis; he'd been accused of being a traitor by both Jacobites and Royalists. Why would that be so? Well, for one thing, he had fought for the Jacobites in one uprising, and then swore allegiance to the English King. Then he had violated his oath, only to recant again. Where did his loyalties lie? It seemed that he was really only out for himself and choose to be loyalist or Jacobite whenever the wind was blowing one way or the other. Was he just being a pragmatist? Certainly, he was that. Was he different from others in the Highlands? Probably not. Many times a clan would hedge its bet and send one son to fight for the King and another son to fight for the Pretender, whoever that might have been. It seemed that maybe this was the best course of action, for no matter what, a part of the clan might survive and thrive. It was certainly the duty of a member of the clan to sacrifice himself for the greater good of the clan. So in that way may be Lord Lovat was only practicing the true religion of the Highlands, which was the religion of survival.

He had, as one could say, lived a full life. Now, he was to be a martyr. It would be his last incarnation.

For him, the chief of a clan to appear upon the scaffold was a sign by King George II that the Jacobites had better give up their forlorn hope of resurrecting the Stuart line or else they would be marched one by one to be hung. No one was exempt; no one was immune; all were subject to the King and his judgment.

For Lord Lovat was many things and many contradictory things. In this way, he was the perfect symbol of Scotland.

Lord Lovat's blood, like that of so many Scots before him, would feed the soil of Scotland and, in the endless cycle, the soil would feed the Scots. This is the story of how the Scottish people arose as a people and how and why they came to fight at Culloden against almost impossible odds. This too is the story of Scotland and of the Scots and why the Scots, to save themselves and to save what they believed to be the true Scotland, had to leave Scotland.

Chapter 2

Scotland is Born

My heart's in the Highlands, my heart is not here,
My heart's in the Highlands, a-chasing the deer;
A-chasing the wild deer, and following the roe,
My heart's in the Highlands, wherever I go.-
Robert Burns

Three thousand million years ago (when you say it that way, it makes the immensity of the number sound more like its true worth, rather than the simple expression of 'three billion years ago), during the period of time called the Archean, somewhere near the South Pole, lava was spewing forth. With it, volcanic rock – granite of the hardest type: Lewisian gneiss – began to be laid down. This rock is the oldest rock of the Continent we now call Europe. It created the islands that are now on the north and west of Scotland. Specifically, from the depths of the earth, the lava came and formed from north to south, the islands of Lewis, Harris, North Uist, Benbecula, South Uist and Barra. The lava formed the backbone of what would become the city of Edinburgh with the castle sitting upon the volcano's mount, with the Royal Mile being a lava flow that spread forth from the mount. This volcanic rock was laid in the crust of the earth, beneath the sea, and slowly it became exposed to the air and to the sun.

As it became exposed to the elements, it moved north past the equator and finally came to rest near the North Pole. As these rocks wandered northwards, they became part of the continent called Laurentia.

Only the very southeastern part of the Island of Skye was part of this eruption, but most it came later, formed from what we now call the post-Caledonian rock. The Island gained most of its expanse from volcanoes that flamed, spewed, smoked, and flowed with lava during the era called the Paleogene, some 66 million years ago. The earth's climate, which had been hot and humid, was changing, becoming drier and cooler. The world now belonged to the mammals, after the cataclysm which killed the dinosaurs had taken place. The beeches, oaks, and conifers grew, as well as abundant amounts of grass. But the Island of Skye, as well as all of Scotland looked a lot different then, because what would become Britain, Ireland, and Norway were all landlocked and part of western Laurasia. So the Island of Skye, like Iceland, which though an undersea volcanic hot spot, was not yet an island and would not become an island for another 35 million years. The Arctic sea was almost completely surrounded by land and was much less salty than today. A land bridge joined Scotland to Greenland and Canada. Greenland was but a tenth of the distance away from Europe that it is today. So had one wanted, one could have walked from Europe to the Americas via Greenland.

The Islands, the Orkneys, the Shetlands, the Hebrides, and the Highlands are closer to the Arctic Circle than they are to the city of London. And even though the land bridge that joined them to Norway is long gone, in many ways these islands are still tied to Norway and Scandinavia in many mystical ways. Often in the history of Scotland, people came from Scandinavia to populate the Isles and Glens of Scotland.

Chapter 3

The First to Walk the Glens of Scotland

The first human ancestors were squirrel-like creatures that lived in trees, analysis of their ankle bones reveal. Purgatorius lived after the dinosaurs were extinct. It is the earliest primate fossil ever discovered, dating to 65 million years ago.
-**Science Magazine, January 20, 2015**

It was here in Scotland, such as it was, and other places during the Paleogene, that a rat-like creature, perhaps, more like a shrew or may be a squirrel-like animal, with a long naked tail and naked feet with long claws, but otherwise covered in fur with long whiskers sprouting from its snout, called Purgatorius, eked out its living in this wonderland, eating insects and berries. Its rodent-like eyes were on the sides of its head. It probably climbed trees or so its fossilized ankle bones tell scientists. Its fossils were first found in Purgatory Hill, Montana, and, thus, its name arose. This shrew-rat scientists think is the forerunner of all primates, so our first ancestor, our first Scot, perchance.

It was not alone, but shared this new world, now free of dinosaurs, with other mammals just starting out on their journeys down the evolutionary track

Later, a creature with a bushy tail, a raccoon shaped hump to its back, a cat-like head and ears, sporting long fingers with long claws on its hands, called Plesiadapis, developed in the Americas, but wandered across the land bridge to Europe. Its eyes still were on the sides of the head so it lacked that essential trait, which we, humans, take for granted, three dimensional vision. It loved the trees and climbed well.

There were gliding creatures shaped like squirrels or lemurs that stretched their skin with their limbs to fly from branch to branch of the trees. There were miniature mice-like animals weighing less than 30 grams. There were all sorts of creatures, but none yet wore a kilt. Generation upon generation of these creatures-the first Scots-lived and died and their blood watered the soil of Scotland.

Chapter 4

Skara Brae

The Neolithic village of Skara Brae was discovered in the winter of 1850. Wild storms ripped the grass from a high dune known as Skara Brae, beside the Bay of Skaill, and exposed an immense midden (refuse heap) and the ruins of ancient stone buildings. The discovery proved to be the best-preserved Neolithic village in western Europe.-**Historic Scotland**

I. A New Land

Nybyggarna

It was long after Purgatorius and Plesiadapis had walked the glens and hills of Scotland. Now, man walked, lived, loved, begat children, and died.

He stood looking out to sea. He could see there on the horizon ragged edges of what must be land interrupting the perfect line of the horizon. It appeared to be some giant island. What could be there? If he could get there, would he be safe from all the others who threatened to kill his tribe? But if he could get there, could they, his enemies, also get there? It looked so far and the waves looked so tall. Could it be that-the distance and the waves-were enough to deter them from following him?

His people had the log canoes they had built from oaks they had felled. These massive canoes were dugout from the trunks of oaks that were thirty or forty feet long. These had brought them fish from the sea, as well as trade with others. But this trade was a two-faced thing: wealth came with trade and thieves came with wealth. It was their wealth that now threatened their lives. The others from another tribe wanted their wealth and would kill to gain it. He feared the others and their lust for things they had not made or wealth they had not earned.

Now, he envisioned a different role for these seafaring trees. They would carry him and his tribe across the waters and to those ragged edges on the horizon. Maybe there he would find the security he craved for his people. Maybe there it would be safe from the others.

How would he convince the members of his tribe to leave this place which was good and go to somewhere else when he knew not whether that new place was better?

He sat down. The wind tousled his hair. The sun felt warm upon his face. He could almost fall asleep, if only the world would let him… He worried. He always worried about them, the others, that other tribe. He wanted his people to be free of the threat that they posed. They were always ready to attack them and to take their women and children, carry off the farms' harvest, rustle their cattle, and leave behind destruction and devastation. There must be a place where they can't get to. A place free of them.

It was days later. The tribe's elders would not let him use the dugout canoes, only the hide-skin boats. Only a few of his tribe had chosen to go with him, to see this new island. They had rowed. It had taken them most of the day to get here.

He climbed up the gentle hill and stood upon its crest. The sea breeze gently tickled the whiskers of his beard and mustache. The reddish auburn of his hair scattered the sunlight. He looked out upon the oval lake that was down the cliff from where he stood. Beyond the lake, a finger's width of land separated the lake from the ocean. The golden sand of the beach, the light blue of the lake, and the cerulean blue of the ocean were offset by the rich green of the sweet grass that spread across the land like a rich, velvety carpet. The grass stretched on and on-a vastness of grass like he had never seen before. He knelt to stroke the grass and its sheer softness pleased his hand. He ground some of the blades of grass in his hand and sniffed the debris. The grass smelled incredibly sweet, full, and earthy. He could see cattle grazing, lowing, nuzzling calves, tossing their heads to shake off flies, and drowsing in the brilliant sunlight.

The scent of the wind carried the salt of the ocean to his nostrils. A few trees with their leaves broke the line of the horizon, but rocks, tons and tons of rocks, littered the shore of the lake and protruded through the green of the grass like so many teeth in a smiling face. The paucity of trees, for there were only a couple of hazel and birch trees, with a willow or two lining the edge of a brook, were all that was left of once vast forests that within the last hundred years or so had finally withered away, told him that rock would have to be the main building material of the village he saw growing up on this hill in his mind. There were stones all around him. He picked one up. And then another. The one in his left had just the right heft and feel to it. It fit his hand as if this stone had been created for his hand. He struck the middle of the width of the larger stone in his other hand and surprisingly the larger rock split into two slabs. He picked up another large stone and he struck that one too. It did it again. Again, the larger stone split into two almost equal slabs. He started picking up large stones and began splitting them into slabs, until he had a tall pile of slabs. He companions watched him and they began to wonder if their leader had drifted off, like some of the older members of their village had done in the past. He smiled at them and they began to murmur that the drifting had begun. He paid them no mind. Now they were sure that his mind was clouded. Finally, after a long time, he laid a line of slabs on the ground. Then, he laid one slab on top of the first line of the slabs, placing the end of the topping slab in the middle of the first slab on the ground. He quickly placed slab upon slab, the end of the topping slab in the middle of the first slab, lay upon layer until he had small wall. The group smiled at him and then at one another. Now they understood.

He stopped his labors. The sun warmed his face as he closed his eyes and he tilted his head to it. His eyes closed, all he could see was red. He heard the gentle lapping of the waves of the ocean against the beach which was about a mile off. Opening his eyes, the beauty of the lake below this cliff of maybe some 50 feet seemed like an endless supply of fresh water.

Something within him said, "Here, here." He felt at home, so comfortable he could lie down in the grass and fall asleep. Everything about this place was so perfect. He stared at the horizon, his eyes wandering the line where sea-aquamarine-blue separated from azure-blue of the sky. He was the first man to behold this sight, but had he known this, he may not have appreciated the fact. Nonetheless, he still appreciated this place, this ideal and archetypical place. He smiled.

The grass would feed the cattle, sheep, goats, and red deer that they would bring with them to his place. It did not matter that this place was miles across the ocean from their home. He had made it here in his hide-skin boat and he would bring the animals, one by one, across the water, to graze here on this lush, verdant green.

He reached down and crumbled the soil in his hand across his fingers. It was rich, lush, and full of life. Here, they would grow crops of wheat and barley. They would farm and the soil would bring forth whatever they planted in abundance. What was left of the forests would be cut down and the land cleared.

He could see women gathering in the berries that grew everywhere. Life would be easier here than their home across the water. They would make beads, they would shape pottery, and what they didn't use themselves, they would trade with those of his tribe who remained behind and those tribes further to the north across that greater stretch of water.

II. The Group

> A group is a social system involving regular interaction among members and a common group identity. This means that the members feel a sense of connectedness and a feeling of belonging to a distinct entity.
> **-Definition of the word 'group' in Sociology**

He turned to the 12 men and eight women who had come with him. He smiled at them and they, in turn, smiled back at him. Without a word spoken, all knew this was the place. There was something so majestic, so serene, so inviting, and so comfortable, about this place that they all felt this and instinctively knew it was home. So it was decided.

Tasks were divided. Some would go back in the hide-skin boats and start bringing the others and would start ferrying the animals across the treacherous water that separated the mainland from this island. Some would stay and start building huts of timber to be their temporary homes. They would also mark out the farm land and the grazing pens.

All knew that later they would have to start digging into the soil while others would gather as many of the flat rocks as possible to start building their homes, workshops, storage places, hearths, bedrooms, kitchens, and the tunnels that would connect them. For his vision was to build their new village in the soil, deep in the soil, so no one would find them. They would cover the homes with hides and then camouflage the homes by putting sod over the hides. Their rooves would hide them. From afar, no one would see or know that there was a village here at all. It would like the rolling green grasslands all around. They would keep the soil from falling in by pushing thousands of the flat slab-rocks into the earthen walls. Each home would be built upon that model and each family would have its own home, but each home would be connected to other homes by tunnels. Though his people were relatively tall, they knew to make the tunnels far shorter than the height of the people such that each person coming into the tunnels would have to bend down or crawl in. This would give protection to the village from outsiders who might want to harm them and loot their goods. Those attackers would be bent over as they entered the tunnels and each homeowner could protect his home by hitting the head of the prostrate attacker to kill him. This then was the protection against them, those who would hurt his people. The sea, the distance, and their hidden homes of stone in the soil-all this would protect them.

They dug into the ground. Each family would have their own home, but each home would be connected to another home and all the homes would be connected to the central communal places-the work shop where they would make the beads and jewelry for export, the room where they would gather and worship and share their lives. The laying of rock slabs, one upon another, continued for weeks.

He died with the last glow of the sunset. He had done what he had set out to do. He had built a community. He had protected his people. He worried no longer.

This community did amazing things. It built stone circles with rocks so heavy only a community working together could move them, stones so precisely set that the stars, the moon, and the sun seemed to be commanded by them for the seasons fell exactly upon certain stone pillars. The community also built large burial chambers, again with precision and exactness that marvels all even today.

This community lasted for 800 or 900 years. Then his children took over and they lived their lives. They had children and then their children died, leaving the world to their children, who had children and died, leaving the world…till the dust of their bones mingled in the earth of their land and then their stories, their lives, and their deaths became interwoven in the tapestry that was the tale and life of Scotland.

BOOK II

"Vanity of vanities,"
says the Preacher.

"Vanity of vanities! All is
vanity."- Ecclesiastes 1:2

CHAPTER 5

THE PICTS

Part I: A Door Opens

> "Ask, and it will be given to you;
> seek, and you will find; knock, and it
> will be opened to you."-**Matthew 7:7**

Malcolm scratched his beard. He knew that he had been given a momentous opportunity. He was to join Colum Cille and journey to Scotland. They were to found a monastery and a center of learning. He had been chosen because of his knowledge of the Picts. Colum Cille, who some knew as Columba, was leaving Ireland in disgrace. Still, even so, he was a man of charisma, learning, and piety. Malcolm had not met him, but still desired to undertake the journey with all of his heart. Malcolm knew his credential, his knowledge of the Picts, was a thing built upon sand. He had stayed but one summer in the land of the Picts, when he was a young boy. His father, a fisherman, had taken him there thinking that the catch might be better. The summer had been hard, they hadn't caught that much. He remembered smoking the fish they did catch. He would never forget the smell of the fire, fueled by peat, for they could find no wood.

So, his knowledge of the Picts was scant, but what he had not experienced directly, he would make up for it. He read voraciously. He talked to others who had had more contact than he with the Picts. He did everything he could such that may be he knew something that would help the learned missionary he would accompany.

"Glory be to God! Thank you for this wonderful opportunity to serve You. I shall not fail with Your help and grace. May You grant me wisdom, patience, and perseverance to carry out your mission and convert Picts." Malcom earnestly prayed.

He looked up and there before him was one of the tallest men he had ever seen. Malcolm was not a short man, but still the form before him towered over him. He had not heard him come up and so at first, he was quite shaken. He appeared clothed in the habit and cowl of a Benedictine monk with his Celtic tonsure and crosier, as was his custom. "Father? Is there anything I can do to help you?" asked Malcolm.

Colum Cille looked down on him benignly and lovingly. He had such a radiance to his face and such a gentle manner. His mere look put Malcom at ease.

"Father Malcolm? I have been told that you know the ways of the Picts. Are you willing to come with me to Scotland? It will be an arduous journey; there will be a great deal of work to be done; it will be dangerous; and there will be great deprivations which we must suffer. We are armed only with prayer to overcome all that will stand in our way." Colum Cille's eyes were a striking blue that pierced Malcolm to his soul; could Colum Cille see directly into his heart? Did he know the truth that Malcolm was a fraud?

Malcom rose from his kneeling position and got on his feet. "Father Colum, I would follow you anywhere, because God shines his countenance upon you."

Part II: The Picts Revealed

> For nothing is hidden that will not be made manifest, nor is anything secret that will not be known and come to light.-**Luke 8:17**

Before Malcom knew it, they were on foot and heading to the port to board ship. He was leaving Ireland! Now, he was going back to that strange land of Scotland where he had spent his youth. There, he had come to learn the ways of the Picts. He had not been able to tell Colum that he had spent just under three months there and then had left. "Any knowledge of the land was better than none. And no one had more knowledge than I," he mused or may be rationalized.

He began educating Colum with bits that he had read, bits that he had heard, and bits that he recalled from that one summer fishing trip with his father. He told Colum how somewhere in the second, or maybe it was the third, century, the Picts had emerged as the unifying tribe of all the northern tribal communities of Scotland. He lectured Colum, and Colum, in his humility, accepted it.

There was not a time that Colum was not studying, reading, or praying. He stayed up late at night, sometimes all night in his studies. He was a man who was obsessed, determined to learn all. What Malcolm did not know was the Colum was reading everything he could about the Picts, not relying only on Malcolm's words, memories, and studies.

"The northern Picts lived north of the great Glen and the southern Picts lived south of the Great Glen to the Antonine Wall. All, but the most Western portion of Scotland was, thus, under the domination of one or the other of the major tribes of the Picts." Malcolm lectured in his flat tone and manner.

"The Picts were the tattooed or painted people that so perplexed the Romans. Along the coasts, the Picts were known to be pirates and quite skillful on the sea. The Romans loathed the sea and could never match the capability of the Picts afloat." As Colum listened to Malcolm, he wondered how all of this knowledge, this information would help him to evangelize amongst the Picts. But still he listened knowing that God's purpose would unfold. Colum had to atone for the lives he had caused to be lost.

Day after day, Malcom continued his lectures as the traveled from Ireland to Scotland. Colum endured what was almost unendurable because Malcolm was a boring teacher. He seemed to have no fire to him, no spirit.

"The Picts were also known to be merchants and would travel to Gaul to trade. Pictish metalwork was highly prized on the continent and demand was high, which allowed the Picts to become relatively wealthy. Brooches in particular were most desirable and the Gauls would pay handsomely for them. The Picts were thus able to amass large hordes of silver on account of their handiwork." Malcolm drew a breath. Colum also breathed a sigh of relief that Malcolm had stopped, even for a moment, his interminable droning.

"The very ancient name of Scotland, Caledonia, is a corruption of the name of one of the Pictish tribes, the Caldones who lived along the Great Glen." Malcolm droned on. Colum had come to realize that some men were not meant to be teachers. Although Colum was quite interested in the subject of the Picts, in his heart he also knew that he was bored. He realized that Malcom was continuing his lecture. "It is said that seven Pictish kingdoms once existed in Scotland. They were Cait or Cat, which appears to have given rise to Caithness; Fib which may have given rise to Fife; Fidach; Fotla, which gave rise to Atholl that is Ath-Folta; Caldones, and Fortriu the cognate of Verturiones of the Romans. I can't remember the name of the last tribe."

Malcolm thought a moment, but still he could not recall the other tribe. "The Romans called the Picts Caldones or Verturiones, often using these names interchangeably, not knowing or caring that these were separate tribes in separate lands of Scotland."

Malcolm taught Colum that the Picts were tribes that lived together as a confederation, joined by their common language, Celtic. They had joined together and buried their feuds amongst themselves to stand against the Romans. Rather than submit, the tribes banded together to withstand the onslaught. The tribes were so successful, they stopped the Romans. The Romans, not used to being beaten, in terror built a wall to keep the barbarians contained. Sometime thereafter, the Picts intermarried with the Gaelic peoples and the Britons and the resulting amalgam was the Scots, or at least the forerunners of the Scots.

"The Picts are farmers living in small communities. They plant wheat, barley, and oats. For vegetables, they raise bitter kale, cabbage, onions, leaks, peas, beans, and turnips. The livestock kept are horses, cattle, pigs, and goats. The wealthy hunt using dogs and falcons. They season their meals with wild garlic, nettles, and watercress." Malcolm then had a thought which diverted him from his train of thought. "You should know that the Picts are pagans who worship many gods and goddesses. No one, who is not a Pict, knows anything about their religion. It is sacred and a secret. Some have said that they are very devout in their way."

Colum looked up at Malcolm. Suddenly, there was a hardness in his eyes. Colum simply said, "No pagan can be devout." He paused and continued to look into Malcolm's eyes. "Only Christians can be devout. No one who worships a god other than the One True God is truly worshipping and, thus, cannot be devout and cannot in any way be viewed in a laudatory manner."

Malcolm recoiled from the chastisement. In his embarrassment, Malcom looked for a topic that would steer Colum away from his faux paus. "Oh, I forgot to mention that sheep and wool were most important things in their culture. Wool is the cloth for the Highlands, both for its cold winters and almost equally cool summers." Malcolm was imparting everything of which he could think. He took pleasure in the fact that, as he talked, he seemed to remember more and more of that summer. He had thought that it had been a waste when he was there as a boy, but now he knew that God had been preparing him for this grand adventure in spirit.

"Do they wear anything else besides wool?" asked Colum.

"Yes, they have some cattle, which means that they have hides which can be worn to ward off the winter's raging winds. As one is never far from the coast in Scotland, they fish, hunt seals, and even venture into the seas to chase whales. They are very industrious." Malcolm smiled. His student was listening. What all this knowledge would do for them once they were there, he did not know, but he thought that Colum would know what it all meant. Further, Colum seemed to want to know everything about the Picts and the new home he was going to forge for them all.

"You have talked much about winter and its ravages. How do they keep warm?"

"Just like us, they burn peat to keep warm. They also use it to dry the wheat or barley which they then turn into something they call 'whiskey', meaning the liquid of life." Malcolm became quiet, which was unusual for him.

Colum seemed to note down in his mind everything that Malcolm said. 'Would these pieces fall into place someday and somewhere?' thought Colum. "Dear Father, please bless this learning to thy use and grace." Colum prayed aloud, catching Malcolm off-guard, who quickly responded with a bowed head and folded hands.

Then it happened. In all this dross, Malcolm hit a vein of gold. "Maybe, I should tell you something about the Dalriadans." He began without realizing how important was what he was about to say. "Not all of Scotland is under control of the Picts. There is a teeny portion of Scotland that is under the Dalriadan Scots that is the Scotti who came from northern Ireland. The Dalriadans were led by King Fergus, who migrated from Ulster to Kintyre and then moved to Argyll in may be the late 490's. King Fergus Mor, that is the Great, was converted to Christianity by St. Patrick and he became the first King of Dalriadan Scots."

'This is the entre to this strange world,' thought Colum. 'Christianity is not wholly unknown in this world.' He then asked Malcolm, "So the Dalriadans are Irish in origin?"

"Well, yes…" Malcolm said not realizing the pearl he was imparting to Colum.

"Could we meet these Dalriadans?"

"Why yes." Malcolm nodded his head affirmatively. "But why?" he asked

CHAPTER 6

St. Columba

"Behold, I am sending you as lambs among wolves; be therefore crafty as snakes and innocent as doves."-**Matthew 10:16**

Part I-The Land of Nod

An I mo chridhe, I mo ghraidh. – (In Iona that is my heart's desire, Iona that is my love.) – **Saint Columba**

A small fleet of coracles, each carrying two or three men, crossed the 2 mile straits that separated the small island, which soon would be called Iona, to which they were travelling from the large island, which one day would be called Mull. Each coracle was but a frame of wickerwork upon which were stretched dried and tanned hides of animals. To look at a coracle, one would think it not seaworthy at all, but the Irish had sailed these flimsy things all across the Irish Sea and even as far as to the Hebrides and the Orkneys. One of these coracles carried Malcolm, guide to Colum Cille to the land of the Picts, another carried Colum himself.

The tall central mountain on the Island of Mull, which would centuries later be called Ben More, spread its base as fingers radiating outwards from a hand into a number of moor-covered peninsulas. But now the Island of Mull was unnamed and was just rugged large hulk of an island off the mainland of the place called Scotia or Caledonia. Malcolm watched as the mountain receded behind them and as the small island ahead of them steadily grew in size.

Peoples, unnamed, or else their names have been lost to history, lived here when the ice sheets advanced from the north pushing soil, pebbles, rocks, and boulders before them. Then one day the ice sheets had retreated from whence they had come, and left it all as detritus, like one last giant wave leaves upon the sandy beach its mark where the high water had once been, leaving a line laced with seaweed, shells, and jellyfish. The tribes had hunted the wooly animals. Once they had caught one, they all ate well. Of course, the hunters, who had brought this bounty forth, ate the best of all. The fires sizzled with the sound of roasting meat, as the smell of grilling meat wafted through the air, making mouths water as the tribe sat around the circle of orange firelight and warmth. Later, people had forged weapons of bronze, the then new wonder metal, which gave out begrudgingly to iron, which was stronger and harder. Iron met needs which could only be met by stronger and harder metals.

Now, this was a place where few could live, because it was so rugged and because it had so few natural harbors. Although most of its inhabitants were Picts, it was part of the Irish kingdom of Dál Riata, also known as Dalriadan.

Colum Cille had been granted this island by the King Conall, who was his distant cousin, continuing the tradition of Ireland where the king granted land, usually a rath, which is a fort, or other secure place, to a holy man to found a monastery or church. Each of his prior monasteries had been founded following this practice. For example, in Daire (Derry), the King of Erin, Aedh, had set aside a royal fort for an abbey. Colum Cille had at first refused the gift, because the fort was held by Mobhi, an evil and dangerous man who was no friend to Christianity. On approaching the fort in Daire, Colum Cille was greeted by some men bringing him the girdle of Mobhi, who had just died. These men, bowing down to Colum

Cille, begged him to establish his church there, to which he readily acceded upon learning of Mobhi's death. This was accounted a miracle.

But it was not a miracle that King Aedh, son of Ainmire, made this grant of land to Colum Cille, though some wished to portray it as such. Rather, it was a gift by one cousin to another. Besides Daire, Colum Cille had founded monasteries or churches in many places, the most famous of which to date was in Cennanus, the "Soft City" in Gallic, better known as Kells, in County Meath. It too had been a fort and it too was a gift.

Now, this would be his new monastery, his new center of learning. It was not in Ireland and that was the point. He was to be exiled from Ireland. What Colum Cille had done was thought to be unpardonable and unforgiveable. This characterization having been made by his spiritual leader, confessor, and mentor, Molaise. The man Colum Cille loved the most, Molaise, had exiled him to live upon this rock in disgrace.

Lest one think that land as such was then privately owned by the monastery, it should be noted that the truer concept was that land was owned by the tribe and all the members of it. The king or chief of the tribe was merely then allowing the holy man to use the land for the monastery or church. This usage was given with the express requirement that the use of the land would be repaid by the monks by their tending to the spiritual needs of the tribe. The monks could use the land so long and only so long as they performed the holy rites such as baptism, confirmation, and the last rites, and only so long as they said mass. The unity between the civil government and the clergy was thus was forged in a bond of reciprocal obligations. The king would protect the church and the monks would protect the souls of the members of the tribe.

Now, Colum Cille stood up in his small coracle. He was of imposing height. He surveyed the small island in front of him. It was as green as his native Ireland and, like Ireland, it boasted few trees. What few trees that it had were yew trees and thus some called the island, Iona. The bright sun silhouetted the island's two hills which gave the island the appearance of a man sleeping on his back, his hands tucked under his neck and his tummy full of beer. Colum Cille turned to his 12 friends and smiled. Each of them returned his smile nodding their heads in approval, Malcolm especially. Colum Cille had found the site for his new monastery.

Still, it was a bittersweet moment for Colum Cille. This was quite a come down for the man who, on his father's side, was descended from an Irish high King, Niall of the Nine Hostages. As he stared ahead and was catching sight of his future, the past still had its sway over him. He remembered studying under Finnian at the Magnum Monasterium on the shores of Galloway. "Can I make this place, this barren place as full of learning and knowledge as Magnum Monasterium?" He recalled his travels to Leinster to study under the aged bard, Gemman. 'I was his star pupil at the monastic school of Clonard Abbey,' he thought. He sighed. He knew he would never be welcome in Ireland again. His exile weighed heavily upon him, but he knew that he had no alternative but to go forward and save as many souls as he possibly could to atone for his great sin. He would never be in the great centers of learning and the great spiritual centers of Ireland again. He would have to construct his own monastery here. 'This will become my great center of learning,' he mused. He smiled. "Maybe exile will bear fruit," he whispered.

At first he thought that he might construct his monastery at the place where he first set foot in Caledonia, the Peninsula of Kintyre. But as Kintyre was still in sight of Ireland, he sought a more remote place. To see Ireland and know that he could never go back there was too much for him to bear. He had continued his search for a more remote place, a place from which he could not see Ireland. This was that more remote place.

They set about making a fire. One would cook, while the others gathered what they could to build crude shelters for the night. The sun set in a spectacular blaze of orange-golden glory. The fire grew in height and they gathered around it.

Colum looked around his circle, his band of monks and friends, who would become his instruments, he corrected himself, "God's instruments", to convert the Northern Picts to Christianity and bring Jesus to this land. "We sit tonight in Ireland, but know it to be something else. It is "God's Footstool" to bring His Word to this heathen land." He knew, even if his followers did not, that this, "God's Footstool", was the name given by Herod the Great to his Temple to Yahweh in Jerusalem. This now was his Salem, his Jerusalem, and from here, this very spot, Christianity and learning would flow unto the ends of Scotland.

At this thought, a slight smile crept over his face. "It is your lot, your duty, and your joy to be God's servants in this holy mission. Think on this: God has given us this place. You might think it a bleak, small stony island, off the shore of an even larger stony, desolate island-far from the shore where we will carry out His holy mission. We are to be evangelists to proselytize His word to unthinking heathens who speak not a word of our language." He stopped there and let this thought sink in-really sink in. He wanted no one to waver in his duty or if one were to waver, he wanted to know now. Likewise, he wanted the doubtful one to know now and renounce the endeavor. None of them betrayed the slightest hint of doubt, not even Malcolm. He waited just a moment more giving them time to weigh their options.

"Tonight, is a special night. We have landed here, on the eve of Pentecost, May 12 in the five hundredth sixty-third year of Our Lord. At Pentecost, God granted each believer a special gift to help spread His Holy Word. So, too, now He will grant each of us a special gift to spread His Word."

He began again. "Let each of us pray silently tonight that God my reveal His plan to each of us. Tomorrow, we will start to build our homes, our chapel, our kitchen, our granary, our storehouse, refectory, and our library. We will build everything out of wattles and rough planks of wood. May God bless our endeavors." He left them to their thoughts and prayers.

Part II-Remembrance

"Venit de Hibernia... praedicaturus verbum Dei" (He came out of Ireland to preach the word of God.)
-Venerable Bede

He slept on the cold ground, a stone for his pillow. He dreamed of his mother, Eithne. Her long hair flowed down her back and always seemed to be blowing in the wind, even when there wasn't the slightest hint of a zephyr. It was his mother, over his father's protests, who had named him Colum, which means dove. She had baptized him with that name and that was that.

He saw his father leaning over him. His father's hand was stroking his face. He did not understand for his father was not usually a gentle man. Father was fiercely proud of his royal descent, his clan, the O'Donnells, and his wife, the beautiful Eithne.

Both of them were now leaning over Colum and they were saying something, but it was whispered so softly that he could not hear. They were smiling and Colum basked in the warmth of their smiles. Something within his head seemed to say to his father, but without words, that he too was proud of his clan and his heritage as the great-great-grandson of Niall of the Nine Hostages, the Irish king of long ago, and he would do nothing to bring shame upon their name. He would strive for glory. He would atone for his sin.

He awoke with a start. "I already have brought shame upon our name and our Clan," he said to the glittering stars hanging in the convex bowl of the heavens above. He got upon his knees and prayed until the dawn started to appear in the east. Tears flowed down his cheeks.

With the rising sun, Malcom rose and saw his master's face. "Why do you cry?"

"I weep for those of mankind who do not know the Lord." Colum whispered, not desiring to disturb the others.

"I see it in your eyes that it is more personal than that." Having said that, Malcom knew he had been impertinent. He averted his eyes to the ground, as if the dust below his feet had particular interest and meaning.

"Ah, Malcom, I do cry for them. But you are right. I cry too for myself. For I too have lapsed in my love for the Lord. And when I have, men have died."

"Tell me about that for I have heard rumors, but feared to ask …until now." Malcom's eyes were still averted. He could not look his maser directly in the eye, but still he wanted to know. Had Colum killed a man as some said?

Colum knew what troubled Malcolm. "It is true. I am responsible for many deaths. I was too self-centered. I was vain. I was too conceited and thought I knew all that was right. I substituted my judgment for my master, Finnian's judgement. I did in defiance what my abbot, Finnian, bade me not do. I broke my vow to him to obey him. I wanted to have a copy of the psalter and so secretly, I made myself a copy. And to defend my vanity, I lead a band of men into battle. I did this to defend my honor, my right, my vanity." The tears flowed freely now and laid down pink clean tracks in the grime that graced Colum's cheeks. Colum looked heavenward. He raised himself up and the fact of his imposing height again struck Malcom, who, even though he was a tall man, was now dwarfed.

Colum began again. "Molasie, my confessor, spoke my judgment. I told him of how I had lusted to have a copy of Finnian's psalter. I labored in secret to produce the copy, telling no one. There was a battle in the North. I was directed by Finnian to pray for the success of Diarmait and his men in battle. In defiance, I prayed against them. Diarmait lost three thousand men, good men, true men, Christian men. Molaise imposed my severe penance: leave Ireland, never to see her again, and preach the Gospel so as to gain as many souls to Christ as were the lives lost at the Battle of Cooldrevny."

"I am here to serve my penance and to do God's work. I am a flawed man. I have sinned greatly. If you would leave me now, I would understand, but if you stay, I know that God will grant you blessings beyond measure." Colum turned his head to look at Malcom. Colum's eyes were beseeching Malcolm to stay.

The thought to leave Colum, to leave this place, and to forsake the mission to the heathens, had never entered Malcom's head. He shook his head vigorously from side to side for he could not speak. "I will not leave you." He said weakly. "I could never leave you."

They sat there in silence as the dawn broke. The clouds like crazy, bony fingers stretched out across the heavens, as if an old woman were awakening in the dark twilight of early morning from the deep sleep of a cold winter's night. The sky was a maze of different shades of grey.

Part III: To Be A Missionary

> "William Carey chides his countrymen for deciding it would be impossible for the Gospel to travel over great distances and to penetrate varied cultures when they are willing

to face the same trials for the sake of commerce."

– William Carey, *An Enquiry Into the Obligations of Christians to Use Means for the Conversion of the Heathens*

Colum had journeyed many days to get to this place called Inverness. His party consisted of Malcolm, Kenneth, and Comgall. They were to visit King Brude. The doors to his castle were bolted shut. Colum kneeled, as he gestured to the other monks to kneel also. He prayed and made the sign of the cross. At the sign of the cross, the doors flew open. Colum and his band of monks got up and walked into the castle. At this, King Brude, in awe, fell to his knees and begged to be baptised. The King then commanded that his people be baptised. This led to all of Caledonia becoming Christian and is one of the many miracles that Colum Cille performed.

Part IV-Incident on Loch Ness

Concerning a certain water beast driven away by the power of the blessed man's prayer.-**St. Adomnan, Vita Sancti Columbae c. 690 AD**

Colum Cille had decided to journey into the Great Glen. It was said that at a great castle, in the middle of the Great Glen, lived a powerful Pictish nobleman by the name of Emcath. He was rumored to be upon his deathbed. It was also rumored that he wished to convert to Christianity before he died. His castle was in a place called Airdchartdan, that is "the castle by the thicket of woods". Some called it Urquhart.

Malcolm was brought by Colum Cille to be his interpreter and guide. Malcolm knew that he was greatly out of his depth. He had never before ventured into the mysterious Great Glen. He had never been to the banks of Loch Ness. Much was said about both the Loch and the Castle, all of it was shrouded in mystery and old tales were told which tales were of evil, of death, of ghosts, of strange beings, of unusual lights, and dense fogs, and all manner of unexplained, scary things.

Colum Cille was determined to convert Emcath, and if possible, his son and his household. Colum Cille could only see this as a great victory for Christ to bring His Message to the heathen people in the middle of the country. It was a great adventure, because no Irishman had ever ventured this far from the coasts of Scotland and so deeply into its interior.

Colum Cille replied simply to Malcolm's entreaties not to go. "I was born to do this! I must atone for what I have done by bringing as many souls to Christ as I can."

The journey to date had been successful. Colum had not reckoned on the possibility that he might meet the famed King Bridei mac Maelchon of the Picts, but coming through one of the lovely glens that composed the Great Glen, there he was with his entourage, in all his splendour and beauty. Bridei had left his fortress at Craig Phadrig was on his way west trying to find Colum Cille. He had heard of Colum and he wanted to be converted.

Colum decided to spend the days that Bridei had required into order to convert him and his people. This had delayed him from moving as fast as he would have liked to Airdchartdan, but he deemed it necessary. Colum could not have been happier. Even if he were to arrive after Emcath's death and, thus, fail to convert him, the journey had been well worth the danger, the fatigue, and the risk.

Somehow, Colum and his small party now found themselves upon the mysterious Loch, Loch Ness, in a small boat in a dense fog. Malcolm repeatedly crossed himself to ward away the malevolent spirits he was sure were swirling in the slight breeze that barely disturbed the fog.

Urquhart Castle loomed out of the strands of mist that wrapped itself in tendrils around the mighty castle's walls, towers, and ramparts. The fog descended down the hill in rolling clouds as if they were giant, indistinguishable, but fierce animals, most substantial, yet ethereal. The greyness of the castle's blocks of stone melted into the grey wisps of the foggy mist concealing the vast structure from all but the most discerning eye. Colum could not see the full extent of the building, but somehow he felted its weighty presence and was impressed. The sounds of the oars of their skiff were muffled, as were every other sound in the grey gloom. Though it was noon, or at least so he thought by his reckoning, little was to be seen as the small boat paddled its way across Loch Ness to the castle's docks.

He dragged his fingers in the cold waters of the Loch, watching the tiny waves, like a miniature wake, spread and subtly vanish into the wispy nebulae. He silently prayed that his mission to those who lived in the castle would be successful and that they would be converted. His lips unconsciously betrayed the words spoken in his mind as he prayed the Lord's Prayer. His slight purring of the prayer set all others, but especially, the now terrified Malcolm to reciting the prayer also. Colum stared out into the misty darkness, sensing but not seeing, something alter the vapor's murk. He felt a shiver pass through his body, upending the small hairs on his neck, as the cold and the fog, the sisters of the winter, seemed to wrap him ever more tightly in their complementary grips. It was then that he saw it. At first, it was so silent, so hushed in its passing that he almost hadn't noticed it. But its passing stirred the water ever so slightly and the waves of its wake tapped up and down his along his wrist and arm above the fingers with which he had caressed the water. The oarsmen, too, had noted its passing and knew not what it was. They turned to look at each other, asking without a word, what had happened. The fog eddied in its wake also and the hint of a colder breeze tickled their faces and beards. Then it hissed as it passed the boat now in the opposite direction. It was first here, then there and then here again. It was a subtle, serpentine, slithering, almost silent, yet still a soft, strange hissing of a sound of a beast that could be faintly heard.

The oarsmen were scared. One stood with his oar at the ready to strike the menace. He could see it now. Colum crossed himself and then crossed the air in front of him to bless the men of the boat. "Fear not. The Lord is with us. He will let no harm to come to us." Malcolm had seen it too, but knew not what he had seen. All the tales, all the frightening, eerie, evil, tales flooded into his mind. His hands were shaking and his whole body was quivering.

The standing oarsman looked straight at Colum half in disbelief, but as Colum gestured with his hand to sit, the man slowly worked his way down, his oar dipping back into the water.

They sat still in the water. For just a moment, a brief moment, the miasma cleared over a tiny patch of the Loch and the water turned glassy. Then out of the fog bank and into the clear air, Colum saw the head of a beast topping a very long, serpentine neck. The head reared high above the water and higher still than the heads of the men sitting in the skiff, tilting its eyes to look at Colum, his men, and their now suddenly extremely, tiny boat. The neck expanded down to a great trunk of the beast which was more than 3 or 4 times greater than the length of the skiff. The skiff rocked as the great beast slithered by in the water. Waves of water crested over the sides of the boat. The men grabbed any projection of the boat they could in order to steady themselves against the violence of yawing, pitching, and rolling of the craft stirred by the beast.

Malcolm let out a scream which pierced the fog, but was quickly stifled by the glare of Colum who in reproach whispered, "God will protect us, Brother Malcolm. Have no fear. You are in God's hands."

And then it was gone.

When they had landed, they were greeted by Virolec, the son of Emcath. "My father awaits you in his chamber. You must come quickly; I fear he will not survive the night."

Colum and Malcolm ascended the stone steps spiraling to the chambers of Emcath. There in a wooden bed, covered with many animal skins, propped up by several pillows was the King of the Northern Picts. He was an old man who was so emaciated that his head already looked like a death skull. He held up his bony hand and gestured with a bare stick of a finger for the two to sit down in the chairs near his bed. His breathing was labored and low.

"You are Colum?" asked the aged and ill King.

"I am, Your Majesty," answered Colum. "I have come to minister to you and to bring you to our Lord and Savior, Jesus Christ. Will you accept the Lord as your God, renouncing all other gods before Him?"

King Emcath slowly nodded his head in the affirmative and Colum and Malcolm began the conversion.

Later, when they were alone with Virolec, after they had converted his whole household to Christianity, they were able to ask about what they had seen on the Loch.

"You have seen what few men in this world have seen. Some have called it a monster; some have called it our guardian. Nonetheless, I know not what it is; only that it is. My father saw it when he was a young man. I saw it once, as a boy, but I have not seen it since then. I will never forget that head rising out of the water on the tallest tree trunk of the neck, swaying and slithering through the water, as some giant snakelike thing. Did God, truly give men, dominion over such a creature?"

Malcolm began to respond and would have responded with the rote answer that the Book of Genesis does, indeed, tell us that man has dominion over all creatures, but he was cut off by Colum, who simply said, "God works in many ways, and often in mysterious ways."

Part VI: A Death in the Abbey

> "…for a holy joyousness that ever beamed from his countenance revealed the gladness with which the Holy Spirit filled his soul."-**Adamnan describing St. Columba**

Colum wandered the glens and the wooded straths of Scotland for more than thirty years preaching the Gospel. He went beyond the Great Glen past Inverness until Aberdeenshire. As his fame spread, as news of his miracles went forth throughout the land, and as Iona grew in prestige, the number of converts increased, the demand for churches rose, and the need for monasteries mushroomed.

Colum traveled far and wide even to Glasgow, where he met St. Mungo, the apostle of Strathclyde. But his greatest joy was in being allowed to return to Ireland. He was invited to the Great Synod of Durmceatt which he attended with King Aidan, a Scottish king.

No matter where he wandered, his home and his heart were in Iona. His was always in prayer or in study. He read voraciously. He wrote many works including The Book of Durrow, the psalter, The Cathach, and The Book of Kells, which he also illustrated. He was always transcribing.

On the very eve of his death, he was engaged in the work of transcription. It was Sunday June 8, 597. Colum, weak and unstable on his feet, climbed the hill overlooking his beloved monastery on Iona. The sun was setting as he reached the top. The sky was ablaze with gold, orange, and red, the clouds were flowing across the sky as if a great river was flooding and the clouds were leaves of autumn swept along with the waters. He said not a word, but prayed. His eyes took in the color, as it changed to red, then purple and finally grey. He raised his hand and made the sign of the cross, blessing his monastery and the monks within.

The bell calling for vespers rang and he hobbled down the hill. He went into the chapel. He was no longer the tall, athletic man who had leapt ashore years before from the coracle and had proclaimed this place the site of his new monastery.

It was later around midnight. Malcolm was in Colum's chambers.

"We should thank God that we have lived a long, full life in His service. When we came to this shore, I thought that I had been banished. I believed that my life and my service to God were at an end. With your help, we have brought the Word of God to the heathen Picts and have converted many, many people to Christ. You have helped me to redeem my pledge to atone for the deaths I caused at the Battle of Cooldrevny." He paused. "Thank you."

Malcolm nodded. "You, Master, have given me far more than I could have ever given you."

"There will be much to do after I am gone. You must continue to lead the conversion of the Picts and the Scots. This monastery must carry on…" Colum's voice faded there. His eyes were far oft, as if he were going asleep. Malcolm thought it wiser to let him trail off to sleep, for there was always tomorrow.

The bells for midnight service began to ring. Colum stirred and began to rise. His feet were unsteady. Malcolm reached out his hands to assist Colum. Colum waved him off and rose unaided to his feet.

Colum limped to the chapel and used the pews to help him to the altar. He knelt before the altar and crossed himself. He began praying and the community prayed also. Sometime, during the service, Colum slumped over, and his soul departed.

Chapter 7

Norsemen

"But the king's heart swells, bulging with courage in battle, where heroes sink down..."-**Sæmundar Edda**

I. The Raid to the West

"Triumph to some and treasure to others"- **Hyundluljod, Old Norse Poem**

In a small fjord, a small hamlet was just starting its day. The smoke was rising in lazy swirls that gyred through the sky ascending to the few puffy clouds that glowed pink with the coming dawn. The woman ran her fingers through her long hair and arched her back as she raised her arms and stretched her fingers while she yawned. In moments, she would begin the day, bring in the water, build the fire, and begin cooking breakfast, but now this moment was hers and hers alone. She loved this moment when her husband made no demands for food, mead, or love and when children were not under foot screaming over the latest deed an evil brother or an evil sister had done to them. This was her moment and she was glad that Frigga had given this to her.

Her husband stirred. One eye opened and she knew her moment was gone. A second eye opened and with it he spoke. "You are the most beautiful woman the gods have ever made." 'Perhaps,' she thought, 'my moment is over rated.' She kissed him and wrapped the furs of their bed around her and snuggled up to her husband. He kissed her back and they made love as the sun topped the mountains to the east.

"Husband, you are incorrigible." She whispered in his ear.

He kissed her neck and held her tightly, almost to the point of hurting her. "I need you so much."

"What is it?" Although she had been married to him for thirteen years and had borne him four children, it was rare that he opened up to her his deepest thoughts. She had known that he had loved her, although he rarely spoke the words of love. This was something new and different and because it was new and different it scared her, while at the same time the intimacy it displayed thrilled her.

"Thor has said we sail today to the west. 'As far as we can sail.' he said. No one has ever sailed west before. He wants to sail for two weeks to the west to see if there is anything out there. Dag says we will all die." She raised her hands to her mouth in terror. She had not known that this was the plan. None of the men had confided this to their wives, mothers, or sisters. The men had decided, conspired, and duped the women. The days of work leading up to this expedition, the refurbishing of the long boats, the gathering of the food, the livestock, and the other necessities of a long voyage, and the loading of the ships, had all proceeded as if the men were to raid east, as they had always done. Not a word had been breathed of going west-toward the setting sun.

He smiled weakly at her. "I will come back to you."

Days later, she stared at the setting sun, towards which his ship had sailed. Another day was done, done except for the evening meal, the cleaning of dishes, the weaving of cloth, the putting of children to bed, except for these tasks, the day was over. He had been gone now for three weeks and would be gone for longer she knew in her heart, but still she longed for him to be there to share this moment as the sun sank into the western sea. To see the golden light turn orange then pink then grey, together, that was what she wanted. The idea took firmer hold of her mind and crystalized more completely. She wanted him there to be with her to share this moment. While she could hope that somewhere to the west, he too was looking at the setting sun and seeing this day end, this gave her little joy for she wanted him here now.

He had told her that he would come back. She heartily believed that this was true. She had to believe that it was true. For if it was not, then what would become of her life? What would happen to her children? If he were gone, then so too would be Thor, their lord, and most of the men of the village. Who knew who would come to carry them off and take their lands, their cattle?

All she knew was that her man and all the men of their village were on some great quest. They would raid to the west and bring home any gold, silver or precious things they could find. They would steal anything and everything of any value from the people they found and they would think nothing of it. If a man cannot defend his goods, his possession, his cattle, and his women, then what good was he? It was better for him and for his women that these things be taken from him and be possessed by someone would defend them.

Part II: To Colonize or to Raid?

> "From the fury of the Northmen
> deliver us, O Lord."-**Medieval Prayer**

Thor lifted his leg over the side of the boat. His deerskin boot sliced through the loch's waters as he scampered up from the surf to the beach. The land was rich; this he could immediately see. Cattle, goats, and sheep grazed lazily as if they had not a care in the world. They certainly did not turn their heads to look at the hairy, bearded men who were jumping out of the boats, swords, shields, and battle axes in hand. Nothing they did seemed to disturb the peace and tranquility of this place, but Thor and his men were on guard anyway. Who knew who or what lurked beyond? How could they know? They only knew that they were not the first men to come this way.

Olaf called to Thor, "What is this place?"

"I truly do not know." Thor shifted his weight from foot to foot. He chided himself for jumping out of the boat into the water. 'Now your boots are wet,' he thought.

"These are the first islands we have encountered since leaving home. They are south and west of our home." He said to no one in particular.

He directed some to build a fire, some to explore further inland, and some to stand guard. "Where there are sheep, there are men who tend them. We do not fear them, but neither should we let our guard down with them." Thor pointed to Godred. "You lead the exploration inland. Note carefully what you see. Do not attack anyone, although defend yourselves."

Godred bowed to Thor. "That I will do. How far do you want us to go?"

"Not more than three miles. Come back as quickly, but as quietly as you can." Thor's mind was now dealing with other thoughts concerning their camp and defense of it.

There were no trees. Not a one. Still, the land was green and verdant.

He still hadn't decided. Should he raid the peoples who lived here? Should he try to live in harmony with them?

Part III: The Kingdom of the Isles

The Norsemen came. Some came as colonists; still many more came as raiders. They first came to the Islands of Shetland and Orkney. They called the Northern Isles- *Norðreyjar*-in their Viking tongue. They came here first for these are the closest lands to Scandinavia.

Then they went down the western coast of Scotland to places like Mull. Then they came to the Outer Hebrides, the main island of which is the Isle of Skye. They called the other islands *Suðreyjar*, or "Southern Isles," which include the Outer Hebrides and Inner Hebrides, that is Iona, Mull, Skye, and Jura.

Time and time again, they raided Iona and all the other monasteries. They took away the golden chalices, the silver crosses, and the treasuries. At some, they killed all the priests. Some monasteries died such as Portmahomak, a rich monastic settlement wiped out by the Vikings around 900 AD; others such as Iona survived and thrived.

But there were some Vikings who wanted to found kingdoms and be new kings.

One such man was Somerled. His name in Old Norse was Sumarliði. Sometime in the mid-twelfth century, almost out of the mists that hang perennially over the moors and mountains of the Highlands, he came. He lived by his wits. It was by his brilliant military maneuvers of conquest and by singular statesmanship through alliance, that he arose to control the Kingdom of the Isles. But like many a great man, he built upon a solid foundation. For like Philip of Macedon, he took what his father had done and made it that much greater. His father, GilleBride, had made a successful marriage alliance with Malcolm, who was the son of Alexander I, the King of Scotland.

When Somerled became a man, Malcolm was fighting to gain his rightful place upon the throne. Somerled did not hesitate, but threw in immediately with Malcolm and defeated the other claimants to the throne.

With Malcolm's blessing, Somerled then set his sights upon the Kingdom of the Isles. The throne was then held by Somerled's brother-in-law, Godred Olafsson. Although the fighting took more than two years, Somerled eventually was victorious and he seized the throne.

He ruled wisely. He early decided to have a council to advise him such that he could dispense justice based upon true knowledge of his kingdom and with true insight into his people and their traditions. His council was comprised of:

1. Four "great men of the royal blood of Clan Donald lineally descended" (Macdonald of Clanranald, Macdonald of Dunnyvaig, MacIain of Ardnamurchan and Macdonald of Keppoch);
2. Four "greatest of the nobles, called lords" (Maclean of Duart, Maclaine of Lochbuie, Macleod of Dunvegan and Macleod of the Lewes);
3. Four "thanes of less living and estate" (Mackinnon of Strath, MacNeil of Barra, MacNeill of Gigha and Macquarrie of Ulva);
4. "Freeholders or men that had their lands in factory" (Mackay of the Rhinns, MacNicol of Scorrybreac, Mackay of Ugadale, Macgillivray in Mull, Macmillan of Knapdale, and MacEacharn of Kilellan).

Somerled ruled the Kingdom of the Isle until his death. Somerled founded the MacDonald Clan or so at least the MacDonalds like to say that he did. They say this for John MacDonald, a descendant of Somerled, became the first Lord of the Isles.

And the blood of Vikings, of the Norsemen, and of the men of the North flows in the veins of the MacDonalds of Clanranald to this very day. And this Norse blood became the blood of Scotland.

Chapter 8

The Declaration of Arbroath

For too long, England tried to wrest control of Scotland from her people and her lords. For, as long as but a hundred of us remain alive, never will we on any conditions be brought under English rule. It is in truth not for glory, nor riches, nor honours that we are fighting, but for freedom — for that alone, which no honest man gives up but with life itself.-**The Declaration of Arbroath in 1320 AD**

Bernard of Kilwinning, the Abbot of Arbroath and the Chancellor of Scotland, sat back in his chair and admired his writing. His was pleased with himself and then realizing that he was pleased with himself, he was embarrassed because he was committing the sin of pride. Nonetheless, the words had flowed easily and quickly from his pen. It was as if they had a life of their own and were born without him having to do much at all to call them forth. He knew in his heart that these words were necessary words; they were inspired words; they were holy words; they were righteous words; and they were words of rebellion.

He had written them for so many reasons. Had he a choice in the matter? Not if he believed that God was calling him to write this letter and this he believed fervently. All those nobles had come and had chosen him to speak for them. They were from all the reaches of Scotland. They represented all the clans; all the people. Four bishops also had commissioned him to write.

So too, had Robert the Bruce, King of Scotland, begged him to write. "No one but you can write this letter to the Pope. You speak for me and you speak for all the people of Scotland!" The king had said.

Bernard was a monk who had stayed true to his calling. He had not become fat, but had remained fit, and still rode his horse miles every day, if he weather held. He hunted like a young man, yet found time to pray and reflect each day. His hair had not thinned, although it had greyed some years ago and lately had turned white. While he had access to great wealth, he spent little to none on himself and distributed as much as possible to the poor and downtrodden, who were abundant in Scotland. He took his position as Abbot seriously, although he often had to flee to preserve his life.

Bernard stared at the letter. "April 6th in the year of our Lord 1320," it began. Bernard could easily read the Latin and thought nothing of it that his mind wrote, spoke, and thought in Latin. To think that after years of warring with Edward I until he died, and then against his son, Edward II, England would still not concede defeat and leave Scotland alone. This was true even after the English losses at the Battles of Loudon Hill and Bannockburn. Not even the capture of the last English stronghold at Berwick had deterred Edward II. Maybe this letter would.

Now, this letter alone was the hope of Scotland. Would it release Scotland from the icy grip of the English? Would Scotland now have its independence? Would Scotland be a sovereign nation?

Bernard was a Benedictine Monk. He took great joy of being in the same order as Colum Cille, now known only as St. Columba. Bernard's Abbey at Arbroath was the most powerful and wealthy abbey in Scotland. Bernard, too, had spent a great part of his life evading the English King, who had tried to hunt him down, because he was such a strong voice for freedom in Scotland. There were times, for over a decade, that he had been disguised and had hidden at other monasteries and other abbeys, but all the while, he had kept the fire of independence alive in his heart. For his loyalty to the cause, when Robert had gained control of the province of Angus, Robert had ousted the English appointed Abbot and had installed Bernard in his stead.

But this had come at a price. Robert had asked the new Abbot to be his diplomat to the King of Norway. After two years, he returned to Scotland with an agreement. Norwegian ambassadors came to Inverness and knelt before Robert in ratification of the Treaty of Inverness. This treaty ended the continuing reciprocal acts of hostility between Norway and Scotland and opened up trade between the two nations.

Now he was asked to do something more for his king and country. He was writing to the Pope-no he was beseeching the Pope-to recognize Scotland as a sovereign and an independent nation. If the Pope recognized Scotland, then the Pope would also have to order England to cease its claim to be overlord of Scotland. This would force Edward II to relinquish his claim to be King of Scotland.

"With my name upon this document, I am committing my wealth, my position, and my life to the freedom and independence of Scotland," Bernard said to no one as the fire crackled in the fireplace and he read more of his letter again. "That is a sobering thought. I could be hanged for this." He had a sudden chill. Whether it was nerves or the chill of a late spring night in Scotland, he could not tell. Still, he got up, took an andiron to stir the ashes, and adjust a log.

He mused. "It was my poem, a stupid poem, which has gotten me into this." In the flush of victory, he had composed a paean about the Battle of Bannockburn. From this, his skills as an author had grown, till now he was regarded as one of the best writers in Scotland. He knew better, but he had no choice now. Too many people believed and were counting on him, for him to belie his own skills.

Eight earls and forty-five barons, fifty-three nobles in all, would sign this letter and affix their wax seals. They would be signing his letter and affixing their seals to his words, his thoughts, and his beliefs. They, too, were committing their wealth, their positions, and their lives to the freedom and independence of Scotland. This was simply momentous. He felt that he was God's conduit, God's agent, and God's servant, all in a way he had never felt before.

All of his life was arching to this pinnacle. All he had ever done had brought him to this point. If he never did anything else, this alone would stand and justify his life and his being.

And so he called for the all the nobles of Scotland to read what he had written and to affix their signatures and seals to this document. And in so affixing, all were committing themselves to God and to Scotland and, if need be, to the gallows. All so Scotland could be a free, independent nation under its own king.

Chapter 9

The Great Cattle Raid

"God helps those who help themselves."-**Dr. Samuel Smiles, Self Help**

Part I: Castle Urquhart and Environs

Somehow, when one thinks of Urquhart Castle, with its commanding views of Loch Ness, sheltered by rugged hills beyond, one can only be taken in by the seeming tranquility of the spot. It is truly beautiful and it is in a truly magnificent place. Its very name only enhances that impression, for Urquhart is derived from the ancient word 'Airdchartdan', which is a combination of the Gaelic word 'air" which means 'by' and Old Welsh 'cardden' which means a 'thicket of wood'.

But Urquhart Castle is a castle-a building built solely to defend its people from raids, sieges, and war. It is a killing building, a killing machine, and no amount of beautification can ever gloss over that.

The Castle is situated on a rocky promontory that juts into the Loch. Across the Loch, mountains soar into the heavens. Green trees line the banks of Loch Ness, providing a belt of vibrant green against the purple of the towering mountains which seem to rise straight-up from the shores of the Loch stretching into the blue heavens.

Surrounding the Castle is the fertile valley of Glen Urquhart. It is succulent with life and the harvests are rich and full. The farmers and shepherds that live here are happy for the valley is well sheltered from the cold blasts of winter, yet because of the Loch, the summers do not become too hot.

Urquhart Castle began, as many castles and villages in Scotland began, as a Pict village. Probably later, it became a Pictish fort. Old tales say that Urquhart castle was the fortress built by Bridei, the son of Maelchon, who was King of the Northern Picts. It was long after, probably around 1230, that a stone castle was built. It was built by the Sir Thomas Durward, after he was granted the lands by King Alexander II, who sought to have the castle built as one of his measures to assert royal sovereignty over the Highlands.

Urquhart Castle figured once quite largely in Scottish history when Edward I, known as 'Long Shanks', captured it when he invaded Scotland in 1296. It was one of his trophies that helped to give him his nickname, 'The Hammer of Scotland'. His strategy in Scotland was the same as had been his strategy in Wales: his Ring of Iron was the castles he built from Conwy, to Caernarfon, to Harlech and so on. Urquhart Castle was to be part of his Ring of Iron strangling the Highlands. He was determined to subjugate the Highlands, destroy the Clans, and eradicate their way of life. This fixed permanently in the English psyche the belief that the English were superior, the Highlanders barbarians, and, thus, the requisite that England must dominant Scotland. Edward's invasions sparked the Scottish Wars of Independence that raged on until 1357, resulting in over fifty years of war, death, disease, famine, hardship, looting, pillaging, and rapine.

It was its position in the Great Glen, central and commanding, that made Urquhart Castle so essential a conquest, that Edward I was lured to it, as would be the clans from the Isles later. It seemed that everyone did all they could to capture it, when they decided to attempt to assert their various and many claims over all the Highlands.

The Castle that the Durwards had built around 1250 had its main buildings on the summit at the extreme southern end of the Castle complex. Beyond the Castle was a valley with a creek running through it. This valley swelled to hills beyond it which looked down upon Urquhart Castle imparting a feeling of vulnerability, which diminished as one walked down the hillside into the valley which seemed to become deeper and deeper until one got to the creek. There, the one small bridge across it became a funnel, a place which men would be crammed together to cross the deep, ravine cut by the creek. This exposed them to the bolts of the crossbows of the Castle, whose range perfectly targeted the bridge and the creek. Then, and only then, did the feeling of doom of the killing fields around the Castle start to make the hairs of the back of a warrior's neck stand in fright.

When the MacDonalds approached the Castle in 1545, this portion of the Castle had fallen into dis-use and disrepair. However, what they faced was still formidable. The Castle had been built on two small hills immediately adjacent to the Loch. Although, the MacDonalds could see right into the Castle complex from the higher hills surrounding the Castle, they faced the fact that there was a wide open killing field leading up to the Castle which was protected by both a moat and a bridge. The Castle gate was exceedingly strong and presented quite an obstacle. Nonetheless, the MacDonalds of the Isles coveted Urquhart Castle and all the goods, cattle, sheep, swine, horses, geese, oats, barley, and other foodstuffs. But most of all, the MacDonalds coveted the suits of armor and the 20 pieces of artillery which were said to protect the Castle.

Part II: Upheaval in the Great Glen

> The Scots "love me worst of any Inglisheman living, by reason that I fande the body of the King of Scotts."- **Lord Dacre** who discovered King James IV's body at Flodden.

How the MacDonalds came to be here and why their lust for the cattle and goods of Urquhart Castle leads one to the story of the Castle.

Urquhart Castle had fallen into a state of ruin in the late 1400's. The Earl of Huntly was administering Urquhart Castle as a royal agent, but he was unable to bring stability to the Great Glen after many years of unrest. The MacLeans, who were allies of the Clan Donald, disputed the ownership of Urquhart Castle, leaving the Earl of Huntly no choice but to appeal to the King. Although the King ruled in favor of the Earl of Huntly, the Earl, greatly impoverished, decided to lease Urquhart Castle to Sir Duncan Grant of Freuchie. Sir Duncan Grant started the restoration of the Castle. His death, in 1485, interrupted his work. He left Urquhart Castle to his grandson, John 'the Red Bard', in his Will.

John performed the herculean task of bringing Urquhart Castle back to her glory. He also ran the estates efficiently and with justice. His handling of this important area of Scotland brought him to the attention of King James IV. King James IV granted John a Lordship; however, the King divided the estate into three parts and named John and his two sons as Barons and gave each of them control over a part. While John was the Baron of Urquhart, he now found that the King required the complete rehabilitation of the Castle and as well as his estate, in addition to providing military service to the King. It was John 'the Red Bard', who built Grant Tower, the five story tower house which stands at the northern edge of the promontory.

King James IV, like so many Scots before him and after him, found the lure of France as an ally against the English to be overwhelmingly tantalizing. While one can think that an alliance between Scotland and France would keep England at bay, it often embroiled Scotland in wars, the center of gravity of which was far, far from her shores. Often, knowing that Scotland would do her bidding, France began adventures on the Continent to ensnare England with armies upon the Continent, and then, France, would invoke the treaty of alliance and request that Scotland go to war against England. The logic was always the same. With England embroiled elsewhere, England must be weak at home and Scotland could peradventure gain English lands at English expense.

This particular conflict arose when King James IV declared war on England to honor his commitment to France under the Auld Alliance. The English King, Henry VIII, was already fighting the French King, Louis XII, in the War of the League of Cambrai defending Italy and Pope against the French. In October of 1511, Henry the VIII had joined what was also known as the Holy League with both Venice and Spain to defend the Papacy against France. Louis XII only had to tell James IV that Henry VIII had reasserted his old claim to be the overlord of Scotland to make

James IV inflamed and ready, willing, and able to fight his ancient enemy: England.

Pope Leo X, threatened James with excommunication, if James broke his peace treaties with England. When James did not desist, Pope Leo X had Cardinal Christopher Bainbridge excommunicate the recalcitrant Prince. Scotland now faced the usual prospect of a war against England, but with the unusual circumstance that Henry VIII was now cast in the role of the protector of the Catholic Church and the Scottish King was cast as an excommunicated monarch.

James responded by sending his Navy to help the fleets of France, as well as sending his envoy, Lord Lyon, Islay Herald to King Henry VIII. On 11th August 1513, the Herald found Henry at his camp in Guinegate, France with Emperor Maximilian outside the walls of the besieged the city of Thérouanne.

"Your Grace, I bring you greetings and salutations from the great King, James IV of Scotland. His letter, I would entrust into your hands and I would await an answer from you." Lord Lyon, Islay Herald bowed to Henry, while proffering James' letter in his outstretched hands.

"What would your King ask of me?" sneered Henry.

"Only that Henry abandons his efforts against this town and goes home. Your actions in attacking France and Louis are in violation of our treaty and are abhorrent to God. Cease now and come to Scotland to ask forgiveness from my Lord and King, James."

Henry twirled and pulled his sword in anger putting the point at the neck of the diplomat. "Your King, if indeed he be a King, has no right to summon me. He was married to my sister, Margaret, and, thus, should be my ally and my friend. He disregards all familial love and affection and tramples all civility."

Warming now to his rhetoric, Henry continued, "I am the very owner of Scotland and he holdeth it of me by homage." Henry stroked his chin and then, slamming his fist on the campaign map spread before him on his table, snarled, "And, now, for a conclusion, recommend me to your master and tell him if he be so hardy to invade my realm or cause to enter one foot of my ground, I shall make him as weary of his part as ever was man that began any such business."

Henry lowered the sword and tossed it in the ground between the diplomat's feet. Lord Lyon gasped a breath of relief. Henry stomped the ground, "Your King is now excommunicated from the Church and is now officially a pagan. I will treat him as the pagan he is. For as Matthew taught in his Gospel, a Christian who errs is naught but a pagan and should be treated accordingly. Go and tell him the Protector of the Church bids him to recant his heresy and to repent his ways or face my sword."

After the diplomat had withdrawn from his tent, Henry wrote to Thomas Howard, Earl of Surrey, his lieutenant general of the Army of the North. "My dear Earl, I have entrusted you with the banners of the Cross of St. George and the Red Dragon of Wales. I know now from James' own diplomat, that James will wage war against England and invade the North. Have your spies cast their net across the Lowlands and determine what Army that comes against you. I shall deliver to you as many men, arms, cannon, and horse that I can spare from this siege. It is now up to you to save England!"

Upon Lord Lyon's report, James IV invaded England with an Army of 30,000.

Part III: The Battle of Flodden

> To tell you plaine,
> twelve thousand were slaine,
> that to the fight did stand;
> And many prisoners tooke that day,
> the best in all Scotland.
> That day made many a fatherlesse childe,
> and many a widow poore;
> And many a Scottish gay Lady,
> sate weeping in her bowre.

Late in 1513, King James IV battled against an English army commanded by the Earl of Surrey. It was a beautiful autumn day, beginning with a hint of frost and a pleasant coolness which the men of both sides greeted with joy as they were clad in their woolen uniforms. September is often thought of as being about as late in the campaign season that one should fight. King James IV should not have fought this day and should not have fought a battle in England against England. Although both armies were the largest that each nation would ever field and, although the casualties were the greatest that both sides would ever suffer, the blood, valor, and weapons of the Scots were not enough to overcome the will of English men fighting for England on English soil. King James IV died upon the fields of Flodden. With his death, died the dream of Scottish domination of England, at least for a while.

Everything to do with Scotland seems to be a contradiction. And this battle, this Battle of Flodden is but another one. The Battle of Flodden was actually fought upon Branxton or Brainston Moor.

Part IV: Great Consequences

> In war, trivial events can have great
> consequences.-**Julius Caesar**

Often times, in the course of human events, there are consequences far beyond the event that precipitated them. In this case, the loss at the Battle of Flodden not only signaled the defeat of Scotland to England, but also it led to great instability in the Highlands.

Donald MacDonald of Lochalsh saw in the defeat at the Battle of Flodden an opportunity, actually a golden opportunity. It was his chance to invade the Great Glen. It was his chance to assert his claim of suzerainty as the Lord of the Isles over the Highlands. He saw that there would be much to loot and further hoped that he might capture the great Castle of Urquhart. So Donald MacDonald of Lochalsh unleashed his Clan upon the Great Glen. They swept forward in a great tide of looting and killing, which tide crested at the walls of Castle Urquhart.

John Grant appealed to the King for recompense for the things that had been looted from his lands and Castle which included pots, pans, kettles, napkins, beds, sheets, blankets, coverings, pillows, fish, flesh, bread, cheese, butter, and all other stuffs of the household, and salt, as well as other things of mounting to least 100 pounds. The MacDonalds carried off 740 bolls of barley, 1040 bolls of oats, some 300 Highland cattle, and over 1000 sheep.

John Grant, however, knew that he had to take further steps. The Red Bard knew that he could not beat the MacDonalds with violence and so he resorted to diplomacy. He married his daughter to Donald Cameron, trusting that an alliance with that clan would give him a powerful family and ally to counterbalance the MacDonalds.

All was well for many years, until the son of John Grant, James, unwisely decided that he should intervene in a succession dispute within the Clanranald. For whatever reason, he decided that he should side with the Huntly and Fraser clans against the MacDonalds of Clanranald. There was a great battle ending the feud known as the Battle of the Shirts. In reprisal for this betrayal by James Grant, the MacDonald Clans of Clanranald, Glengarry, Keppoch, and MacIian swept forward again into the Great Glen with the intent to devastate James Grants' estates and, in particular, Castle Urquhart. As before, the MacDonalds carried off vast treasure, including three great boats, 3,377 sheep, 2,355 heads of cattle, 2,204 goats, 395 horses, 122 swine, 64 geese, 3,206 bolles of oats, 1427 bolles of barley, 60 ells of cloth, 12 feather beds with bolsters, blankets, sheets, as well as tables and other items of furniture, a chest of silver containing over 300 pounds of coin, and all 20 pieces of artillery, complete with all their gun powder and shot, as well as many stands of armor.

The MacDonalds were not content yet. They tore down the iron gates of the gatehouse of Castle Urquhart and carried away its doors and locks. Deciding also that they needed to brew beer, they took the brewing vats and other equipment, as well as six roasting spirits, five pots and six pans.

What had begun as the Great Raid had now become the Great Cattle Drive. Beside the banks of Loch Ness, the MacDonalds drove men and animals, while the wagons, full of the suits of armor and iron gates, creaked heavy on their wheels as armor and weapons clinked one against the other. Along the road to Eilean Donan Castle, they herded the vast flocks of sheep and goats, 'til they reached the banks of the Kyle of Lochalsh. They divided the spoils and each of the great families of the Clan of MacDonald went their way back to their homes of the Isle of Sky, Glengarry, Keppoch, and MacIian. They went back home bearing much loot and sporting broad smiles.

The romance of this adventure is the romance of the Highlands. Reaving cattle-that is cattle rustling-was an art form. Men living a life, which anywhere else would be considered banditry and make them outlaws, was considered the highest form of defense of one's Clan from outsiders. The cycle of feuds, stealing, looting, revenge deaths, were met by more stealing, looting, and revenge deaths, continued generation after generation. For once set in motion, hatred grows with each new act of violence, one against the other. The fact that they may have been Christian men living in a Christian country, did not dissuade them from following this life where the greatest glory was to pay back your enemy for wrongs done in the past, whether real or imagined. Each Clan had an enemy and that enemy had to be reduced and destroyed. All took the code of the feud as being the only possible way of life. Hundreds of years could pass by and yet that initial evil act, done centuries ago, was still alive, still vibrant, and still needing to be revenged.

Chapter 10

The Massacre of Glencoe

"We look to Scotland for all our ideas of civilisation." – **Voltaire**

Part I: The Making of a Vow

Man's inhumanity to man Makes countless thousands mourn! - **Robert Burns**

"What is probably the greatest of all feuds is that of the dirty dog Campbells, who barked beneath the table of the English to get crumbs or tidbits of meat and joyfully licked the hands of the English scum, against the true Highlanders, the devout Christian Clan MacDonald." So began my grandfather in the telling of the tale of the feud between our clans. I was but 9 or 10 years old when I remember this telling, but I am sure that I heard it years before that, maybe even as I suckled at my mother's breast. It was like the wind, you could feel it, it was present, but you could never see it. All the men of my clan who had fallen at the sword point of the Campbells, the very fact that our name and clan identity had once been stolen by them, the betrayals, the lies, the very evil which was Campbell, had been a part of the very fabric of my life, of my being, and of my psyche from the very moment of my birth.

The greatest insult of it all was their unholy alliance with the devils, the English. To think that they took the side of our hated enemy, the scourge of all mankind, the Protestant cause which knew no bounds to its grasping greediness, the English, who had stolen our land, had raped our women, had enslaved us, and had stolen our nation while it was aborning. This was beyond all comprehension and understanding. It was beyond being able to turn the other check and meekly submit. Jesus Christ Himself could not forgive them for what they did.

I sat by the fire, whilst its warmth coursed through my body driving out the damp chill of the Highland winter. By my side were my two best friends, Ranald, the chief's son, and his cousin, Mary. We had been inseparable friends for as long as I could remember. Ranald, known to all as Young Ranald, was about three months younger than I. His mother had died giving him life. So the chief declared that my mother would suckle him along with me. This gave my mother great status within our clan and made me, in essence, his brother. We shared the same toys, we shared the same bed, and my mother read us our bedtime stories together.

When were about five, Mary came to live with the Ranald, the chief, as his ward. She was a member of the MacDonalds of Keppoch. She had been betrothed to Young Ranald at birth, because the Clanranalds and the Keppochs always married one another. Since the day she came, she was our playmate and close friend.

Mary had red-auburn hair, light reddish freckles, dairy-milk skin, greenish eyes, and the grandest sense of humor that God ever allowed to walk the earth. She was always ready with a prank; she was an imp.

She had the utterly annoying habit of doing mischief and getting away with it. Once she stole butter and buns from the kitchen, when the cook was not looking. Ranald and I had been in the kitchen shortly before the theft had occurred. When asked whether she knew who had taken the pilfered food, Mary innocently said, "Last time I was in the kitchen, the butter and buns were there." A true enough statement as far as it went, but the implication was that someone else had purloined the food. As we were the last ones seen in the kitchen, we were the ones punished.

We were playing hide and seek a few months afterwards when Mary said, "By the way, I took the buns and butter!" She fluttered her green eyes, laughed, and ran off leaving us to marvel over her statement.

Lest you think her callous, she was not. She was the kindest, gentlest person I have ever known. She was also the most considerate person. She just had this impish quality to her that sometimes made her have fun at our expense.

Another time, it was summer. We might have been six or seven years old. Unlike the usual Highlands day, this one was hot, very hot. The Highland cattle were lowing and their tongues were hanging out from the heat and thirst. One of the stables hands suggested that we get the cows a drink. We wandered with buckets to the far pond. When we arrived, we were all hot, tired, and thirsty. We bent down to get drinks. As we did so, Mary filled her bucket with cold water and threw a bucket on us!

We cupped our hands and threw water at her in retaliation. Then it was war-water war! We splashed each other and we screamed with joy and surprise at the coldness of the water. All thoughts of taking care of the cattle fled from our minds. We were intent on getting each other wet.

After a while, Mary suggested that that we go swimming in the pond as we were wet already and the day was so hot. We striped off our clothes. Ranald and I had never seen a girl without clothes before and neither had Mary seen a boy. She was quite intrigued with our anatomy. We marveled that she had nothing down there. Then we all ran into the pond and splashed and screamed some more. Not long afterward, the stable hand came looking for us wondering where the water was for the cattle. Seeing us naked in the pond, he ran off.

We jumped out of the pond and we were in the midst of dressing, when my mother came up. "What's ye been doing Jamie? You and Ranald should have enough sense to know ye can't go naked around a girl!" With that, we were dragged off by my mother, who pulled us along by our ears. We were royally tanned for our "indecent actions". My mother suggested to Mary, who was about 2 years younger than we, that the 'bad, older boys had made her do it', to which she merely looked at the ground, never correcting my mother!

As much as she infuriated us, we both loved being with her. Her sense of adventure, her willingness to go anywhere and do anything, allowed her to keep up with us (and sometimes to surpass us!) She was brave; she was funny; she was not a delicate, little girl.

The long nights of winter wound their way from the very early sunset in but the mid-afternoon, through the supper of boiled oats and weak tea, till the evening was passed in bawdy song and story with a tad of whiskey circulated amongst the men folk, whilst the words magical and mournful filled the air like the smoke of so many pipes. It was then that my grandfather would speak of the Campbells and swear us all to undying hatred, an oath of terrible blood, a vow of vengeance so vile that it curdled the blood like a hysterical scream of the Baccanalia. We hunched over low in the dimming light of the fire as the embers burned out one by one. We were men of the dark night thinking of dark things to be done by men who were damned by man and God for their crimes. My mind was impressionable and I was imprinted by these images and oaths. I have never escaped their spell. My oath held sway over me then and holds sway over me even now, years and years later.

My grandfather would pull his tartan closer around him as the temperature dropped, which only beckoned us to move closer to him. He would lower his voice and this swept us in as conspirators. There in the orange glow whilst the fire hissed and crackled, a log might fall or break under its own weight as the fire ate it up. With each sputter, a voice might say an "aye", or a foot might stamp the ground, or a hand might reach for a dirk to be ready to find the gut of a Campbell.

These nights were spent in Duntulm Castle. I recall the windswept cliff, upon which Duntulm Castle was built, was devoid of trees. The Castle looks out upon the Isles of Tulm and Harris, from whence the finest tweed comes. Harris is so very mountainous, but from here in Duntulm Castle, it appears to be but small bumps upon the horizon, when it is clear enough for them to be seen floating in the distance.

This Castle was the seat of the MacDonalds. It was built they say in the 14th century, but really came into its own in 1618 when Donald Gorm Og, now known as Sir Donald MacDonald of Sleat, was granted the rights to it, as long as he kept in it repair. He added another tower and reinforced the structure and it was then a formidable bulwark against the MacLeods, when the MacDonalds and the MacLeods were feuding.

I grew up there in this windswept, lonely coast of the Isle of Skye. I learned to fight there; I grew into my first claymore. As I grew up, my uncle's leg, wounded a long time ago in some fight with Angus Campbell, got the better of him. He hobbled more. He could not effectively wield his claymore and would have been vulnerable in a fight. He took me under his wing, because he was my father's brother and because he had promised my father while my father lay dying from the same fight with the Campbells, which had claimed my uncle's leg, that he would raise me and raise me right.

I shared my grandfather's and my father's name: James Augustus MacEachern, which I counted the most honoured, proudest name in the world. It was my shield and my sword. I was a MacDonald; I was Lord of the Horse. I had the heritage of the seas and the land-my clan motto was: Per mare, per terras, by land and by sea. With my uncle, Daniel Alexander Liam McEachern, I felt that nothing was impossible; we were invincible. Someday we would have our revenge upon the Campbells who had taken so much from my family.

My grandfather started the story. "Boy, ne'er forget that we're descended from Viking Kings. We're royalty. Remember our father, Somerled, the first Lord of the Isles, one of the greatest of all the Lords. Lord of Argyll, Lord of the Hebrides, Lord of Kintyre, the Norse King of the Sudreys. Your blood courses with his blood." To say that grandfather was proud would be the greatest understatement. He relished being a Viking descendant, a Highlander, and once the second to a Clan chief.

He gestured around the room to all the men who stood at arms ready to serve. "We've vassals aplenty."

The smoke of his pipe swirled, danced, and wove itself into wreaths of mist that faded into the darkness away from the fire. His arms were still strong and his mind was clear, but his old bones pained him with every movement.

My grandfather had been at Glencoe in 1692 and had fought for the King James in 1715. He had raised me with my uncle after my father had fallen in Lord Mar's defeat in 1719. It was at the same battle that uncle had taken a musket ball in the right knee fired by a Campbell. It had shattered the knee cap and he had been maimed thereafter. Lord Ranald had let the old man retain his position as chief of the horses, although he could not ride.

The MacEachern family, my family, of the Isle of Skye made swords for hundreds of years. These were the famous "Islay Hilts". The "claidheamth mhór" (claymore - great sword) was up to eight feet long, so heavy that it made a two handed grip necessary for most men to wield it, and had a dull rounded point. This was a slashing weapon, not a thrusting weapon.

My grandfather had forged my claymore, my father's claymore, the Lord's claymore, and his own. They were considered the finest weapons anyone in clan had. He had taught his sons the craft and then had retired from making the fearsome weapons. While he raised me, he never let me forget my father and always told me stories of my father to keep his memory alive. I owed all that I was to my grandfather and my uncle.

At some point, my grandfather told me, that the very earliest known reference to McEachern name is a Celtic Cross raised in memory of Colin and Katherine McEachern sometime around 1500, in Kintyre, Scotland. The Mull of Kintyre is the south westernmost tip of the Kintyre peninsula in southwest Scotland. From here, the Antrim coast of Ireland is visible on a calm and clear day, which happens occasionally.

It was grandfather, who had arranged for my mother to suckle the young Ranald, forging that special bond-stronger than the bond between brothers-that existed in men who had been suckled by the same mother. It was this which had given me a special position in the clan for the Young Ranald truly loved me and we were the best of friends.

"I'll fight to redeem your knee." It came out before I knew what I was saying.

"What lad?"

"I'll fight to redeem your knee." I reaffirmed my vow. Having said it, I could not take it back; much like the smoke once expelled from your lungs can not be put back into the tobacco.

"There's my lad," he said as he clapped me upon the back.

Part II: Being a Winner

> I would prefer even to fail with
> honor than win by cheating.-**Sophocles**

The one thing I have not mentioned yet is that the Campbells, as evil as they are, always seem to wind up winning or be on the winning side. It is uncanny. It is clear that they have a pact with the devil. They must be in league with the devil for no God fearing man could ever choose so unerringly well. They ne'er falter, ne'er make a mis-alliance, ne'er duped, nor seem to have any bad luck. It is ungodly, they are.

It does not matter that the MacDonalds had large tracts of land and held sway over the Islands of the Hebrides. Somehow, little by little they took our ancestral lands in the Argyll. Was not Somerled the Lord of Argyll? Yes, he was, but nonetheless, somehow, we lost it. And we lost it to those half-devils, the Campbells.

For three hundred years, little by little, acre by acre, here a farm, there a sheep meadow, we lost land to the Campbells. MacDonald land became Campbell land. And sometimes, MacDonalds became Campbells, whether willingly or not. With my sept, it was unwillingly. They enslaved us, renamed us, and now we were MacEacherns, or MacEachains, a nasty diminutive, telling all of our impoverished and low estate.

How did they do it? Well, they backed the right man when disputes were had over who was to be king. They used the law and courts when they could. They found legal niceties and turns of words that said one thing pure, clean, and clear, and yet somehow made the words stand on their heads and do cartwheels to come around and say something that no right-thinking man could ever discern from them. When the law failed them, they showed that ruthless side that no other Highlander ever seemed to have in such a quantity. Stealthy killing, poison, assassins in the night, seductive, willing women hiding dirks in their skirts-whatever came to hand, whatever trick they could think of. Cunning beyond the fox, evil beyond the devil, that's what the Campbells were and are.

They would never face us in a real battle. But the feud went on and on, like a pot on the stove simmering and simmering, ready to boil over.

By every tool that came to hand, the feud continued. When William became King of England in 1689, the Campbells found it expedient to become Protestants. This sat well with William and more power began to accrue to them. The MacDonalds had remained loyal to the Catholic Church and saw the Campbell conversion for what it was-a power play, pure and simple. But William saw it not, and the Campbells became his lap dogs.

Part III: A Good Night's Work

There was one tale which my grandfather spoke of only when the memory of it so weighed upon his mind that he had to get it out. He always began the story the same way. He read the infamous order that had sentenced the MacDonalds to death.

> *You are hereby ordered to fall upon the rebells, the McDonalds of Glenco, and put all to the sword under seventy. You are to have a speciall care that the old Fox and his sones doe upon no account escape your hands, you are to secure all the avenues that no man escape. This you are to putt in execution att fyve of the clock precisely; and by that time, or very shortly after it, I'll strive to be att you with a stronger party: if I doe not come to you att fyve, you are not to tarry for me, but to fall on. This is by the Kings speciall command, for the good & safety of the Country, that these miscreants be cutt off root and branch. See that this be putt in execution without feud or favour, else you may expect to be dealt with as one not true to King nor Government, nor a man fitt to carry Commissione in the Kings service. Expecting you will not faill in the full-filling hereof, as you love your selfe, I subscribe these with my hand att Balicholis Feb: 12, 1692. For their Majesties service*

> *(signed) R. Duncanson*
> *To*   *Capt.*
> *Robert*   *Campbell*
> *of Glenlyon*

He began again the old worn story, like a wagon wheel fitting into the rut of the road, or the horse knowing the way home.

"Snow had been falling all night. One of the wonders of snow is the total silence that comes with a heavy snow. All sound is muffled. One can be out in the night in the snow, not hearing anything but the fall of each flake as it tumbles from the sky. I was out of the snow going to the necessary. It was late night. I was marveling at how the flakes came out of the sky and alighted on my face.

"While it was cold, yet I still felt comforted. There was a sense of being the first man in the world, the first man to ever see the branches of the trees with an inch or two of snow laden on their branches, and the first man to feel the sweet coldness of the night swirling with dancing flakes. My feet sunk into the snow and the skin of my ankles and calves tried to shrink away from the wet coldness of the snow.

"I turned around and saw candlelight pouring out the windows. The yellow-orange candlelight danced upon the blue –white purity of the snow, as the flakes gyred in the wind and swept along the ground one following the other as if they were some winter's daisy chain. I was enjoying the sight when it suddenly struck me that there was far too much light pouring forth from the windows and the candelabra were dancing from window to window. The bounding wind was muffing all sound-all was still-when just a wee cry broke forth from the house. Then another and another. Followed by hideous screams. Blood curdling screams. I knew then that death was afoot and suspected the Campbells were behind it.

"I rushed towards the Castle. It was then that MacDonalds spewed forth from every orifice of the house screaming: 'Flee!' 'Murder.' 'The Campbells are killing everyone'.

"I was turned around as a body hit me, which sent me spinning to ground, and deep into the snow. A moment later, I was shaking the snow off when the whoosh of a sword's blade cut the air above my head. I recoiled in terror to see Ian Campbell swinging his claymore once more at my head. I rolled. Ducked. Kicked my foot in a sweeping movement and brought him down on the flat of his back. I pulled my dirk from my sock and thrust for his gut. I caught his side. He howled and dropped his claymore. Quickly, I rose and sliced for his throat, but he flung up his hand. My blade caught his arm forcing it to cut across his jaw and tearing him up 'teen the eye and ear. I got up, grabbed his claymore, and ran into the darkness of the forest away from the Castle. No steps did I hear upon my heels, but sweat was pouring out of my body despite the bitter bite of the frigid night.

"I did not see anyone. I thought the Campbells must have killed all the MacDonalds in Glencoe.

"The night gloomed in around me. The snow combined with the forest to smother any sound. I did not know in what direction to flee. I was thoroughly out of breath and wanted beyond anything else to sit down, catch my wind, and cry. Cry for my family who were now dead, cry for the fear of my own death looming before me, cry for the despair I felt in the dank of the night, but then to cry for vengeance upon the Campbells, who had violated all decency by using the cover of hospitality to commit foul murder. We had let them in. We had given them entre to our home. We had given them the keys to our kingdom. Our friendship, our graciousness, our politeness had been used against us in the most devious, demonic way. We had been duped. We had been cheated. We had been gulled. How could we ever recover from this? Was there anyone left? Was I the last one? Did the future of the clan rest upon my shoulders?

"It was morning. How that happened I do not know. I had been running and running. But somehow, I ended up asleep in the snow.

"'Jamie! Jamie! Awake son! McIain MacDonald has been slain!' My lazy eyes fluttered awake.

"'What?' I asked.

"'Our chief is dead!'

"It took me some time to re-orient myself to the place, the time, and the person before me.

"'What?' I asked again, still in the shock of disbelief. Wasn't last night a nightmare, just a zephyr of a night terror that fades with the bright of the sun?

"Of course, it was a nightmare. The truest of all nightmares. Thirty-eight MacDonalds were slain that night. The Campbells had caught them in their beds, bound them, took them out into the snow, and then had slain them one by one. Mothers suckling their babies were scattered to the night and the snow with many a mother freezing to death by morning. Some of the clan was hunted down the next days. This is the crime of Murder that the Campbells visited upon their hosts the MacDonalds of Glencoe upon orders of King William. No true MacDonald can e'er forgive or forget this crime against man, nature, and God."

He stopped telling the tale. The fire had grown low, but not a man stirred till Young Ranald of Clan Ranald MacDonald, whispered from a dark corner, "Death to the Campbells and death to the English!"

Part IV: Closer Than Brothers

> Oh that you were like a brother to
> me who nursed at my mother's breasts!
> If I found you outside, I would kiss
> you, and none would despise me. -**Song
> of Solomon 8:1**

I was brought up with Young Ranald, as he was called. We were as if brothers, suckled by the same mother. We played together in the Highlands. We rolled and wrestled in the peaty soil covered in tough and ragged grass. We gazed upon the heather-coated mountain sides of stony peaks that rose some 3,000 or so feet above our heads. We watched the clouds and thought fantastic animals formed, breathed, lived, and died in the blue skies and white-clouded heavens. We beat our wooden swords upon each other's targe, our Scottish round shields, and thought of the raids we would pull grabbing the cows and sheep of the clans with which we were feuding. Mary, too, would join in our battles and she too had her wooden sword and targe.

We did our chores. We sheared the sheep and pulled ticks from their wool. We learned that the economy of the Highlands was based upon wool and livestock, our coos, that is our Highland cows. Trade, barter, and exchange were the way of the Highlands, for no one had money.

We sat in the nights and heard the pibrochs played upon the bagpipes and dreamed of our ancestors who had been heroes. The sagas told around the fire burned into our brains and filled us with pride as well as an abiding desire to be better than our ancestors and outshine them all. The sonorous sound of the bagpipes lilted on the evening air, swelled, and spilled here and then there. There is nothing like the mournful sound of the bagpipe as it wafts across the moors and glens to disappear like a tendril of moonlight or like a beat of the wing of a butterfly flitting from flower to flower in haphazard industry.

We were schooled together. It was during our schooling that we saw less and less of Mary. Our distant relative, Father Hugh MacDonald taught us. I must make this clear; he was not the man who would be Bishop of the

Scots. One unfortunate quality of the Scots is that we are all named alike. It is for this reason that many attach their homeland's name to their name.

Father Hugh MacDonald had been aboard to France, Italy, and the Holy Land. He knew Latin and Greek, as did many of the Highlands Scots who were to be lords and chiefs. Beyond that, he spoke French and Spanish, Italian, German, and Hebrew. He had read the antiquities and so thought that we must also. Cicero, Plutarch, Caesar (Gallia est omnis divisa in partes tres...), all the ancient greats were drilled into our heads. We conjugated verbs and parsed syntax. Father Hugh, as we were allowed to call him, was a man who had been brought up Catholic, but found that to get an education he had to profess the Episcopalian way to enter university in Aberdeen. King's College, which until the middle 17th century had been Catholic, was now Protestant, but was now a typical Renaissance university like that of Paris or Bologna. Remaining true to his faith, he entered The Scanlan in the Braes of Glenlivet. He was the son of Mary, the daughter of Ranald MacDonald of Kinlochmodiart (see there's the homeland name attached!) and of Alexander MacDonald of Morar (again with the homeland). We adored the man and he treated us as prized pupils, even though in reality we were his only pupils.

But he prepared us well for we were able to attend the University in Edinburgh and then later the Scots College in Paris.

We traveled abroad to Rome. It was Rome where we met our destiny.

BOOK III

VANITY OF VANITIES REDUX!

Chapter 11

The Eternal City is Aflame with Intrigue

> Rome is the city of echoes, the city of illusions, and the city of yearning.
> - **Giotto di Bondone**

Part I: The Making of a Pretender

Bonnie Prince Charles was born in Rome, Italy, in the Palazzo Muti on December 31, 1720. His home had been given by the Pope to his father, Prince James, who would be King James VIII, if he ever recovered the throne. Prince James was also known as the Pretender, because he was the son of the deposed and exiled King James VII of Scotland.

So to put it succinctly, Bonnie Prince Charles, was Italian born, spoke no Gaelic, had never been to Scotland, owned no home, and lived on the charity of the Pope. Still, he was to lead the Scots to reclaim the throne for James VIII, who had fled Scotland after an abortive attempt to lead the Rising against the English. This certainly was not an inspiring start.

Perhaps, it was fitting that Charles was born in a home given by Pope Clement XI, for he would become the last great hope of the Scot Catholics. Perhaps, it was fitting that Charles was born on December 31st, for again he would become the last great hope of the Scot Catholics... The last of his kind, at the end of an era. Perhaps, it was fitting that he was named grandly and almost pompously, Charles Edward Louis John Casimir Sylvester Severino Maria Stuart, which combined the Scot last name of Stuart with what would be the important countries of his life, Italy and France. Finally, perhaps it was fitting that he was born in Italy, for it filled him with dreams of martial glory like the Romans.

Bonnie Prince Charles was a tall, young man. Everyone described him as handsome, probably due to his fair complexion and his small regal nose. He was always immaculately groomed and dressed; some would say that he was vain. Although he adopted the kilt well after arriving in Scotland, he is always remembered in his kilt, with a tartan short coat without the plaid, and a dashing blue bonnet upon his head, his chest bearing the magnificent Star of St. Andrew. He wore a white periwig, but brushed his brown hair forward around his the sides of the periwig. His most impressive characteristics were how charming, charismatic, energetic, and brave he was. Nonetheless, he was saddled with the nickname, the Young Pretender, which faintly echoed of the taint borne by his father.

As the Young Pretender, he had a destiny to fulfil, whether or not he chose to do so. His parents felt deeply and painfully that what had been taken from them by an ungrateful people through a thankless parliament was their birthright. It was their gift from God. Further, they felt that no man had the power to take it from them, ever, under any conditions, or under any circumstances. They were God's chosen ones. They were God's anointed ones to rule. They knew it, much like the Romans knew from the gods that they were to conquer the world to bring civilization to all men.

His mother, Princess Clementina Maria Sobieski of Poland, being the granddaughter of John III Sobieski, the victor over the Ottoman Turks at the Battle of Vienna, felt that her lineage, alone, that is being the granddaughter of John III Sobieski, was more than enough reason (assuming that she needed a reason, which in her mind she did not) for her to be entitled to the throne and for the Parliament to have been wrong to cast aside her husband's claims. She was one of the wealthiest women in Europe and she longed suspected that it was her wealth, and not her beauty, that had attracted James Francis Stuart, the so-called the Old Pretender. But she spoke this not, for she had her reasons. Through him, she would rule a nation. This meant that she would be a queen, something she would never be in her native Poland. But she would not be just any queen and not just queen of Scotland. Because Scotland was part of the Union, she would be queen of the United Kingdom, which is both Scotland and England, the most powerful nation in the world. She liked that: queen of the most power country in the world. And she liked this more: her weak husband would accede to her every wish. "Grandfather would be pleased," she thought.

Charles' father, of course, agreed with his wife that he should be king, but they agreed on little else. Charles' parents argued constantly about everything, except that they should be upon the throne. They staunchly believed that they were the legitimate heirs. They also agreed on one thing more: Parliament could not remove a king, for they also staunchly believed in the Divine Right of Kings. Finally, they agreed on one thing more: that a Catholic, not a Protestant, should be on the throne of Scotland. The constant fighting between father and mother only served to heighten the combative and morose nature of Charles' father.

As Prince James aged and Charles grew in stature, James began to be called (not to his face of course!) the Old Pretender. Charles gained the name of the Young Pretender.

The Old Pretender had not been of any help to restore the waning fortunes of the Stuart claim in 1715. He had landed in Scotland some months after the Lord of Mar had bungled his military campaign to reclaim Scotland for the Stuart dynasty. When James did land, it was mid-winter; the Highland clans had gone home for the winter. Everyone knew that no one conducted a military campaign in the winter, except perhaps the Old Pretender. Further, he landed alone, without any of the promised French aid. It certainly could not come as a surprise when no one rallied to him after Lord of Mar's defeat. After a drek and dismal winter, the Old Pretender, his tail between his legs, had sailed to back France, leaving Scotland. He never returned to Scotland.

The Old Pretender's failure made him only the more morose and combative. Further, it left his son with a legacy of failure and with a taint of dishonor.

Prince Charles' earliest memories were of the ongoing arguments of his parents, which always had the same theme.

"If only...I am sick of your insipid lamentations over 'if only'!" This was his mother's battle cry.

"But… if only the Act of Settlement had not been passed…" The Old Pretender's voice died away under the withering look of his ill-disposed wife.

"If only the Act of Settlement! You fool! That is like saying if only God had not made the seas, we would not have had a flood!" She glared at her husband, Medusa-like, hoping against hope that her stare alone would silence him.

"Yes…if only Parliament had not decreed that the crown would pass to the heathen Protestant heirs of the Electress of Hanover!" He begged his wife to listen to him.

"You are merely stating the obvious, husband! Tell me something new! Give me a plan to get us back on the throne! Say something that will inspire me! Well! Do it!" She challenged him.

"I am supposed to be a Queen-a Queen reigning over the United Kingdom. And where is my realm? It's this filthy, little apartment in an off-the-beaten-track of Rome. And it is rented for us! We own nothing! Where are my palaces? Where are my jewels? Where are my ladies in waiting? Where are my parties? My balls? The fine dinners? Courtiers standing around our court? Where? Where? I don't see them!" Waving her hand as if playing to a crowd of thousands, she surveyed her non-existent domain. Her practiced look of disdain, of cynical, critical, demeaning, disdain was showered upon her cowering husband.

"Well…if only…if…well…" he sputtered.

"I see." She tossed her head and sighed. Her manner revealed her complete indifference to what he was trying to explain. "I've heard it all before." She wheeled on her heel and left the room, the crinkling of her dress' voluminous bulk drowning his further protestations.

The Old Pretender was not up to the challenge and he knew it. Something had gone out of him in 1715 and he never re-captured it.

Charles grew up not in Scotland, but in Rome and Bologna. He grew up not knowing the Highlands. He grew up not knowing the smell of peat burning, the dampness of the moors, the burning taste of whiskey from the still, the feel of a kilt's wool, the weight of a caber, the sound of sheep bleating, or the sound of the bagpipes. He grew up not knowing the people he was to rule. His childhood was one of wealth, pleasure, privilege, and distance from Scotland. Like most English, to him, the land of Scotland was a cold, craggy, barren, unpleasant, rocky region, swept by winds and suffering the worst weather, populated by almost barbarian Highlanders, speaking a tongue unrefined and obscure, and their shaggy cows.

He knew not the fierce Highlanders who had passionate loyalty to clan and kin, who loved their ancestors, bathed themselves in epic sagas of feuds held, battles won, cattle reaving raids embarked, bagpipe music unique to their clan or family, called pibrochs, played in tribute to heroes long-dead, but surely not forgotten.

Still his parents groomed him, best as they could, to be the rebel leader of the Scots against the English, to be the champion of Catholicism against the heresy of Protestantism, and to be the paragon of the family Stuart. Bonnie Prince Charles would right the wrongs against the Stuart clan and would restore the rightful Stuarts to the throne regaining the lost and denied glory. All that had gone wrong would be made a right.

But his childhood was still one that prepared him for his role. He dreamed of Scotland. He read voraciously every military book upon which he could lay his hands. He exercised daily and practiced with weapons. Whatever was a deficiency in his father, he wanted to transform in himself and make it strength. He would not go to Scotland in the winter. He would have French aid. He would confer with the chiefs of the clans in advance and line up the chieftains on his side. He tended to each detail.

Part II: A Knight's Tale

Heere bigynneth the Knyghtes
Tale.-**Chaucer**

Cavaliere Angelo Giovanni Vincenzo Piccolomoni was not a handsome man. He was short with swarthy skin, a large aquiline nose, and black curly hair. He liked to think of himself as being a little rotund, but most people would describe him as being portly. Although he had the title of "Cavaliere" which means Knight, he had no money and he had no real training in any profession. He'd gotten on in life by being a pleasant man who did not make waves. He was the type of man whom women ignored, never giving him a second look. That was unfortunate, because he was a good conversationalist and had a pleasant smile.

For some time, Cavaliere Angelo Giovanni Vincenzo Piccolomoni had been acting as the personal secretary, as he was now styling himself, for he was really only a low-level clerk for a merchant, a merchant he rarely saw. Recently, the merchant told him that his business was bad and he would have to let Cavaliere Piccolomoni go. Cavaliere Piccolomoni, as was the case with many members of minor noble families in Italy, had fallen upon hard times. You had to have a patron to rebuild your family's position and wealth. Cavaliere Piccolomoni then attached himself to James VIII. How that came about warrants repeating here.

Cavaliere Piccolomoni had a cousin who was a priest. This cousin, Alessandro, had been a boyhood friend of the man who became Pope Benedict XIV on August 17, 1740. His cousin was now the personal secretary (a real personal secretary-one with power and authority) to Pope Benedict. Of course, as personal secretary, Father Alessandro had the ear of Pope Benedict and, as a boyhood friend, had his confidence also.

Benedict faced being Pope at a time when the world, or at least a good part of it was at war. Spain and France were at War with England over the Austrian Succession, which was the question of Maria Theresa's succession to the realms of the House of Hapsburg. There were those who argued that Maria Theresa, as a mere woman, could not inherit her father's throne under Salic Law. Prussia was behind this maneuver, aided and abetted by France. England, joined by the Dutch Republic, both of which were the traditional enemies of France, took the opposite stance. The nations of Europe lined up one side against the other, with the Electorate of Bavaria with France and Prussia, and the Kingdom of Sardinia and the Electorate of Saxony with England. Spain, who had been at war with England since the prior year of 1739, ostensibly over colonies, slaves, and trade, became involved due to her alliance with France and the unity of the Bourbon monarchies. King George was at war not only with France and Spain, and their allies in Europe, but also was facing the threat of the French and the Indians in North America.

Benedict saw this nearly world war as a grave threat to his Catholic Church and to his Papacy. In just a very short time, he came to heavily rely upon his childhood friend.

It was then that Cavaliere Piccolomoni, nearly impoverished, asked his cousin for help. "Alessandro, isn't there something the Pope could do for me? Won't you ask your old friend to help me? Isn't there something I can do to aid the Church? Does the Pope need a courier or something?" Piccolomoni looked up to his cousin with his large brown puppy dog eyes. Father Alessandro could only feel pity for the man who was begging him for help.

A priest, who was at the same time a relative, found it hard to turn his back upon a person in need, especially, when that person is both a relative and a man promising that a portion of the salary of his new position would find its way back to Father Alessandro's hand. This same priest knew that, while he could think of nothing at the moment poor Piccolomoni could do, it was wise to file away in his mind this poor relative for some future use by the Pope.

It was sometime later that Father Alessandro arranged for a Papal visit for Piccolomoni. Something had come up. The Pope had been furnishing an apartment to the Old Pretender. With the war heating up, France had floated a trial balloon that maybe, just maybe, the Old Pretender or his son could start a rebellion in Scotland and thereby divert troops away from the battlefields on the continent where English troops were confronting (and winning against) French troops.

Pope Benedict, somewhat to Alessandro's surprise, found Piccolomoni, as intelligent and as obliging as Alessandro said.

"This is a grave time for the Papacy, my son," Benedict said as Piccolomoni, as a supplicant, knelt before him. "There are forces at work that are trying to destroy the mother Catholic Church."

"Yes, Holy Father. Is there something I can do to aid your Holiness?" Piccolomoni asked his eyes wide and expectant, not knowing where the question would lead.

"What skills have you? Father Alessandro says you have a fair hand, that you speak several languages, that you are discreet, and that, above all, you are devout. Is this all true?"

Piccolomoni knew this was the moment not to hold back with false or even real modesty. "Yes, Holy Father. I can converse in French, Spanish…" Piccolomoni was hoping for an assignment, an easy assignment, with the French, whose food was so good, but, of course, not the equal of Italian food, or with the Spanish, whose wine was so good, but, of course, not the equal of Italian wine. In life, there are times when you do something that you can't explain and you know as you do it that you are doing the wrong thing, but still your mouth continues to speak long, long, long after it should have ceased speaking. "…and English…Holy Father."

Benedict's eyes twinkled and brightened. "I have something for you, something very important, something very necessary for the Church. You will be the personal secretary to a King."

Piccolomoni was overjoyed. 'Secretary to King,' he whispered to himself. 'How could I have ever dreamed to aspire to such a lofty position?' Visions of wonderful foods spread before him, wines ever flowing like fountains, and soft cushions of rich silk upon which to rest his head. It was all coming true. "Oh, Your Holiness, thank you. How can I ever thank you?"

"My son, you will be my insight into the royal court and you will report back to Father Alessandro all that you hear, all that you write, and all that is in the correspondence your liege will receive. I must know all. I may also call upon you to support certain propositions I might make to your King. Do you understand? Do you swear by all that is Holy that you will carry out this sacred mission for the Mother Church?"

Visions were still dancing in his head, visions that included wealth and riches flowing from a king to him, and he heard himself utter, "Yes, Your Holiness" as if he, Piccolomoni, were someone else and someone far distant. "When do I begin?"

"Don't you even want to know with whom I will place you?" Benedict was rising from his chair signaling that the audience was over.

"Yes, Holy Father."

"Father Alessandro will give you the details." Pope Benedict XIV extended his hand and Piccolomoni kissed his ring.

When the Pope had left the room, Father Alessandro spoke. "You will be King James VIII personal secretary. I will provide you with a Papal Letter of Introduction. You will be a gift from the Holy Father to King James VIII of Scotland."

It was then that Piccolomoni's visions of wealth, food, wine, flowers abounding, splashing fountains, and rich silk and velvet pillows came crashing down. Everyone knew that King James VIII was broke.

Part III: Pact with the Devil

> For what shall it profit a man, if he
> shall gaine the whole world, and lose
> his owne soule? – **Mark 8:36**

Elsewhere in Rome, Lady Frances Townsend Foster was alighting from a carriage. She was a young woman of 20 and was in Rome with her brother, Robert Markham Foster, the Baronet of Werrington in Staffordshire. She was an extremely beautiful woman with a peaches and cream complexion. She had light brown freckles and long flowing blonde hair which set off her blue eyes. She wore the latest Paris fashion, whose low-cut dresses revealed her ample curves. While she appeared to be demure, there was a little sparkle to her eyes that said something slightly different. Inwardly, she was quite aware of the effect that she had upon men and used it carefully to get what she wanted. Although she proclaimed to one and all that she was in Rome to view the art and learn about the Renaissance, she and her brother, the Baronet, were there on a mission from King George II: get as close as possible to the Old Pretender and find out his plans.

Lady Foster had come to the attention of King George II, as most women had come to the attention of King George II. His roving eye had darted from young female to young female in his court and came to rest upon her ample bosom. Later, after a strenuous bout of lovemaking, he came to realize that she was extremely quick witted, as well as being completely loyal to him.

"Your Majesty," she purred into his ear, "I could be of great use to you, if I were to be sent to either Paris or Rome." She batted her eyes and continued, "I have a way with men. They like to tell me things. Intimate things, indiscrete things, and, certainly, inappropriate things." She got up slowly from the bed making sure that the King could not miss seeing her voluptuous derrière. She stopped and turned her head around, while she slightly turned her body such that the side of her bosom was also able to be viewed by the King. "I can make any man love me and I can make any man tell me what you might want to know."

Without taking his eyes off of her Venus-like form, he thoughtfully cradled his chin with his left hand. "And what do you propose?"

"Why it is simple! I shall become your spy and you shall reward me handsomely. You shall shower a title upon my brother and give him an estate."

"Do you have an estate in mind?" asked the breathless King.

She laughed. She tossed her long blonde hair with her right hand, turned around, and smiled at him. Her entire body was his to visually drink in. "There is a vacant baronetcy in Werrington in Staffordshire. That will do nicely." She bent down and started to pick up her clothes, while her hands modestly began covering her body.

Gesturing to her not to clothe herself, the King was convinced. "As you ask, so shall it be done."

Part IV: A Mole in the Garden

> "In shallow holes, moles make
> fools of dragons"- **Old Proverb**

It was a few days later. Father Alessandro had arranged the meeting with King James. Cavaliere Piccolomoni was in his finest clothes. (He had spent the night before with needle and thread in hand stitching a split seam there and a small little hole here.) They walked briskly from the Basilica di San Pietro across St. Peter's Square. The fact that it was the world's largest Basilica and was built by the finest architects including Michelangelo, was a source of pride for every Italian. Of course it was a most holy place, because the body of St. Peter was buried beneath the Basilica. As they walked across St. Peter's Square, they both looked up at the windows of the Papal apartment, although both knew that there would be nothing to see.

"You, Cavaliere, are one of only a select few who has ever been through the Bronze Door." Father Alessandro said pointing to where three Swiss Guards, in their hugely colorful and flamboyant uniforms with their long swords and giant halberds, stood standing by the massive and tall door. This door led to the steps of the Scala RegiaScala Regia, designed by Bernini, and then to the Papal apartments.

Piccolomoni felt a surge of pride at these words. "To think, I am one of the few, the select, to have visited the Pope's apartments." He smiled.

They fell into an easy step which then became a marching cadence as they walked down the Via della Conciliazone. Near the end of it, they passed the Church of Santa Maria in Transpontina, a Carmelite Church. It was said that this was the site of an Egyptian pyramid, which Pope Alexander VI demolished. This pyramid was called Meta Romuli and it marked the northwestern most boundary of ancient Rome. This Meta Romuli was thought to be the tomb of Romulus. The Church was later demolished in order to create a clear line of fire for the cannon of Castel de Sant'Angelo. In time, the church was re-built, but in a manner such that it was below the line of fire, and, thus, its dome is fore-shortened.

They continued on past the arches of the Passetto de Borgo, the secret passageway from the Papal apartments to the Castel Sant'Angelo. They did not reflect upon the irony that the Pope would flee from the Vatican to the Castel which was, in reality, a mausoleum built for the Emperor Hadrian in 139 AD. So to save one's self from death, one had to venture into a mausoleum!

The Castel was an immense and imposing round structure surrounded by a crenelated wall. The wall was flanked on either side by square towers which reached only two more stories in height over the wall, and thus, looked squat and mis-shapened. From their heights, Papal flags flew straight out to the side in the strong wind. The flag was two squares side by side. The first square was bright yellow which flared like a flame against the cloudless blue sky, while the white one held the image of the Papal coat of arms, the crossed-keys of St. Peter overlaid upon the Papal tiara, called the triregnum, which is three crowns in one, replete with Christian symbolism.

"So how did the Castel become a sacred site for Christians?" Piccolomoni asked Father Alessandro as they turned off the Via della Conciliazone to take the bridge across the Tiber River.

"In 509 A.D., the most marvelous miracle occurred here," enthused Father Alessandro. "The Black Plague was decimating the city. The dead were so many that the living could not bury them. The stench of death reeked throughout all the streets of Rome. It appeared that there would never be an end to this scourge of death. Men and women threw their hands up to the heavens despairing of their fate and losing their faith in God. It was a true crisis! It was then that a black angel appeared at the top of the Castel. Its sword was drawn and was pointing to the heavens. The dark grey and black clouds swirling and twisting in evil forms suddenly parted and a shaft of brilliant sunlight shone upon the Angel. The Angel's sword glistened in the brilliant sunlight. Next, the Angel slowly and deliberately sheathed her sword. With that, every citizen of Rome knew that the Black Plague was over! God had heard our prayers and had answered them! Glory be to God!"

The Romans in ancient times had built a bridge in front of the Castel to connect it with the rest of Rome. That bridge had long been destroyed. They now walked across an open bridge which had beautiful statues of Angels. "Bernini celebrated that miracle in this beautiful bridge which he built." Father Alessandro waved his hand in a gesture of beholding the beautiful statues.

After crossing the bridge, they took the Via di Panico which cut at an angle to reach the Via dei Coronari. It had gained its name, Coronari, from all the shops along the sides that sold Rosaries to pilgrims who journeyed to St. Peter's Basilica. The homes along the sides of the street were ancient, but beautiful and fashionable. It was in one of those houses that James had set up his royal chambers.

Cavaliere Piccolomoni had bowed grandly when he was introduced to the King in exile. "Your Majesty, I am your servant. I would be glad to be at your service."

James waved his hand in a flourish towards a chair. "Please, sit."

Piccolomoni did as he was asked. "It is an honor and a privilege to meet you, your Majesty."

"Tell me about yourself and your qualifications," the King looked directly into the eyes of Piccolomoni, as if he could read the young man's soul.

"Well, I read, write, and speak English, as well as French, Spanish, and Latin. I am discreet and trustworthy." Father Alessandro smiled as his protégé parroted his words perfectly.

"I see. Have you ever served as a personal secretary before?" King James looked severely at Piccolomoni.

Piccolomoni, his coaching by Father Alessandro having covered this eventuality, smiled at the King and said, "Why, of course, I served Cardinal Marcellino Corio until his untimely death last February 20th." Again, Father Alessandro smiled as his protégé spoke. "It would be an honor and a privilege to serve the greatest of all Catholic Majesties." Father Alessandro could not have been happier with Piccolomoni's performance for Piccolomoni had lied convincingly: Piccolomoni had not served with Cardinal Corio, but that lie could not be found out now. Father Alessandro was much more confident in his choice of Piccolomoni and inwardly could not be more satisfied.

James, who had just finished another argument with his wife, was somehow flattered by Piccolomoni's blandest of compliments. "You are a gift from the Holy Father. And I have been assured that you are discreet and honest. You shall begin immediately." With that, King James, the Old Pretender, got up from his chair and waved off both priest and newly appointed secretary.

Father Alessandro and Cavaliere Piccolomoni were leaving the chambers of King James VIII. Father Alessandro whispered in Piccolomoni's ear. "Remember that you are serving the Holy Father. You loyalty lies with the Church. Don't get too infatuated with your royals!"

Piccolomoni bowed his head to signal his agreement. Although he had misgivings about his new position, Piccolomoni knew that his cousin had done all he could for him. "I am truly appreciative of all that you have done for me. Thank you Father."

Part V: Doors Opened and Closed

> "Never open the door to a lesser evil, for other and greater ones invariably slink in after it."
> — **Baltasar Gracián (The Art of Worldly Wisdom)**

Now months later, Lady Foster and her brother were in Rome. Although she was a dutiful sister, she was not the dutiful sister of a newly made Baronet, for the Baronetcy had not yet been publicly made known. To date, they had tried unsuccessfully to obtain an audience with Pope Benedict. It might have been the fact that they were Protestants or it might have been the fact that they were suspected of being messengers on behalf of a Protestant King; nevertheless, the Vatican doors had not yet been opened to them.

Although they had dropped hints as to their proclivity to support the Jacobite Cause, the doors to James VIII had not yet been opened so far.

Finally, the doors to polite society, that is English Society abroad in Rome, had not opened to them either. The rumors of Lady Foster bedding the husbands of the aristocracy had arrived in Rome afore her and the rumors of her support for the Jacobite Cause only further alienated her from society.

The first door not opening was a real obstacle to be overcome, but overcome it would be. The second door she was sure would open to her, once the Old Pretender learned that the third door was closed to her.

Lady Foster was doing some shopping for new clothes and accessories. Now, she went to a store which was considered the finest milliner in all of Rome. Sometimes in life, chance or fortune or serendipity takes control of events and what you most earnestly hope for happens, just not in a way that you thought it would. In the same store at the same time was Princess Clementina Maria Sobieski with several of her ladies in waiting. The proprietor of the store, Giovanni Scala Michelangelo Rotini, and his daughter, Maria, were waiting upon the Princess. Lady Foster did not immediately recognize the Princess.

"My dear, Princess, this gown would look exceedingly lovely upon you and I have dresses for your ladies in waiting which would complement yours." Giovanni Scala Michelangelo Rotini, known to all as Michelangelo, bowed as low as he possibly could while spreading his hands into wide arcs to his sides, being as obsequious and as ingratiating as he possibly could be. At this, the pretty ears of Lady Foster perked up. The ladies in waiting were giggling and making silly jokes with one another, partly in English and partly in Polish, thinking that no one would understand them. They all seemed to deal with the fact that Michelangelo Rontini was quite rotund and they punned upon his name and his girth. With that, Lady Foster had a hunch that the Princess was the Princess Clementina Maria Sobieski, the wife of the Old Pretender.

She walked over to the Princess and curtsied deeply. In her finest French, Lady Foster began: "My dear Princess, if I may be so bold and forward, I am Lady Foster. I know that you do not know me, but like you,

I am in exile in Rome, because of the evil King George II. Unfortunately, someone betrayed me and my brother to the King and he learned of our Jacobite leanings. I stand before you only to give you my support and my love." All the while that she was saying this, Lady Foster had kept her eyes subserviently looking at the ground slightly in front of her forward foot. She was awaiting an order from the Princess before she made eye contact.

The Princess, extremely impressed with the beautiful French, which was spoken by a woman who was clearly English, let down her guard. "Ma chère," she began in French and then switched to English, "I thank you for your support and your love. It has been quite hard for me and for my husband, James, to be happy in this strange land. We only wish that we could be back in Scotland. Perhaps, with your support and love, that may yet still happen. Please look up."

Lady Foster slowly tilted her head up to look at the Princess. She batted her eyelashes to draw attention to her flashing blue eyes. "Thank you, Your Grace. I shall tell my brother of your words. I only wish that he could have met you also."

"Well, I, too, would have liked to have met your brother. I am having a soirée and would like to invite you both to come. I will send a footman to you bearing an invitation, if you will but give me your address," offered the Princess.

Part VI: Beauty and the Beast

> Remember that there are two kinds of beauty: one of the soul and the other of the body. That of the soul displays its radiance in intelligence, in chastity, in good conduct, in generosity, and in good breeding, and all these qualities may exist in an ugly man. And when we focus our attention upon that beauty, not upon the physical, love generally arises with great violence and intensity. – *Miguel de Cervantes*

The soiree was most elegant and clearly cost more than King James VIII could afford to pay, but he denied his wife nothing, feeling that he had much to atone for. Their exile was his fault and he knew that she knew it.

Lady and Lord Foster arrived promptly, breaking the social convention that seemed to demand that the most important people arrived late. Lady Foster had talked her brother into it believing that this might be their opportunity, their only opportunity, to get so close to James VIII and she wanted to make the most of it.

They were greeted immediately. "Cavaliere Angelo Giovanni Vincenzo Piccolomoni, at your service. I am the personal secretary to his Majesty James VIII of Scotland." Piccolomoni bowed deeply to Lady Foster. As he did, his eyes danced across her ample bosom and perhaps lingered a moment too long for polite society. She, on the other hand, immediately noticed his large nose, his shortness, and his lack of physical beauty. She noticed, but was so practiced in the art of seduction that she did not betray a hint of this with her looks or her voice.

"My dear Cavaliere, I am so pleased to meet you." Her voice was as mellifluous as the sweetest honey. She fluttered her eyelids, which only called attention to the softest pools of Tyrennian blues, Piccolomoni had ever seen. He was already in love, or at least, deeply in lust.

She gazed upon him: truly he was not a handsome man. He was too short, too dark, had a large and bulbous nose, and oily black hair. Not the sort of man she would choose for herself to be a lover, but sometimes, as now, the choice was made for her. From the moment he had said that he was the King's personal secretary, she had determined to seduce him and bed him, which meant she would make him a slave to her beauty and her sexuality.

Part VII: On Becoming Indispensable

> To be without some of the things you want is an indispensable part of happiness.-**Proverb**

It had been a fortnight since the soiree. Lady Foster had become a fixture in the presence of the Queen, as Lady Foster had taken to calling her, to ingratiate herself with the Queen even more. She paid especial attention to the Queen's ladies in waiting, giving them little gifts each time she visited, so that with time they all came to like her and enjoy her company. In short, Lady Foster became indispensable in the House of King James. She played whist so well; she gambled excessively, and more to the Queen's liking, Lady Foster lost large amounts of money to the Queen, and lost them gracefully. The Queen began to believe that she might be able to finance the Rising herself just from her winnings from this one English lady. She welcomed Lady Foster into her group. And as they played, because it was forbidden to talk about the cards or the play, they talked about other things. It was these other things that Lady Foster listened to most carefully, hoping for a nugget or two. It was worth it to lose money to gain the confidence of the Queen, because as the days passed, the Queen said more and more of what she should have said less and less.

Lady Foster also did all she could to encourage the attention of "Piccolo" as she endearingly called him. It did not take much to excite his attention. A whisper here, a shy fluttering of the eyes there, a quick look over a shoulder, a note passed by a lady in waiting: all the tricks of the book were used in the 'war' to gain his heart, his interest, and his confidence. And day by day, Lady Foster gained more and more access to Piccolo and to the Queen.

Piccolo became ever more entranced with Lady Foster. He was almost at the point of screwing up his courage to suggest a liaison. Meanwhile, Lady Foster was growing exceedingly impatient. She wanted the affair to become full blown; she knew she could ensnare him, if only she could bed him. But he seemed too shy and too unsure of himself. She was practiced enough to also know that if she moved too fast, if she fanned his ardor too quickly, the dreamy illusion of their relationship might yield before the sunlight of day. He might ask questions, such as: "Why would the most beautiful of women lower herself to consort with an ugly man like me?" And in the 'why' would come doubt, and with doubt, would come self-reflection and introspection, and with self-reflection and introspection would come realization that she wanted him for some ulterior purpose.

In casting around for that ulterior purpose, he might hit upon the real reason, he might not; but he would be concentrating on things other than the affair and he might then pull back.

Piccolomoni saw Father Alessandro each Tuesday at 4:00pm. They met in a small café which was non-descript in all manners that a café can be non-descript: food, beverage, clientele, bar tender, bar maids, furniture, location, and, most importantly of all, cleanliness. In short, it had nothing to recommend it and much to discourage patrons from frequenting it. Thus, for Father Alessandro, it was perfect. He would see no one there and no one would see Father Alessandro as he met with Piccolomoni.

"Well, what have you to tell me?" Father Alessandro roughly inquired. He was tired. The day was hot. Nothing had gone well today. He had a headache. The wine was bad and the food was worse.

"King James still is casting about for funding for his Rising. He has recently become acquainted with Aeneas MacDonald, a banker from Paris, who has banking friends and contacts that have agreed to raise funds for the venture," Piccolomoni confided.

"He has not really assembled a team of experts to assist him. He has met a few military men, but they are not apparently of the highest quality. A French cavalryman or two." Piccolomoni continued. He quaffed his wine and looked imploringly at Father Alessandro.

"I see." Father Alessandro motioned the bar maid over. "Another wine for him. A brandy, a good brandy, for me." He looked up at the bar maid, ignoring hers breasts that almost flopped out of her blouse, with a stern look in his eyes. It was as if to say that it had better be good or he would have her flogged. She shuddered when she realized the seriousness of his look. She hurried off. Then whispered female and hushed male voices were heard emanating from behind the bar.

"Anything else?" Father Alessandro asked, not really expecting anything, but making the effort so his report to the Holy Father would be complete.

"Uh, one thing. I do not know what to make of it…There is this woman…An English lady… She met the Queen in a milliner's shop…she loses a lot of money in cards…She is now close to the Queen…" His voice trailed off. Father Alessandro had been watching where the bar maid had gone, hoping to see her return quickly with his brandy. He was paying little attention until the words seeped in "English", "lots of money", and "close to the Queen." He quickly turned around and looked squarely at Piccolomoni. "Who? What? When?" He spit the words out.

"Lady Foster, she is a Jacobite. She met the Queen quite recently and now is the Queen's favorite. But there is something about her…" He trailed off again. Piccolomoni instinctively knew he should not tell Father Alessandro that he was bewitched by her and wanted to bed her. Not because Father Alessandro was a priest, but because he sensed that Father Alessandro would somehow someway ruin his relationship with her. He thought now that he should not have even mentioned her. 'What if he orders me not to make love to her?' He panicked with the thought.

"Get to know her and know her well. Do anything you can to get close to her. Make sure she is what she says she is. Do anything. Do you understand?" Father Alessandro demanded of him.

"I will," Piccolomoni weakly answered. Inwardly he smiled. 'Anything includes bedding her. Of course, only to get information for the Holy See.' He laughed to himself, but hid it by drinking his wine. "Yes, Father." He said aloud.

Part VIII: Dangerous Liaisons

> "Don't marry for money,
> you can borrow it cheaper."
> **—Scottish Proverb**

Piccolomoni spent the next several days arranging everything for a liaison. He had rented a magnificent palace for the affair; he had obtained discreet servants, the best wines, delicate meats, fruits, and even some caviar. All had to be perfect. He had written the invitation and had awaited her answer.

Hours later, a note in the finest feminine hand arrived. He broke the wax seal and opened it. He saw one word-amor-and clasped the note to his heart. His prayers had been answered. She was coming. He was in love. He was thrilled that love and duty had coincided.

Chapter 12

Bliaðhna Theàrlaich (Charles' Year)

'Will ye no come back again?' – **Scottish Lament after Charles Edward Stuart returned to France following the failure of the 1745 uprising.**

Part I: King James VII Has "Forfaulit the Croun'

How had this sad tale of the Stuarts begun? It had all begun with Bonnie Prince Charles' grandfather, James II of England and the VII of Scotland. For three brief years, he had ruled Scotland and England. His passion for Catholicism had driven him to try to bring Protestant England, kicking and screaming, back to the Catholic fold. He acted as a despot, a divine right despot. In following his passion to convert England to Catholicism, he had alienated his subjects in England and with them, his Parliament. Perhaps, it was he decision to appoint commissioners to exercise powers throughout his realm. Perhaps, it was his choice of commissioners. Perhaps, it was his decision to delegate viceregal powers to his commissioners. Wherever the fault lay, his commissioners relentlessly embarked upon a ruthless and barbarous persecution of a Protestant sect known as the Covenanters. Many died. His reign became known as the "Killing Times".

Parliament, driven to distraction, had invited James' daughter, Princess Mary and her husband, the Dutch Protestant, William II, the Prince of Orange to jointly rule over Scotland and England. They had accepted. How could they not? Of course, this is the way the story got reported in the history books. The true story behind these events is more convoluted and complex. Certain members of Parliament invited William of Orange to invade England. In one of life's ironies, after William's successful invasion of England in 1688, William, who was not the king and was not even in any position of authority in England, had convened Parliament in an irregular manner. Once convened, William and Mary then requested Parliament to ask them, William and Mary, to jointly rule over the combined Kingdoms, to which Parliament quickly acquiesced. James could not believe that his daughter and his son-in-law, who was also his nephew and, thus, Mary's cousin too, could repudiate him and could manipulate the circumstances so. This complex and convoluted situation which involved disputes over religion, strained familial relations, different views on the rights of monarchs and the rights of men, was beyond the understanding of James II of England and VII of Scotland. He was perplexed further when he learned that Parliament had taken this action of asking for the dual monarchy because he, James II, was deemed to "have fled the country" leaving it without a head.

Part II: Trapped in a Bygone Era

> They think it a most Sublime Virtue to pay a Servile and Abject Obedience to Commands of their Chieftains, altho' in opposition to their Sovereign, and the laws of the Kingdom…The Virtue next to this, in esteem amongst them, is the Love they bear to that particular Branch of which they are a part, and in a Second Degree to the whole Clan, or

Name, by assisting each other (rightly or wrongly) against any other Clan, with whom they are at Variance, and great Barbarities are often committed by One, to revenge the Quarrels of Another.-**British General Wade on the Scots**

Charles inherited his grandfather's tangled mess and also his father's failure to cut through that Gordian knot. The knot had become more tightly tied when England and Scotland signed the Articles of Union and became the United Kingdom of Great Britain. The fact that it was Queen Anne, the sister of Mary, that is another Stuart, who firmly tied the knot firmly binding Scotland to England forming the United Kingdom, only made it harder for James and his son, Charles to fathom.

Charles faced the almost impossible task that to win the war he had to win the hearts of his countrymen. This he could do only if he convinced them that his father had no intention to re-establish the arbitrary powers that had been exercised by his grandfather. He had to demonstrate that the Glorious Revolution had justly removed the arbitrary powers, but unjustly removed the man who exercised them. A Stuart restoration was remote, neigh impossible, if he could not convince adherents of the correctness of his cause. His father would be king, but would not be the king his grandfather had been.

The Cause was one of David versus Goliath. England was one of the world's great powers, if not the greatest power. The Highlanders alone could not beat England's military might. It would take more, much, much more. While the Highlanders were as rugged as the foreboding, almost forbidding mountains of northern Scotland, as raw, natural, and aloof, as was the isolation of the Highlands from the rest of the world, as sharp as the rocks that made up much of the rugged coasts and isles that seemed to resist exploration and economic exploitation, they were few in number. What courage they possessed made up some for their want of numbers, the fierceness of their weapons again made up some for the want of numbers. But what they lacked was a great deal, too. They lacked clothing, equipment, discipline, supplies, and most of all cannon, powder, and shot.

How could he, as an unknown young man, mend the ways of the Highlands? These clans were riven by feuds of generations in the making. Time and time again, one clan had raided another clan, stealing cattle, goats, sheep, and more. These raids were not forgotten nor were they forgiven. What one clan had done to another was as hallowed or enshrined as what that self-same-victim clan had done in retribution, so no evil done was ever forgotten and no vengeance ever taken was enough. They lived almost in the medieval past, perhaps barbaric to the modern eye of the seventeenth century. They were anachronistic throw backs in the age of Technology and Science known as the Enlightenment.

He needed the clans to fight for him. The clans were the building blocks of the military units he would need to raise an army. Each clan could contribute a regiment or two of Highlanders, retainers, septs, and if they were fifty thousand Highlanders of military age and bearing, he could expect an army of thirty thousand or so to rise up within the United Kingdom. This would dwarf the forces that the English had in Scotland which were about 2,500 men.

Part III: The Pretender Learns the Tools of His Trade

> "By failing to prepare, you are preparing to fail." – **Benjamin Franklin**

The upbringing of Charles by his parents did little to prepare him to be the leader of a nation, let alone a nation at war. It was up to Charles and he did his utmost to become prepared.

By age six, he could read English, French, and Latin. He loved music, as well as horseback riding. He was proficient with a gun, but he loved the cross-bow.

He grew up to be handsome, perhaps somewhat effeminate in his looks, the femininity of which was accentuated by his very high and squared forehead, which contrasted with his small triangular-shaped chin.

His brown eyes, which were piercing, were set beneath perfectly arched eyebrows. He always wore a white periwig.

His looks, however, belied a man with a mission, an all-consuming purpose: to be king. He knew from his earliest years he was born to rule. He knew too that to rule, he would have to fight. He read every book he could lay his hands upon about conducting war, warfare, military campaigns, and battle. He hunted and rode horseback extensively to harden his body and make him fit for war. He was determined and extremely self-disciplined.

"I will make myself as Spartan," he said to himself. "I will come home with this shield or upon it."

He did this in spite of his father's gloomy nature. While his father was called "old Melancholy", no one could but be but uplifted by Charles. He was too happy, confident, and sunny of disposition to ever let a melancholy thought flicker across his brain. He was born to lead and he knew it. His father's failure would not be his fate. He would not go to Scotland too late. 'If I get my chance, no when I get my chance, and I know that I will get my chance, I will not fail. I will be there in Scotland to kindle the flame,' he thought.

"I'll be there from the first. I will not hang back and let others do what I should do," he vowed.

It was at the siege of Gaeta in 1734 that he tasted the experience of war for the first time. He was thirteen, just short of fourteen. He went forward, far beyond what his advisors thought safe for a boy. He spent a day in the trenches observing and being under artillery fire. The war was one of those obscure wars about the Polish Succession with the Hapsburgs under siege by the armies of the Bourbons under the Duke of Parma. The politics of the war did not matter to him; what mattered was to see what war was really like; to watch the arc of the cannon fire; to see how the men stood the test of battle; how they stood up under fire; how they made themselves ready to go forward into the hail of musket balls, grape and canister. The boy did not waver; he was not frightened. He went as far forward as he could, until the troops would not let him go any further for fear that he would get hurt. They had to restrain him, even though they knew touching the young king to be was forbidden and punishable.

Living in Rome was living in the land of intrigue, the world of the spy, the home of the rogue and the assassin. The Pope gave refuge to the King, thrilled to have a Catholic thorn which he could thrust into the English side whenever he wanted. The Pope could threaten Protestantism continually by just keeping King James VIII with but a minimum expenditure of funds. 'The cost of a King, his rich wife, and son was far less than that of maintaining an army, and far more effective,' the Pope reflected. So the King languished in Rome, his clouds of melancholy ever gathering, his wife ever harping, and his son ever dreaming.

Highland lords and chieftains visited the King in exile and brought news of the Highlands. "If but the King come to the highlands with money, lots of money, and French support, preferably French troops, then the Highlands would rise up," they told the King.

A frequent guest was Lord George Murray, who vowed support in return for command of the King's army. That he was a capable soldier, no one doubted. That he was a gifted commander, he assured the King he was. His service to King George of Hanover had been exemplary, but still it was disconcerting, for it was service to King George, the enemy. Could Lord George Murray be trusted?

So too, word came that Ranald Chief of the MacDonalds of Clanranald might support King James. As Lord of the Isles and virtually sovereign of the Isle of Skye, Ranald wielded considerable influence, not only over his own clan, but also over much of the Highlands. With Ranald, success was not assured, but without him, failure was assured.

It became a waiting game. When would the moment be right? It would take the removal of the British forces from Scotland in general, but the Highlands in particular. It would take England at war on the Continent, with a power with a navy threatening invasion. It would take an ally willing to invest in the enterprise, not just gold, but troops, weapons, supplies, transport, and ships. It would take an ally who would support a Catholic King in Scotland and possibly over Great Britain. It would take a France. And not just France alone. Could Ireland too be enticed?

The Pope could whisper in the French ear, but the Pope knew that in this, the eighteenth century, the Pope was no longer a King maker. 'But who knew what might be accomplished by stealth and secret?' The Pope mused. 'The right Bishop or Cardinal could journey to Ireland and preach out loud the Gospel, while privately whispering the Pope's encouragement that Ireland help free Scotland from the Protestant yoke. But the whispers must be done quietly enough not to arouse English suspicion.' The musing continued and started to sort themselves into a plan. The whispers merely had to be done in the right ear and at the right time.

Part IV: Of Art and Artists

Spericus archetypum, globus hic monstrat macrocosmum. (This spherical ball shows the Macrocosmic archetype.)-**Inscription on the floor of Westminster Abbey.**

The Prince met Young Ranald, the son of Chief Ranald of the MacDonalds of Clanranald in a French restaurant. It was a chance meeting, or so Young Ranald thought. The Prince was not a man to leave things to chance, if he could. The Prince wanted to test the mettle of the son of the man most crucial to his enterprise.

They were the same age and soon found they were 'molto simpatico', as they say in Rome. They shared the same sense of humor. They shared the same love of fencing, shooting, and hunting, while being men who loved to read and think, but most of all they shared the same passion for a Scotland free of England, free of Protestantism, and free to have its Stuart line restored to the monarchy.

Young men, sharing the same passions, fed each other's souls and their words encouraged and re-enforced each other's belief, making uncertainty dance away as a wisp of fog is burned off by the morning sun.

"Your Majesty," young Ranald began, "I saw a painting in London once, which stirred my soul. I have never forgotten it."

Prince Charles leaned in to better hear. "Why did it inspire your soul?"

"Your Majesty, it was by a German Painter, Hans Holbein. Its subject was two young, wealthy men and is called 'The Ambassadors'".

The Prince started to look away. "Why should this interest me?"

"Because the painting is more than a portrait of two young men seemingly at the height of their power, wealth, and influence. Who they are is interesting, but barely scratches the surface of understanding this complex and complicated work of art, no, it is a masterpiece of art." Ranald caught his breath. "On the left is Jean de Dintville, the ambassador from Francis I of the France to Henry the Eighth. His mission was to try to avert war between France and England and to try to keep England in the Catholic fold. Henry, at the time of painting, was quarreling with the Pope over Henry's marriage to Anne Boleyn and was on the verge of establishing The Church of England."

Charles sipped his tea. It was clear that his interest had not yet been awakened. Ranald saw this and decided that he must enthuse the Prince with his passion.

"On the right is Georges de Selve, at the time of the painting, he is soon to be Bishop of Lavaur. Between them is a table. On the top of the table are instruments of science for things such as for measuring time, and determining the sunrise, globes, one of the earth and one of the heavens. This displays man's intellect and understanding. Below is a shelf upon which are among other things a lute and a hymnal of Martin Luther's hymns..."

"Why would Holbein include Martin Luther?" The Prince set down his tea cup down and stared at Ranald.

"The lute right above the hymnal has a broken string. Holbein is saying that Martin Luther has brought discord into the world and has upset the natural order. This concept is reinforced by the unusual skull in the painting. This skull can only be seen by one who is standing on the very right of the painting and perhaps from several steps above the painting. If one stands in front of the painting, it appears as an amorphous blob. It is not recognizable."

"A skull? Is the painting a vanitas?" The Prince asked as he brought his left hand to his mouth in awakening understanding.

"Yes, my Prince. The Vanity of Vanities is that all passeth away, all is illusion, and all is beyond the full understanding of man. What we strive for in life must be of real eternal value. What are these men striving for? All their science, education, and learning do not exempt them from death's icy grip. It is there right at their feet and they can barely see it for it too has a quality of illusion. It is distorted and does not seem to be what it really is, until you see if from an unusual angle and direction." Ranald let his words sink in.

"What then is the answer?" sighed the Prince. His eyes were as wide as those of a child asking his mother a question.

"The artist tells us in his painting. Hidden away, barely visible in the upper left corner is a crucifix. It is partly covered by a green curtain which is the backdrop for the entire painting. If you are again standing on the very right of the painting, it forms a perfect angle with the skull: the skull is as much below one's sight line as the crucifix is above. God is the answer. Faith in God is the answer. But it is the God of the Holy Mother Church, not the God of the heathen Protestants. Again, the lute's broken string is a sign that the music of Luther is discordant with God's will. You my Prince, must restore Catholicism to Scotland. That is your higher purpose. You must come to Scotland and free your people from the tyranny of England and the oppression of the Protestants."

It was days later that I met the Prince.

Part V: The Birth of Venus

> Do not let a flattering woman coax
> and wheedle you and deceive you; she
> is after your barn.-**Hesiod**

Lady Foster tossed her head to shake her hair off of her breasts. She glistened with sweat from love making. The silver moonlight of a full moon streamed in through the open windows, the silk curtains having been tied back so the air of the night could flow in. Piccolomoni gazed upon her naked form spell-bound and transfixed. She was more beautiful than any of the nudes in any of the paintings he had ever seen. Her breasts were full and round. Her stomach was flat. Her blonde hair against her milk white skin, which was covered with the perspiration of love-making, shone like a delicate dusting of a snowfall when no one has set foot upon it. She turned to make sure that he could see her full length, not being modest at all. Her pubic hair curled in little ringlets. She wanted him to drink her in; she wanted him to remember this night forever; she wanted to ensnare him once and for all. She would use every trick she had ever learned about the weakness of a man in the sight of a naked woman. She would make love to him until she had drained every drop of his vital fluid from him, knowing that to satisfy him as he had never been satisfied before would enslave him.

He began to talk. He wanted to impress her and so he started to talk of King James. She looked into his eyes dreamily as if she was utterly enthralled with his wisdom, his savoir faire, his masculinity, and his skills as a lover.

"James has gotten a banker, a one Aeneas MacDonald to help finance his Rising. As if that is ever going to happen! He believes the Pope will contribute also. That will never happen. But if nothing else, the Pope will command King Louis of France to lend his support. The Pope enjoys spending other monarch's money. Funny thing, Lord George Murray has become a regular in the Prince's circle, as has Young Ranald MacDonald, son of Hugh MacDonald, Chief of the Clanranald."

"Picco dear, you know how much affairs of state bore me. Tell me what the ladies were wearing." Lady Foster knew not to appear too eager. She could ask later anything she wanted, but it was best if she feigned a complete absence of interest in the subjects which were truly of most of interest to her.

Piccolomoni drank in her naked form. He wanted her to lie there on her side revealing her breasts, her pubis, and her thighs forever. He searched his mind for more to talk about. "Darling, you know that the only woman I notice is you," he lied. In actuality, like most men, the only thing about women's clothing he noted was where the dress left off and the skin began. The curves of the breast always drew his attention, but the color of the dress, the material, the cut or style, eluded him completely.

He turned over to get a better view of her. "I know you are a Jacobite." He said lazily.

"Yes, my knight, not in shining amour, but my naked knight." She cooed the words, urging him on.

"You maybe should take a greater interest in what is going on." He replied.

"Oh, if you really think I should..." her voice trailed off dreamily.

"James is about as morose a man as there could be. But his son, he is so dynamic. He could get the job done, if he only could get the chance." Piccolomoni made direct eye contact and began to lose himself in the pools of blue that were vibrant in the moonlight. A soft breeze blew the curtains apart and even more moonlight flooded in. The effect on her naked skin was dazzling. Lady Foster could not have planned it better herself.

"Tell me all about it…and when you are finished we will make love until you beg me not to move anymore…" she promised in the moonlight. Piccolomoni needed no more encouragement to unburden himself of everything he knew about the King, the Prince, their co-conspirators, the Queen, the Pope, and King Louis.

Part VI: A Letter

James was at his desk dictating to Piccolomoni, his personal secretary, who was writing furiously. In his mind the time was becoming right to try again to win back Scotland for the Stuarts. He knew his letter was grandly important. He was writing to the King of France. "Is this not the right time?" James waved his hand in the air to emphasize his question. Piccolomoni knew well enough by now not to answer his King's questions, but merely wrote on.

"A few ships, some equipment for 5,000 men, some of your finest infantry, 25 cannon, and 500,000 livres would suffice to convince the Highlands to Rise. We have obtained the support of some Paris bankers lead by Aeneas MacDonald. Pope Benedict has given his blessing to this mission as a holy crusade. If it would please your Grace, I would have my son, Prince Charles, who We have named our Regent as of December a year ago, proceed to Paris to assist in the final preparations. He and his band of men could leave any day now, for all is ready here." James stopped there. "You know Piccolomoni, make it all sound grander, and more diplomatic. Do your magic with words." His hand dismissively left it all to Piccolomoni, who was thinking only of bedding Lady Foster later that afternoon.

"I shall have a draft tomorrow morning, your Majesty."

Part VII: A Second Letter

It was later that next evening. Lady Foster had left the sleeping Piccolomoni and had bathed to get the "slime" as she called it of "that vulgar man" as she called him, off of her. She took pen in hand and wrote the message the British diplomat in Rome who would send her intelligence on to the Royal Navy. Her job was now done. Her counterpart in Paris would have to find out the exact day and time the Prince would sail, but for now, she had served her King and her country. She could feel the baronetcy being conferred.

Chapter 13

Ad Caledonia!

> But pleasures are like poppies spread;
> You seize the flower, its bloom is shed.
> Or like the snow falls in the river,
> A moment white--then melts forever.
> **- Robert Burns**

Part I: A Story of Two Ships

> Ships that pass in the night, and speak each other in passing, only a signal shown, and a distant voice in the darkness; So on the ocean of life, we pass and speak one another, only a look and a voice, then darkness again and a silence.-**Henry Wadsworth Longfellow**

We had left Paris in groups of ones, two, and three, all of us were disguised, We met up outside Paris near Aubergenville, which had nothing to recommend it and thus, having nothing to recommend it, made it just the perfect place to meet. The town was quite pretty, because around 70 years ago, in 1671, a great number of trees were planted in the park of the castle, including, birches, elms, wild cherry trees, chestnuts and 400 fir trees.

We were riding to St. Malo to meet Antoine Walsh, a famed privateer who had promised to provide a frigate to take the Prince and his entourage to Scotland.

The word privateer played over and over in my mind. I knew there was a difference between a pirate and privateer. I even explained the difference to Ranald. "Pirates are the scourge of the sea. They loot, steal, and commit rapine totally outside of the law. Privateering, on the other hand, was a distinguished practice," I drawled, "whereby a sovereign grants a commission and official recognition to private armed vessels to prey on enemy shipping." I knew though that many a privateer turned pirate after the war was over, because the lure of taking cargoes on the open seas was just too great and too lucrative. What would this Antoine Walsh look like? I began to imagine all sorts of possibilities. Visions of Edward Teach, the infamous Blackbeard, filled my mind. I was sure that Antoine Walsh would have a big, bushy, black beard, and would wear a tattered tricorn hat. The further we got from Paris and the nearer we got to St. Malo, the more maleficent my visions of Antoine Walsh grew.

The walls of St. Malo glistened in the morning sun of a perfect day in the province of Brittany in north-western France. She was a port that was tres belle, as the French would say, because her beautiful spires soared into the skies. The tallest one was that of the magnificent Cathedral. The sky was a gorgeous shade of robin's egg shell blue. It was as if the hands of man were reaching up to the heavens. St. Malo was on a star shaped island in the River Rance and had the most beautiful beach with ochre sand just outside the walls. Her docks jutted out from a sheltered harbor into the estuary of the river. If one did not look too closely, one would have imagined that this was almost an ideal port city.

This vision contrasted with the reality of St. Malo and its past. Because it was on the English Channel, it had been a home for notorious corsairs and pirates who preyed upon English ships with great audacity and regularity. It thus had an unsavoury taint, which the town could not shake.

A small band of men wended their way to St. Malo. They pulled their hoods down over their faces to cover themselves as best they could. It really didn't matter, for in St. Malo, no one really noticed this small caravan, because no one really wanted to notice them. What did it matter if a few more unsavoury individuals came into this unsavoury town? The group blended in as best they could as they entered the gate through walls and made their way to the docks. They were looking for a particular man in a particular place.

I was with this group of men. Who were they? Well, we were the Seven Men of Moidart, Young Ranald, the Prince, several servants, and me. The Seven Men of Moidart was the Council of the Prince. They would help him bring about the Rising, as we were starting to call it, organize his regency government, and form the army that would be necessary to fight the English. For we all knew that the English would not allow the Prince upon Scottish soil without a fight. In the English view, the Stuarts were not welcome in Northern Britain, as the English were now calling Scotland, and most certainly a Stuart would not be welcome on the throne of Scotland.

It was an unusual group, this Seven Men of Moidart; of the Seven, only two were Scots, Aeneas MacDonald, the Paris banker, who was to help with the finances, and William Murray, the Marquis of Tullibardine. William Murray had fought for the Stuarts in the Uprising of 1715. Some called him the Second Duke of Atholl. The rest of our group was composed of four Irishmen and one Englishman. The Irish contingent was composed of Colonel John William O'Sullivan who had served in the French army, the Reverend George Kelly, an Episcopalian clergyman, Sir Thomas Sheridan, who had been one of the Prince's tutors; and Sir John MacDonnell, a cavalry officer in the French army. Our lone Englishman was Francis Strickland, who had once been the royal tutor to the Prince. Three of our group were quite elderly and truth be told, quite frail: Sir Thomas Sheridan, who was the prince's tutor and under governor, and a veteran cavalry officer; Sir John MacDonald, who also was a veteran cavalry officer for the French; and William Murray, the Marquis of Tullibardine. The only one who would prove himself of worth when the fighting began, in my opinion, was John O'Sullivan.

Perhaps the most famous of them was William Murray, the Marquis of Tullibardine. He was the eldest surviving son of the first Duke of Atholl and was thought that he would bring the Clan Murray with him. He had begun his career in the Royal navy. Later, he was the first join the banner of the Chevalier, James Francis Edward Stuart in 1715. Although his father, the second Marquis of Tullibardine and the first Duke of Atholl, did not join in the uprising, Lord William Murray, the Marquis of Tullibardine, was able to bring the bulk of the men of Atholl to the side of the Old Pretender. He had led the left wing of the rebel forces at the Battle of Sheriffmuir. For his part in the rebellion, he was stripped of his titles and lost his estates, which are given to his younger brother, James. He had recommended to the Prince his brother, George, as a commander of the Jacobite forces to be.

Still, it was not a group you would have thought would be the inner council of a regent about to form a nation. There was not a single statesman among them. The only common language which they all spoke was English; the Prince could not speak Gaelic. How they would fare would be seen, but my first impression was not a positive one.

Once we had entered the gates of St. Malo, I began to inquire where we could find Mr. Antoine Walsh. I had been chosen, not because my French was the best, but because I was deemed to be the least memorable. Aeneas MacDonald, the Paris banker, for example, spoke French with a Gaelic accent, even though he had been in Paris since he was young. His white hair and white beard, though made his face had to forget. The Prince was deemed to be too recognizable. The Irish spoke French with a brogue. Our sole Englishmen spoke no French. So I was left.

We made our ways to the docks and to the warehouses belonging to Antoine Walsh. Unfortunately, he was nowhere to be found. I ventured aboard one of his merchantman and found the captain working his men to load the ship. To my question of where Mr. Walsh was, the captain advised me that he was in Bon Anse Saint-Nazaire. Surveying the group behind me, the captain winked at me and said, "The ship for which you are looking is there too!"

We began our journey cross country at the base of the Bretagne peninsula. We could have gone back to Rennes and thence southwest to Bon Anse Saint-Nazaire, which would have placed us on better roads. We eschewed that route, thinking it more likely that anyone looking for us would go by the best routes. Our 'back roads' route took us to Dinan, where we spent the night.

I became the butt of many jokes, because one of the barmaids took a liking to me. She wore a very low cut blouse. At every chance she got, she bent over our table to make sure that I could see her ample bosom. At first, the others tried to ignore it, but it became so frequent, and it was so clear that I was the intended "victim" of her desire, snickers began to emerge accompanied by pointed fingers. Among Scots, an evening spent singing lusty songs and making bawdy jokes is the national pastime. I had to take the whole thing light-heartedly, or else, I would face the wrath of my compatriots.

Our next stop was Caulnes. Here we intended to spend one night, but, because William Murray, Marquis of Tullibardine became so ill with a bout of gout, we had to stay three days, while he recovered.

We passed through multiple little villages such as Gael, Mauron, Serent, and Nivillac as we made our way to Bon Anse Saint-Nazaire. Each French country inn seemed to be the same. They all had the long baguettes of bread, the same good cheese, lots of red wine, and the same stew, whether it contained lamb, beef, or pork. The French women all seem to flirt with us, although I guess that was their way of trying to get a more generous tip.

As before, I began to imagine what the mysterious Antoine Walsh might look like. The Prince told me that Walsh had Irish ancestors. Beyond that, I had little to go on. Somehow, the incongruous vision of a red headed, red freckled, but black bearded pirate kept filling my head. To say the least, I could hardly wait to meet the man.

At Bon Anse Saint-Nazaire, we were greeted by beautiful beaches of a golden color. Had we been tourists, we might have wanted to stay for several days in the seaside town. Of course, we inquired after Mr. Antoine Walsh. Although we had expected that he might visit us that first evening, it was not until the next morning that he arrived.

Instantly, my visions of the privateer Antoine Walsh were dashed as if a fine cut crystal goblet had been thrown to the stone floor. First, he was clean shaven-no black beard! Second, he bore no red freckles nor did he have red hair! Third, he looked as unremarkable as any English shopkeeper would have looked. He wore a jacket and a waistcoat and had a large watch on a chain slung across the front. My visions of a ferocious man with fire eating eyes met the reality of a somewhat portly and diminutive gentleman of impeccable fashion, manners, and taste. The famous privateer was certainly not the ideal pirate.

Very quickly, he sat down with Aeneas MacDonald to finalize the arrangements for our frigate. Aeneas MacDonald had been appointed by the Old Pretender to be our commissary officer. Antoine Walsh was at Jacobite, as well as a shrewd businessman. These two tendencies were clearly in opposition to one another, but one was winning out over the other.

William Murray, Marquis of Tullibardine, hobbled over on his cane, bent down, and whispered to Ranald. I could barely hear what he said, but what he said was quite surprising. The Marquis gestured to make Ranald come closer. I moved a little closer, but was still outside the circle. "It seems that our Prince has been involved in some intrigue. For the last several months, he has been writing to a Monsieur Legrand under the pen name 'J. Douglas'. Monsieur Legrand is none other than Antoine Walsh. Antoine Walsh has the highest credit in the court of Louis XV. After the battle of Fontenoy, Louis XV promised support to the Old Pretender. King Louis XV was well aware of the Prince's intentions through Lord Clare, an Irish-French Officer, and King Louis XV promised that he would secure two ships for the Prince. When Antoine suggested that he would be willing to put his frigate, Le Du Teillay, at the disposal of the Jacobite cause, the King felt that it was necessary to lend one of his warships. That is how we have come to have L'Elisabeth and her 64 guns. In addition, the King has promised some £400,000 in gold, weapons, uniforms, guns, and other equipment, as well as troops. So you see, our Mr. Walsh is quite important to our cause."

The Marquis could see that I was quite interested. He beckoned me to join the close circle. "The Walsh family were a wealthy merchant family in Wexford. Around the 1680s, Antoine's grandfather, Philip, left Ireland and came to France. He established the shipping business. His son, James, joined the French Navy." The Marquis clearly relished telling the story and he knew how to tell it well. The long pause that he now took only wetted our appetites for more.

"It seems that Antoine Walsh's father, James, became a captain in the French Navy. It was aboard his ship that James II had fled from Kinsdale to France in 1690. "Antoine is doing this in memory of his father. He is giving us the ship for a song," the Marquis said. Although the Marquis was infirm and elderly, his mind was the sharpest of the Seven.

True to his word, Walsh had made ready the frigate. Her crew, 67 men strong, all volunteers, some Irish, some Scots, a couple of English, but mostly French, were ready and waiting for us. She was named "Le du Teillay" which means 'from or of Teillay', a town dear to Mr. Walsh in Breton. She was armed with 18 guns and 24 swivels. She was beautiful, in my opinion, as a full-fledged landlubber. She had three masts and seemed to fly with the wind. Antoine Walsh had also arranged for us to meet the French man of war, "L'Elisabeth," at Belle-Ile.

We left the next day, July 3rd, which was a beautiful Friday. We expected to be at Belle-Ile in a couple of days, but the winds were contrary and it took us a week. When we reached Belle-Ile, the L'Elisabeth was not there yet.

Belle-Ile is the largest island off the coast of Brittany. She lives up to her name because she has wonderful beaches. We landed at Le Palais, which is the main town on the island. Le Palais is noted for La Citadel Vauban, and is supposed to be an example-a masterpiece of an example-of the military architecture of Sébastien Le Prestre de Vauban, whose military treatise on building stone fortresses was read in military schools the world over. The local inhabitants spoke his name with all and reverence, but, frankly, it meant nothing to me. It appeared to be a strong fort in the classic star pattern that was so popular at the time.

Part II: Preparations

> The way to secure peace is to be prepared for war.-**Benjamin Franklin**

In Portsmouth, on July 3, 1745, Captain Percy Brett was readying his Royal Majesty's frigate, Lion, for sea. Orders had come from the Admiralty in the traditional packet envelope, sealed with blue wax and blue ribbons. The outside was marked both "Captain's Eyes Only" and "Most Secret and Confidential-To Be Opened at Sea Only". This thick packet was accompanied by another packet, likewise sealed in blue wax and blue ribbons, marked "Captain's Eyes Only". This he opened immediately.

Through traditional language, he was ordered to go to sea 'soonest' possible. He was admonished not to open the other orders until not only underway, but also until out of sight of land. Captain Brett had never seen such orders, even though he had been a post captain for seven years. Later, he merely told his second in command, First Lieutenant Hastings, and his ship's sailing master, Mr. Marston, that they had important orders of which he would inform them once at sea.

Part III: What Fills a Ship's Hull

L'Elisabeth finally arrived early on July 13, which was none too soon, because we were all going a little crazy on this island waiting to begin our true mission. Loading a ship, or lading her, as the sailors called it, is quite an enterprise. There are miles upon miles of cables, some as thick as a man's thigh, and ropes that must be put in, of course, there are guns, shot, powder kegs, cloth to make the cartridge sacks, canvass for the sails, oil cloth, wool blankets, goats, a few cattle, kegs of salt meats, water kegs, extra spars, board lumber, tools, marines, their side arms, their muskets, small arms and muskets for the crew, powder and shot for the small arms and the muskets, powder flasks, then there are the accoutrements for the captain, his kegs of wines and sherry, his fine foods, his furniture, his charts and chart tables, and so on through a myriad of other items too numerous to name. Although we hurried her loading, we were not ready to set sail until Thursday, July 15, 1745.

I had learned more about Antoine Walsh and the more than I knew, the more impressed I became with the man. It seems that Walsh had deliberately sought out the interview with the Prince. He had also enjoined a friend of his, Walter Rutledge, a wealthy Irish merchant out of Dunkirk, to place himself before the French king, as a privateer. Rutledge was granted letters of marque and was entrusted with the King's ship, L'Elisabeth. The letters of marque came with the condition that merchant Rutledge pay all the running expenses of the ship, as well as her crew's pay. She would have to be very successful at privateering in order to clear a profit, but still Walsh had convinced Rutledge that ferrying the Prince, his entourage, funds for the Rising, troops and equipage, for which he would receive little more than costs was well worth the effort.

L'Elisabeth was a much more impressive ship than Le Du Teillay. L'Elisabeth was armed with 64 guns. She carried 100 French Marines, enlisted by Lord Clare, and in her hold some 2000 muskets, 500 broad swords, as well as a great sum of money, all through the resourcefulness of Lord Clare.

This then was our little fleet to sail to Scotland. We had hoped for more French support, but the French fleet had been badly damaged in some storms and the Prince was impatient. We left Belle Isle with the hope that warships would follow us.

Our Captain of the fleet was Monsieur L'Oe. We had dinner aboard L'Elisabeth in his cabins the night before we were to depart. The Captain had a reputation of being a gourmet; however, his girth betrayed him as a gourmand. He showered us with course after course of delicious food each paired with an extraordinary wine. He kept up a lively discourse about his days at sea beginning when he was just a little boy. He repeatedly said, "I hate the English. They raided my town and slew women and children, the men being away at sea, including me, and they killed my mother." He raised his glass to toast, "To my sacred mother and all mothers everywhere!"

The Prince also raised his glass in a toast, "To our glorious allies and friends, the ever brave French!" To which everyone stood and raised their glasses, "To the brave French!"

The dinner lasted well into the night with toast being met by toast as each of the Seven Men of Moidart felt compelled to outdo each other in effusive praise of the French, their ships, their crews, and their cannons. I was taken with this spectacle and thought that no enterprise had ever begun in so much hope, camaraderie, and true alliance between two peoples. I became more and more convinced that success would crown our endeavors and that James Stuart would sit upon the throne of Scotland and restore our Scottish freedoms, including the right to worship as we pleased. I raise my glass and toasted, "To the restoration of the Stuarts and to the restoration of Catholicism in the Highlands!" All cheered and replied, "To the Stuarts and to Catholicism!"

One of the things I learned about being at sea is how difficult it is to climb down the rope ladder and the steps alongside of the hull, called the battens, from the deck of a warship to the waiting gig below, especially when one is at least semi-drunk. The night was extremely dark, the rope was wet and yet sticky with tar, and my hands and feet were uncertain in their grip. The possibility of falling from the side of a ship somehow clarifies one's mind and improves co-ordination and concentration.

A modern sailing ship is truly a marvel. It is an amalgam of miles upon miles of cables and ropes, stretched this way and that, connecting yards upon yards of canvass sails to what seem like hundreds of feet of tall masts. There are so many men needed to climb the rigging and carefully hand over hand "walk" themselves across the yardarms to riff the sails so as to catch the wind just right. All these men, all these ropes, all that canvass, all the masts respond to the word and will of one man: the captain. By his design, his ship bounds over the waters and goes where he says. Everyone and everything is at his will. He is the 'god' behind the machine, the deus ex machina.

There is something so special about being aboard a ship at sea. This was especially true for me, a man of the land, in general, and the Highlands, in particular. The sibilant hissing sound of the semi-transparent, semi-luminescent spray of wetness slapped the sleek sides of the hull as the bow sluices through the sun-shimmer'd sapphire-satin seas. Perhaps that conveys it, but I think not.

A ship is a spectrum of sensory stimulations. It is an atrium of auditory actions. The ropes swing and hit the masts with different banging and flapping sounds. The cables sing in the breeze with different pitches depending upon their tension. The water, as it rushes by, slaps the hull and emits churning, bubbling sounds, while the waves crash, splash, and thud against the hull. With gun drill, the cannon blast, roar, and explode, nearly deafening one and causing all to seek to place pieces of cloth in their ears, which means that the orders must be shouted. The canvass sails beat in the wind, or ripple as the wind ebbs and flows. The sailors sing shanties as they hone the deck with holystones making the wood glisten in the sun.

The cacophony of sounds is graced by the play of light. When one ascends the stairs from the hold, one emerges from the depths of black Hades into brilliant yellow sunshine that dazzles the eyes and makes them squint and hurt. There are millions little suns bouncing off the tops of the waves that flutter and shimmer. There is the play of colors which daze the mind. As the ship's bow slashes the seas, the dark blue is roiled into light sky blues and foamy whites. The brown of the hull is gaily painted with a line of red just at the water line, below which at some points, the copper sheeting protecting the hull can jut into the sunlight. The main strips of colors across the hull are golds, blues, and whites, the colors of Royal France. There on the deck patches of polished bronze appear in the bells and the compass. The cannon are a glossy coal black but hide behind doors. One's eye is always lead heavenwards by the thrust of the masts where the clouds are ever changing from whites to greys, to steel blues, only to blaze with yellows, oranges, and reds at sunset, and then fading to purples, greys, and finally blacks.

If one is not visually inclined, then one might feel the treasury of textures that surround one. First, the ever present hemp ropes feel prickly and rough. In contrast, the smoothness of the handrails, feels cool and comforting. Yet there are boards of wood which are roughhewn and might prick you with a splinter. One grabs at all times to keep one's balance causing one to look at each hand hold lest one wrap one's fingers around something sharp. The cables are covered in lard that the hand slips and slides along them. Others are coated in sticky tar that holds your hand to it. One's face is often lashed by the stinging salt spray. Your eyes tear because of the slicing wind, which snaps any loose fringe of your clothes. Each metal has its own peculiar qualities. The bronze of the bell is polished. The cast iron of the cannon is blacked but has small ridges, valleys, hills, and plateaus to it. Finally, the glass of the compass binnacle case squeaks as you rub your finger across it.

Beyond the feel of the ship, is its taste, its terrible, bile curdling taste. While one would think one could only taste the salt of the sea, one would be mistaken. Hardtack is eaten and unlike bread is has but little flavor. After a while though, it becomes alive with weevils and worms. The meat from the kegs is at first fresh and beefy, or lamby, but salty, succulent, and savory, but soon spoils, becomes gelatinous and changes from lamb or beef to a liquidified mash which almost makes you gage. Wine is a necessary item to kill the meat flavor. Our ship had a fine selection of Bordeaux, Pinot Noir, Champagne, and brandies which became a staple of one's sustenance.

But the one sensory sensation, which you wish most of all were not, is the smell. If you have never left land, then you do not know how truly bad it is. First, the crew, which rarely if ever bathes, wears the same unwashed clothes for day after day. The odor of sweat, aged sweat, is caked upon the men. This is accented by the world of the bilge. The bilges slosh waters so old, tainted, refuse filled, that if water could rot, then the bilges would be the most rotten, decrepit waters in the world. The wood of the ship acts like a sponge sweeping up, engorging itself upon each and every scent, such that the wood itself has the imprint of every fire aboard, every meal, every fart, every drop of sweat that ever poured out of a pore, every drop of pus, piss, or ooze of any kind, from man or animal. Then there are the animals, their wool wet always, their droppings, their fetid hay containing everything that came out of them. Beneath the decks, the kegs of the meats spoiled added their wafting maliciousness to the air, which also contained the ripe smell of vegetable stink as they sour and turn to mush, as well as the wisps of heavy, burnt lard. Here was the oil spilled; there a gutted cow had bled; here a chicken had made its droppings; there amputations of legs and arms had graced the eating tables, and so on and so on. In this manner, the history of the ship could be told if there was a nose capable of reading the pages of scents in this library of odor. Once smelled, never forgotten.

There is a tension being at sea. At first I could not discern it. But it was there, hanging around our necks like a watery millstone.

You look across the vast expanse of the sea. The ship cuts through the water and there is a white wake surrounding your vessel. Rolling waves come from the north and hit you broadsides (I had learned a new word). A ship moves in three directions at once. There is pitch, which means that the bow moves up and down. There is yaw, which is the ship's bow jostling from starboard to larboard (right to left for you landlubbers!) Finally, there is roll, which is the ship tilting or rolling on its keel, tipping from side to side. The ship all the while is plowing forward.

I found that I had to flail about as I watched. I was most gawky. Arms out at all angles, knees bent ready to pounce upon a step-I was a scare crow of the sea! A foot might aim for one step and then find itself climbing up a wall as the deck rolled hard!

But these, while disturbing to one's stomach, these are not the issue of which I speak. Far oft you see the horizon and it encircles you. The clouds go scudding through the skies. The wind fills the sails and all of the ship's hull creaks, groans, cracks, and shudders, while elsewhere the ship pings, clangs, bangs, knocks, and sighs, as cupboard doors, the gun ports, and the great doors swing open and close, if not secured or battened. All of this is unsettling. But still this is not the issue.

You are surrounded by the vastness of the seas, the waves, the rolling of the seas, and blues, various shades of blues, sky, azure, Tyrennian, royal, navy that blends into greens and greys. You are alone. There is nothing familiar, there is nothing secure. You are at the mercy of the elements-wind and water. You could die. You will drown if the ship goes down. That's it: the threat of death by water.

Give me a good horse, dry land, the glens, the straths, the moors, the bens or meadows and solid rock. God help me, give me the sheep too! Anything to be upon the land.

Part IV: England Expects Every Man to Do His Duty

> This England never did, nor
> never shall, Lie at the proud foot of a
> conqueror- **Shakespeare**

The full moon shone over the waters of the English Channel. HMS Lion was making good time as the wind was fresh. This would have been an enjoyable cruise if it had been for pleasure. But Captain Percy Brett was waiting for the right time to inform his officers of their deadly and dangerous mission.

"First Lieutenant Mr. Marston, Sailing Master Hastings, I intend now to advise you of our orders." Captain Percy Brett began in his finest Etonian accent, which he heavily affected with a strong nasal component. Captain Brett as Post Captain of some seniority had hoped to bring his old Sailing Master and his first Mate aboard, but someone in the Admiralty, who must have been a carter cousin to Mr. Marston, had interfered. Captain Brett was stuck with men he did not like and who were somewhat insubordinate to him. Not so much as to cause him to take action, but enough to make his life miserable. 'Mr. Marston will be aboard the first prize we take,' Captain Brett silently vowed.

"Prince Charles and his entourage are going to make a break for Scotland. We are to intercept them, if they come by way of the Lizard." Captain Brett let the import of his words sink in. "Any questions?"

"How do we know this?" Lieutenant Marston asked.

"The Admiralty through its spies in Rome and Paris has advised us that the breakout is imminent. That should be enough for us to do our duty." Captain Brett did not like his Lieutenant's question. 'What does it matter how our orders come to us?' He thought to himself.

"Captain, I have charted the Lizard and environs," the Sailing Master began. 'Oh, God, no, not another one of his endless lectures,' thought Captain Brett, who maintained a completely blank expression on his face. "The English Channel is the busiest stretch of ocean in all the world. Even with us at war with France, a great deal of trade passes through here from America, and of course there are the Dutch, the Swedes, the Russians, and the Norwegians." Mr. Hasting coughed and then continued. "The typical nor'east wind helps us. Ships going up channel must fight the wind. Ships sailing down the channel, like us, are swept to the west and then are pinned near the Lizard, making our job easier. I'll plot the shoals in the area, Sir."

"Thank you, Mr. Hastings," Captain Brett smiled, because he really meant that. This was the first time the old Sailing Master, whose breath smelled so bad, because his teeth seemed to be decaying right before his eyes, had acted like a real officer of this ship. "Mr. Marston, make sure that Doctor Bradford is prepared for action. Also make sure that the Gunnery Master Johns has made enough cloth powder gun cartridge bags. I expect a fight."

Captain Brett dismissed both men with a nod of his hat and resumed his position in the place of honor upon the ship. He enjoyed the solitude. 'I do not know how Marston will hold up in a real fight,' he thought.

Part V: Another Night's Good Work

The soiree had been invigorating. Lady Foster tousled her hair, as she and her brother left the chambers of King James and Princess Clementina Maria. It had been an exciting evening, and she was not ready to end it now. Though their mission was over now, they still enjoyed being at a party thrown by a King.

"What should we do now?" She turned to her brother and caught him yawning. "Oh, you're no good for anything." She joshed him.

"I could go for some *baccarat* à deux tableaux." He smiled at her.

"Oh, you could *always* play cards!" She rejoined.

"We could go to a club and …" He began.

"But your clubs do not let women in, except if they are scantily clad or less…" Her voiced trailed off.

"But that's what makes them worth looking at!" He joked. "Besides, you know they would make an exception for you!" He emphasized the word 'you'.

They walked the street arm in arm. They were happy and still enjoyed the buzz of the champagne of the King.

She started to sing a little ditty. After a while he whistled along. They were swinging arms as if they were children. They did not notice the two men who had turned out of the alley they had just passed.

The night air was exhilarating and the moonlight was silvery from a full moon. She stretched her chin up to drink in the air just as the wire of the garrote wrapped itself around her neck. Her brother's call was cut short as another wire was pulled, cutting into veins and arteries alike. Within moments, two bodies hit the cobblestone pavement and two shadows melted back into the alleys.

Part VI: Once The Party's Over

Piccolomoni met Father Alessandro that Tuesday at 4:00pm as was their custom. They met in the same small café which was non-descript in all manners that a café can be non-descript. Father Alessandro began the mental catalogue of the items he felt were lacking: food, beverage, clientele, bar tender, bar maids, furniture, location, and most importantly of all cleanliness. In short, it still had nothing to recommend it and still had much to discourage patrons from frequenting it. Thus, for Father Alessandro, it was still perfect.

"Piccolo, you have completed your mission," Father Alessandro began. "The Holy Father has need of you elsewhere. Are you ready?"

Piccolomoni had a long look on his face, as if he were ready to cry. "She's gone."

"Yes, my son, I heard." Father Alessandro was consoling and tender. "She's gone."

"Why? Why did God take her away from me?" Piccolomoni averted his head, but still Father Alessandro could see a tear crease his cheek.

"God works in strange and mysterious ways..." Father Alessandro in a rote manner started to say.

"Did you have something to do with it?" Piccolomoni's eyes were sharp now and flashed with anger.

"Me? Son, you think I would have something to do with murder?" Father Alessandro protested.

"Yes, did you have her killed?"

"Of course not!" Father Alessandro looked Piccolomoni straight in the eye. It was a trick he had learned years before. If you looked someone straight in the eye as you told a lie, not only would they avert their eyes from you, but also they would believe what you had just told them. "No, my son, I would never do that to you."

They both sipped their wine for a while saying nothing. The café maid visited their table a couple of times to check on them, but Father Alessandro waved her away each time.

The clock on the wall keep ticked away the seconds which became minutes, and then finally a half hour.

"Father Alessandro, what would you have me do?" Piccolomoni weakly asked.

"Come, my son, you have work to do for the Holy Father. You will come with me now. We'll send later for your things. You have a new assignment which will require your skills."

They got up together. Father Alessandro threw some coins on the table-a generous tip to the café girl. He put his arm around his cousin and escorted him into the sunlight of the small square outside the café.

"You have done fine work for the Holy Father. He is pleased. He wants you to..." Father Alessandro's voice drifted off into the distance as the two men wended their way through the alley ways of Rome.

Part VII: A Scare Upon the Seas

> You can either be the bird who's too afraid to fly or the one who's too busy flying to feel scared.-**Unknown**

The day after we set sail, we had a scare. Seven ships were sighted in the northwest. Were they friend or foe? They were sailing south and so, after a while, we thought they might be some ships from Brest.

The next day, we saw those same seven ships again. We sailed for a squall and lost them in it. We counted ourselves as being lucky.

About noon on 19 July, we heard heavy firing in the northeast. Not too long after, eight sail hove into view. It appeared that they were giving us chase. They made ready to chase us down the windward. We called to L'Elisabeth and Captain L'Oe ordered all sail, as well as to clear for action.

One of the eight was clearly a double-decker and we thought we could make out English colors. She was crowding on all sail and making way to overhaul us. But she was hull down, so she was miles from being able to fire at us.

We sailed all night wondering whether the English fleet would catch up with us. Our men had been at battle stations, ready for action throughout the night and into the early morning. The ships chaplain gave absolution to everyone.

We were just rounding the Lizard in Cornwall England. "Sails, ho!" came the cry from one of the lookouts. We all scanned at the horizon, but could see nothing. The lookout had caught sight of the double decker again, but could not make out the seven sail we thought might be behind her.

The cold wind curled off the grey seas in the predawn light. The taffrail lanthorns had been shrouded with cloth such that only a slit broke the blackness of the night. The binnacle and compass were similarly lighted by but a brief parting of shrouding, letting just a hint of orange of candle out into the darkness so the helmsman could steer. He paced the quarter deck, where by tradition only the captain of the ship could stand, but as a Prince, leeway was allowed him. He stared into the night and one might think that his eyes could pierce the gloom and see the future ahead of him, but no, like mortal eyes, they could not.

At about 11 AM, Captain Walsh ordered that all men should be given some wine and bread to keep up their strength. As the morning faded into the early afternoon, Captain L'Oe and the Captain Walsh ordered their ships to haul close in order to discuss what could be done. Shouting through speaking tube, Captain Monsieur L'Oe, ordered our ship, Le Du Teillay, to hang back while he went forward with L'Elisabeth. Walsh was our Captain and he began to obey Captain Monsieur L'Oe's command. The Prince came up above decks at the cry of the lookout and shouted, "We should forge together as a squadron; we are stronger together!" Walsh turned to the Prince, "With all due respect Your Majesty, I am in command of the ship and Captain Monsieur L'Oe is in command of the fleet. The ship will do what I order it to do." The Prince looked from man-to-man, his eyes inquiring what he should do. The Marquis, reading the Regent's mind, said, "Your Majesty, we should leave the sailing to the experts and rely upon God and his mercy."

Captains L'Oe and Walsh then agreed that the plan would be that L'Elisabeth would engage the English ship, and after she had fired a broadside, she would board the English vessel, which would be the signal for our ship, Le Du Teillay, to come alongside of the English ship, fix, and grapple her, and then 50 of our men would board her and between our two crews overcome her.

Around 2:00pm, it became clear that the English ship was merely trying to delay us until the rest of his squadron came up. We now understood that the eight of them intended to overwhelm us by sheer firepower. We then clewed our sails and tried to flee away. The English ship somehow was faster than either of our ships.

The sails kept coming straight for L'Elisabeth. Our ships began to beat to quarters and both became a flurry of activity. The small boys, who were the powder monkeys, went into the ship's hold and brought up the bags of powder. The gun masters started selecting the roundest and truest cannonballs for the fight. Captain Walsh ordered ball and chain shot for our first broadsides adhering to the French tactical thought of taking out the masts and sails of our adversaries to slow them down. Ball and chain shot was a particularly apt choice for this endeavor. Two cannonballs were attached one to the other by a length of chain, which when fired from the cannon whipped around in a circular motion slicing through the canvas of sails and the wood of masts-hopefully bringing down a mast or two. In this fashion, the French sought to disable their opponent by slowing them down such that it became easier to hit them and sink them or if necessary, flee from them.

Walsh was giving a flurry of orders for the handling of the ship's sails, rigging, and cannon which was totally foreign to my understanding. The result of these orders was that our ship began to speed up in comparison to our sister ship, L'Elisabeth. On the horizon now, we could see the outline of the ship, but still could not tell whether it was an English warship or not.

Time seemed to move both very slowly and very fast simultaneously. Sawdust was spread over the decks of the ship. "Why?" I asked.

"To sop up the blood and make it easier to clean the decks afterwards," answered the Marquis, who I then remembered had begun his career as a warrior at sea.

Part VI: Rum and Silk

"Mr. Marston, advance the rum issue to six bells."

"Yes, Sir. Do you intend to 'Splice the Mainbrace' to encourage them, Sir?" Mr. Marston advised the Captain.

"No, Mr. Marston, that'd make them too glib-eyed to see the Frenchie. I need them ready, willing, but most of all able." Captain Brett rarely joked, so Mr. Marston was unsure of whether he should smile. Captain Brett seeing the unsettled look upon Mr. Marston's face thought his jest had gone awry and brought back things to complete control. "See to it, Mr. Marston."

The Lion was closing in upon the two suspected French ships. Captain Brett felt it in his bones that the Prince was aboard one of them. He turned to one of his Midshipmen, "Mr. Clarke, be so good as to ask Gunnery Master Johns to converse with me." Mr. Clarke ran off a little too excitedly. Captain Brett forgave the 15 year old boy his enthusiasm at being in his first fight.

Gunnery Master Johns was of Dutch descent, but was an experienced and excellent artilleryman. His dress was always impeccable, but his toilette left something to be desired. Apparently, he had adopted the French fashion and did not bathe, but used 'eau de cologne'.

"Mr. Johns, I intend to engage the larger of the two vessels. The Prince, I would think would be aboard the larger and better appointed ship. I intend to take the weather gauge and I want every shot betwixt hull and sail. I think her a French frigate of about our size, but as they never do live firing practice, I think our rate and accuracy of fire will tell the day." Captain Brett waved his hand in a dismissal of the Gunnery Master.

"Mr. Marston, have the fires staunched. Mr. Clarke, would you be so good as to get my brace of pistols from my cabin. Also, if you have a silk shirt, put it on. It's easier for the doctor to pull a ball from a man, if the shirt is silk."

Part VII: Gun Ports Open!

I could see the form became bigger and bigger. Then her colors became clear. It was an English warship. She seemed to be bigger than L'Elisabeth. Red coated marines filled the rigging of the English ship.

Everything seemed to flow in slow motion. We were now on the far side of L'Elisabeth, so as to have her protect us. Our guns thus could not bear upon the English frigate.

"All right you sea rats," cried Mr. Johns aboard the HMS Lion. Below decks, all had been cleared for action. The hammocks had been stowed. All furniture moved aside from the great cabin. Powder monkeys had brought cloth cartridge bags to settle near the guns. Gun-captains had selected the roundest balls for they would fly the truest to their target.

The gun-captains were directed to open the pans of the flintlock strikes to fill with powder. "Cock locks," Johns ordered. The gun-captains pulled the lanyards to make the strikers taut, ready to jerk on the up-roll.

"Wait for it!" Johns ordered. "Wait for it!" The ship began her ascend up the wall of water and once at the top would settle for a moment before gliding down the hill again. "On the up roll fire!" Johns commanded. And at that special instance when the ship was at the crest of the roll, the entire broadside fired in almost perfect unison.

Part VIII: Fire at Night

> "Hours are Time's shafts, and one comes winged with death." – **Scottish Clock Motto**

The British ship's cannon fired first. Waterspouts fell all around L'Elisabeth, while a few cannon balls found the hull, leaving star-shaped holes. She fired in reply and I could see some ball and chain shot swinging through the air. Some holes opened in the English canvas, but no masts were hit. The English ship fired a second broadside and again the bulk of her balls found their way home to hull, sail, and this time, masts, our masts.

By about half past five o'clock, the English ship was abeam of the L'Elisabeth. The Lion had the weather gauge and then quickly and smartly clewed up her foresail, and hoisted her standing jib to which the L'Elisabeth tried to respond in kind, but way too slowly. The English ship sprinted ahead of L'Elisabeth. She then turned and caught L'Elisabeth with a full port broadside that raked her stem to stern. L'Elisabeth lost a fair portion of her crew in that one broadside. The horrible sight of bodies being cut in half, blood washing the decks, arms torn off, legs splintered into pieces, hull-wood blasted to splinters that hit the men making them into porcupines, is one sight that I hope I will never see again. L'Elisabeth was disabled, but started to give a ragged fire back.

The English ship, the Lion, as we could read her transom, was between us now. She fired her starboard broadside against us. It seemed that before we could fire our broadside, the English had loaded and had fired another one. We fired and seemed to have little effect on her-our guns were just too little to have much effect on her hull. The Lion in turn fired a third broadside, but she was just too high in her aim. Her cannon balls passed between our masts and through our sails, but with little effect and almost no carnage being committed against us. It was then that her Marines in their flaming red coats began raking our decks with their muskets. Captain Walsh immediately saw the danger to the Prince.

"Get below Sir!" Captain Walsh used his body to shield the Prince while he shepherded him to a hatchway and out of harm's way.

It was then that Captain L'Oe turned his ship to the southeast and away from us. In turn, the Lion went after her. The two ships placed themselves abreast of one another, so that the Englishman fired his starboard and the L'Elisabeth her port batteries, pounding each other mercilessly. Somehow, the firing of the L'Elisabeth was getting better as the contest continued. We kept waiting for the L'Elisabeth to board the English ship, which would be our signal to board also, but L'Elisabeth never made the first move to board. The 33 pounders of the English ship were so fearsome that we did not approach her, unless the Elisabeth had done so first. We followed in the wake of the L'Elisabeth to render assistance when we could, but no chance ever came.

Night fell and still the two ships-one French, one English-battered each other. The cannon, flaming and flaring with orange and yellow explosions, showering iron and death upon each other, blazed in the night. The groans of the wounded and dying were unbearable.

Finally, about 10:00 pm, the firing stopped on both sides. Whether it was utter exhaustion, lack of ammunition, or just plain darkness, I do not know. We hove close to the L'Elisabeth. I expected the gallant Captain L'Oe to respond to our hail. To our surprise, it was his flag-captain, M. Bar who responded. "Captain L'Oe is seriously wounded. He is not expected to survive the night." The bad news continued. "Our ship is badly damaged, we fear we might sink. Send over a cutter full of men to help us refit and return to France. We cannot go on."

A voice rang out in the still night. "This is Captain Percy Brett of His Majesty's ship, Lion. Strike your colors and surrender to us. You will be honorably treated."

To this, Flag-Captain Bar replied in perfect unaccented English: "Captain Brett, this is Flag-Captain Bar of His Royal Majesty, Louis XV's ship, the L'Elisabeth. Strike your colors to me and you will be treated honorably. If you do not, our 64 guns will recommence firing and there will be no quarter."

Unbeknownst to Captain Bar, the Lion had suffered as much or more damage as the L'Elisabeth had in the encounter. Several minutes went by. Hushed voices could be heard arguing. Finally, the response came, "Captain Bar, I, Captain Percy Brett, will surrender my sword to you."

Captain Bar was thrilled that his bluff had worked.

Now, after some time passed, Captain Bar was unable to muster enough men to send a cutter over to the Lion to accept the surrender. As time ticked away, Captain Brett became nervous. Again, voices could be heard arguing aboard the Lion. Then, her colors were rehoisted above. She had recanted her surrender.

The night wore on. Both Captain L'Oe and his brother died of their wounds. More than 200 of the crew of L'Elisabeth were killed or wounded. She was no longer an effective fighting ship. She might be able to limp home to France, but she was unable to continue to escort or protect us in a contest.

Part IX. A Landing

> The LORD IS MY SHEPHERD; I
> SHALL NOT WANT.-**Psalm 23**

The morrow would tell the tale. All those days spent in France, thinking, hoping, praying, and begging, had come to this. A night dark and fraught with so much gloom being broken by the merest hint of aurora, the goddess of dawn, trying ever so hard to bend her pink fingers over the horizon and seize the day from the depths of night. He shuddered not so much from what he faced, but from the cold night air. He wrapped himself tighter in his cloak remembering that Scotland, his new home, could be very cold even in July. 'Why, it even snowed one August,' he reminisced, 'when I was a child.' But then he remembered that he had been told this and that he had not experienced it. His thought died in the gloom of this day so drek, dank, and dreary. If he were a man who believed in omens, then he might have started the ship back for France, for surely this night was a portent of defeat. But he believed not in signs, but in himself, his cause, and the strength of his men. 'If I am good enough, if I believe enough, then God will reward me. I am the one, true Prince of Scotland.' He thought.

'Will the Highlands welcome me?' It was a strange time for doubt to creep into a man's soul. For so long, in France and throughout the voyage, he evinced but only the greatest certainty that all would proceed well. Now? Would the Highlands greet him and send him her sons to build his army? Would the cause of the Catholic King rally the men of the Highlands? Would the promise of freedom to worship in their own way, freedom to live in the traditions of the clans, and freedom from the shackles of Protestant England and its King, who wanted only rapine, plunder, and conquest, be enough to win Scotland?

He walked the quarterdeck in the night. He had paid no attention to the men at the side of the ship casting the chip and noting the speed in knots of his vessel. He had not noticed the men throwing the lead plumb line o're the side to gauge the depth. He had not noticed the men in the rigging, reefing in the sails to cut speed as they approached. He had not noticed, till one of the sailors called out the ancient cry, "Land ho!"

Some moments later, he was in a long boat, surrounded by his men. Everything was muffled. Oars in oarlocks were padded, men's feet were swaddled in cloth, lanterns were wrapped in cloth such that only the barest slit of light emanated forth in the night. Men spoke in whispers the words of which were carried by the zephyr breeze but a few feet. Not a sound was carried to the ears of waiting enemies.

The dawn loomed in the east just ahead of the ship. This little vessel was sailing into the sunrise. Was this a better omen? It was July 22, 1745. Prince Charles Edward Stuart, the royal exile, was making landfall at Barra Head on the southernmost tip of the Outer Hebrides. "I have waited for this day all of my life." He announced to his small crew. He reached down and scooped up a handful of sand and seawater. He fondled it in his hand. "I have touched Scotland finally."

Chapter 14

The Raising of the Crimson and White

> It is not in the stars to hold our destiny but in ourselves.-**William Shakespeare**

Part I: The Smuggler Comes Ashore

The heat of mid-summer's day was rising. The sun bright in yellow had chased all hints of clouds from the sky. The bow of the frigate Le Du Teillay was cutting through the blue sparkling water of Loch nan Uamb turning it to white foam frothing up the sides of the ship and splitting in a V shape away from the sides of the brown frigate. The le Du Teillay with her three masts and 80 foot length gliding on the calm waters was a rare sight beheld by the seminarians residing on the islands in the Gaotal Bay. Did they know that it was a ship of war and not a merchantman? Did they guess that the Young Pretender, Bonnie Prince Charles, was the valuable cargo? Did they sense that a war was coming to the Highlands from that cresting ship riding the blue waters?

Late on that day, July 25, 1745, Le Du Teillay was at anchor off a small stretch of beach at the head of the Loch. A small party consisting of a "priest" and his entourage walked the road from the beach to a poor little town set beside some rich meadows. There the grazing Highland cattle with their reddish-brown shaggy fur draping down lowed softly as they ate. The cattle walked slowly tilting their large horns to look at the "priest" as he and his party made their way from the beach to the home of Angus Mac Donald of Borrodale.

As the men walked, some of the curious farmers and townsmen came up. "Who ye be?" They asked.

"We're looking for Angus McDonald. We've a rich job of a trade to make with him," said one of the party, winking his eye hinting that they were smugglers evading the Crown's duties.

The Prince was clothed in the garb of the student of the Scot's College of Paris with a black coat, stockings and a hat, with black shoes adorned with shiny brass buckles, looking all the part of a very rich "priest".

"He's not at home," chanted the townsfolk. "But he be returned this evening."

"Tell him to come to us aboard our ship," intoned the winking smuggler.

Later, it was not Angus, but his son, Robert, who made his way to the 'smugglers' ship. Coming aboard, he was taken to a tent erected amidships, where to his surprise he learned the rich "priest" was the Prince.

"Your Majesty," he said bowing and stammering. "You've come home."

Part II: The Bishop Bows to a "Priest"

> "I do renounce and disown any allegiance as due to any Protestant king, prince, or state, or obedience to any of their inferior officers."-**Oath of a Priest**

The Prince's ship lay at anchor off the beach for the next two weeks as word of his landing in Scotland slowly made the rounds of the Highlands. It took time for the men of the Highlands to make their way through the glens, over the lochs, around the mountains to the seashore where the Prince stayed.

The first among them was Angus Beg MacDonald of Dalilea. "If you join me, you shall be an officer," promised the Prince.

When his brother, Alasdair, known as the Bard, toasted the Prince's health in Gaelic, the Prince made him his tutor of Gaelic, right on the spot, for the Prince knew not a word of his native language.

Next arrived Donald Kinlochmoidart, whose mother was the sister of Cameron of Lochiel. "Go to your mother," the Prince urged. "Tell her that she must persuade her brother to join me, for without Cameron of Lochiel and his men, our caused shall surely fail, but with him success is ensured."

On August 3, 1745, Hugh MacDonald, the Catholic Bishop of Scotland, the only Catholic Bishop in Scotland, made his way to the lonely beach. There riding the rising and falling waves of the Loch was the French Frigate Le Du Teillay. It made such an impressive sight with its 18 cannon and 24 swivels blazing in the sunlight. She was a sight one rarely saw on this distant island in the far western reaches of Scotland.

On board, the Bishop approached the tent where the "priest" was surrounded by his entourage and some of the locals.

"Father, welcome to Scotland. What is your mission from his eminence?" asked the Bishop continuing the ruse of the identity of the Prince.

"Come to my quarters," beckoned the 'priest' as the 'priest' bowing, kissed the Bishop's ring.

Once in the Prince's private quarters and after the Prince had laid out his plans, the Prince asked the Bishop, "What think you of all of this?"

"Because you have asked, Your Majesty, I will answer, but I am sure that you will not like it." The Bishop clenched his jaw and halted there awaiting the Prince's command.

"Go on," the Prince ordered.

"Your Majesty, I have risked much, merely by coming here and talking to you. I should not trade my office as Bishop. I should remain neutral and remain ready to feed my flock and sustain its spiritual needs. I have come, however, because my love of Scotland and my love of you are so great." The Bishop halted there.

The Prince sensing that the Bishop needed further prompting nodded his head. "I see and I understand." He paused a moment, the silence emphasizing the gravitas of what he was about to say. "I, too, have risked much. If I am found, then I will be hanged, drawn, and quartered. Still, I beg you to proceed. What say you about my plans?" The Prince searched into the eyes of the Bishop earnestly-almost begging the cleric to continue his commentary.

"You have come only with seven men; you have come with little money; you have come with no French troops; you have come with no cannons; no weapons; no fodder; nor food, nor equipment, nor uniforms. You have come with nothing." Unwittingly, the Bishop had fallen into the cadence of the sermon. "Yet, like Pompey, you expect to stomp your feet and have legions appear from the soil of the Highlands fully equipped, armed, and uniformed with muskets, cannons, broad swords, and dirks. This is the Highlands. It is a poor countryside. Yet ye expect men to come from all over the Highlands and rally to Your Cause, but you approach them with empty hands. Sire, at the risk of being impudent, what possessed you to come now?"

The Prince scowled. Anger flashed across his face. The veins in his neck popped large and grand. "Never let it be said that We would turn our backs upon our people. Never will We abandon this Enterprise and let the yoke of oppression ring the necks of our people. We have come now to allow the one true Faith to be practiced by all those who yearn God's grace and blessing. We will not be deterred by petty annoyances. We will create all that We need from all that there is in Scotland. If We could get but six good men, We would continue on the fight for ever from each Glen, hiding in the mountains, and swooping down upon the lands of the English like Assyrians upon the fold. We will never ever give up as long as God grants us breath!"

The Prince turned and smashed his fist on the table. He picked up a glass of wine and quaffed it in one toss. He turned back to the Bishop and began again. "My father came to Scotland in 1715. He came too late in the campaign season, with no men, no money, and long after his forces here in Scotland had been defeated and his best general killed. Sensing defeat and doom all around him, he left before the Highlands could rally around him. The Uprising of 1715 failed and failed bitterly. Can I leave now?" The Prince paused. "If I leave now, what will happen?"

The look in the Prince's eyes turned from one of anger to one of pain and sorrow. "I am living in the taint, the stink, and the odor of that defeat.

If I leave now, then there will never be a time for the Rising again. No one will ever follow me or any Stuart. It is now or never."

Part III: The Sky Darkens

> If the skies fall, one may hope to
> catch larks.**-Francois Rabelais**

Hugh MacDonald, Bishop of Scotland, was upon his knees praying. His common sense was at war with his spiritual sense. "Oh God, let Christian warriors rally, as Joshua at Jericho. May the Highlanders, like so many Israelites, march around and around the walls and let them come tumbling down." Meanwhile his rational side saw no great outpouring of men and matériel from the Highlands.

Only yesterday, word had come from one of the two crucial Chiefs, MacLoed of Dunvegan who had rebuffed the Prince's call to arms. MacLoed characterized the Rising as being a 'Don Quixote Expedition'.

Later, the other Chief, Alexander MacDonald had come to Prince. "I would not have come, but for the shoddy way that MacLoed of Dunvegan responded to your call. For I, too, have my doubts, my deep and abiding doubts, but I have come to give you a fair hearing."

Alexander MacDonald did not bow to the Prince, nor did he call him 'Your Majesty'. The Prince almost snarled at the lack of proper dignity being shown him by Alexander MacDonald, but he restrained himself. He smiled weakly.

"The time is now. England is involved in a continental war. The homeland is stripped of forces. Scotland is held, if at all, by just a few thousand untried and untested men. Yes, they are led by General Sir John Cope, but I am sure that he will prove not that difficult to overcome."

"Do ye have money?" Lord MacDonald interrupted.

"We have some. I am sure that…" The Prince tried to continue.

"Have ye French troops?" MacDonald broke in again.

"We have none yet, but I have been promised…" The Prince was still having difficulty restraining himself from lashing out at this old man who was obstructing his plans.

"Did King Louis sign a treaty with ye?" MacDonald fairly attacked the Prince.

"No, but His Majesty has promised…"

"The road to Hell is paved with promises." Lord MacDonald spat. "Ye haven't got anything. Ye got no men with ye. Ye expect the Highlands to be your army, but ye come with no money, no supplies, no arms, and no cannon. Ye come with open hands begging, that's all."

"Our situation is better than…" The Prince stammered.

"Better than what? Ye got nothing and ye expect everything. We're the ones who bear the whip, when you have scuttled back off to France when ye lose and it looks to me like ye will lose. Go home lad, go home."

"I am come home, sir… I am persuaded that my faithful Highlanders will stand by me." The Prince's eyes were flashing with anger that even the old Lord could not miss.

"I'll leave ye now. But I cannot order my clan to follow ye. I'll not invoke the power of pit and gallows to bring them out!" Lord Alexander MacDonald backed away and left the Prince's presence.

Elsewhere and meanwhile, Hugh MacDonald continued to pray. "Lord, is this truly what the Prince faces? Is he engaged in something that cannot succeed? Will you not grant him victory and success? Is he not Your chosen one to lead Scotland back to the Catholic fold? Must Scotland suffer more?" His heart said no; his mind said yes.

As the Bishop prayed, the Council of Seven, the Seven of Moidart, were meeting with the Prince.

"Your Cause is lost, Majesty. We've just had word that Cameron of Lochiel will not join. Young Ranald of Clanranald hangs back and is undecided. His father, the Clan Chief of the MacDonalds of Clanranald of the Isle of Skye has said he will not turn the Clan out. Worse, he has forbidden his son to join. Young Ranald faces the wrath of his father if he joins and even if he joins, who will follow him?" argued William Murray, the Marquis of Tullibardine of the Council of Seven. Marquis William Murray was in his 57th year. He was one of the older men of the Council and many of them deferred to him. He started his military career in the Navy, but had been involved in several campaigns in the Army after that. All of this made his opinion one that could not be ignored.

The Prince was downcast. "Never had We imagined that the Highlands was a nest of old women, more interested in their knitting and their comfort, sitting by the fire, waiting for their oatmeal porridge to be warm. We had been told, year after year, first in Rome, then in Paris, that the Highlands were men at arms, who would rally to their King broad swords in hand, crosses burning, plaid wrapped, bagpipes blaring, ready to fight for God, Country, and King. And now they do nothing?"

Your Majesty, the Enterprise has failed…" The Marquis Murray stammered.

The Prince glowered at him. "How dare you! We shall say when and if the Enterprise has a failed! And not you! We have not yet begun! We have not yet met our people!"

"But your Majesty, without Cameron, without Clanranald, all the lesser Chiefs will hang back…" The Marquis Murray stammered again.

"Dare you to interrupt me?!" The Prince's eyes, squinted small-bore, and then almost burned holes in the flesh of Marquis Murray. All of the Council was cowered and quiet.

"The Le Du Teillay shall set sail for France today. It will return with gold, men, French arms, and her sister ship will also be so laden. King Louis has promised." Prince Charles lied. "We will not give up. We will not give in. We will continue on." He pounded his fist into his open palm accenting each word.

The Bishop, who was hanging back, was quiet. Till now, he had not said a word. He turned to Young Ranald. "I implore you, by the Grace of God, get you some men and be the bodyguard for the Prince. He will stay whether or not you join. You must protect him a while until he knows the truth or until the Highlands erupt in support for him."

Young Ranald, smarting that his father had forbade him and feeling the weight of those conversations in Rome and Paris that had so encouraged the Prince to come to Scotland, could only nod his head in assent. His guilt and shame ensnared him, but still this only complemented his blood which ran hot to kill English and throw them out of his beloved Highlands.

Part IV: The Eve of Glenfinnan

The Le Du Teillay unloaded. The French Captain, knowing the realities of war, donated his swivel guns and some other ordinance. Ultimately, he had to up anchor and sail away, leaving the Prince and a meager pile of supplies to their fate.

Angus Beg MacDonald offered his house to the Prince and his Seven Men. There in early August 1745, they finalized their plans to gather the Clans at Glenfinnan. The Council decided August 19, a Monday, would be time enough for the word to fly to the corners of the Highlands and to allow the Clans to march to Glenfinnan. Although this was done in absolute secrecy, within a week, the word had made its way to the government.

On the evening of August 18, the Prince and the Seven with Young Ranald and his men, as a bodyguard, made their way to the home of MacDonald of Glenaladale by the waters of Loch Shiel. As the sun set, Young Ranald and the Prince walked along the banks of the Loch. The waters lapped the bank and formed a gentle symphony of tinkling watery notes. The Prince waxed nostalgic. "Ranald, I have not thanked you for staying. I do appreciate it. Your loyalty has touched me."

"Thank you, Sire." Ranald bowed to his Regent and then, slowly straightening up, looked at the orange sunlight dancing on the waters, breaking up the small circles of orange and then reforming into a stairway climbing across the Loch to the sun.

"If I may, Sire, what of tomorrow?"

"I have resigned myself to my fate. The Clans will come and we will be successful or Scotland will choose not to be free and not to be Catholic. Que sera, sera."

Ranald kicked a stone into the Loch. "Can it be that simple, Sire?"

"I have done all I can. It is now in God's hands. Tomorrow we shall sail to Glenfinnan. God grant us success. Pray you also for God's blessing upon us."

Part V: A Meeting

Later that evening Donald Cameron of Lochiel came alone to the Prince.

"Donald," the Prince said thinking that familiarity might be the best course, "many of the Highland Chiefs look to you. Though they may be loyal to our Cause, they have pledged to wait until you have given your word, one way or the other."

"My Prince," Donald Cameron began, bowing as he started. "I wish not to bring any offence to thee, but if I can't see the foreign aid, the aid of France, her troops, her ships, and her money, I cannot think to bring the men of my Clan or countenance any other Clan to support the Rising."

Prince Charles put his arm around the older clan chief. "Without you, I am nothing, our Cause is nothing, and no Stuart will ever rule Scotland again."

"Aye, that is so." Donald Cameron allowed.

"Then help me make it so. Now, this time is the most propitious time to Rise." The Prince hung back hoping the Cameron would ask why and thus become enthralled with the logic, by convincing himself.

"Why, my Grace?" Cameron leaned forward.

The Prince smiled thinking that he was reeling in a great fish, which did not know yet that it was hooked. "Where is the British Army?"

"Why, virtually all of it is overseas. Most of it is in Flanders with the King's son, William, the Duke of Cumberland fighting against Marshal de Saxe." Cameron answered the question not knowing whether the Prince was truly asking for information.

"Rightly," the Prince said. The Prince was leading the lamb to slaughter. "How good a general is Marshal de Saxe?"

"Why he is the best, they say." Cameron began to see where the Prince was heading.

"How many troops are there in Scotland?" The Prince said with a broad grin.

"Why General Cope has only a few raw recruits that haven't yet been trained." Cameron now clearly saw the geometry of the Prince's argument.

"It seems to me that once we prevail over those few loyalist militia, which are without training and are few in number, my father will be able to prevail upon Louis to give us the aid, the men, and the material, we need. I think, too, the Jacobites in England will rally to our Cause."

"I'll think this over, Sire and will give you my answer in the morning."

Part VI: The Day of Glenfinnan

It was quiet, too quiet, strangely quiet, almost eerily quiet. It was 11 AM in the morning and but for the Prince, and his small party, consisting of the Seven Men Moidart, Ranald and his men, including me, as bodyguard, all of whom had come in three small boats, there was not a soul around.

Glenfinnan is a valley with wet flatlands leading inwards from the Loch. Hills surrounded on all sides, except for the Loch. It now crossed the minds of Ranald, his men, and the Seven that they were in a perfect place to be ambushed. Someone asked, "Has God deserted us?"

The Prince made his way to the tenant farmer's small hut and waited. He wondered, "What will the day bring?"

Sometime after noon, Allan Ruadh Mac Donald, the half-brother of the Bishop, appeared with just over 150 men. While greeting Allan Ruadh MacDonald, the Prince thought, "So far only the Bishop, who had so counseled against the Endeavor, has been the one to come through and obtain support for me." Then the eerie silence wrapped itself again around the valley. All were caught in a hot summer's day funk.

Ranald entered the farmhouse. "I've placed my men and those of Allan Ruadh MacDonald around as a guard. I am concerned that we are vulnerable."

The Prince hardly stirred from his examination of the rough planks of the table. He did not look up, he merely nodded his assent.

The hot summer day continued and no one spoke. The heat engulfed the men in their wool plaid. Many shrank into the shadows to seek out some relief from the sun and its boiling heat. The sun started its downward slope towards the West. An hour went by. Then, a second hour. Nothing was stirring. Not a sound could be heard. The men thought that maybe the Enterprise had failed and wondered whether it was time to pick up their things and vanish back into the glens, hills, and lochs of the Highlands. Yet they remained, quiet, waiting, expectant, and sweating, as hope started to fail.

A third hour past. Men began looking at each other wondering whether the time to leave had come. All started to feel the heavy millstone of doubt begin to crush and grind their resolve. They were risking their lives by being there. Sweat was running down their backs, flowing from their armpits wetting their shirts. Several unwound their plaid and lay it on the ground leaving their shirts wide open and unbuckled. The heat was oppressive. August in the Highlands can be as hot as the outer cornices of Hell or cold with snow that can swirl with whipping winds that blow. Today, it was only the heat of the Sahara. Some men slumped and closed their eyes. Slumber overcame their guard. If the English came, they would've easily overcome the sleeping Scots and captured the Regent.

Then faintly, barely audible, a mere zephyr of sound carried on the still air. Not even a breeze was available to break the heat or carry the sound. Heads tilted to hear, to catch that barest hint of… What was it? Was it the English? Were we betrayed? Hands grasped dirk, broadsword, targe, and musket.

Then, wafting on a rare breeze, louder at one moment, softer in the next, rising now, falling now, came the wail of bagpipes. Cheers erupted from the MacDonalds as they saw Donald Cameron of Lochiel at the head of a column of 700 men of the Clan Cameron.

The Prince ran across the River Finnan to greet Cameron and to give permission for his men to venture beyond the lands of the Clan Cameron. Cheers chorused from MacDonalds to Camerons to MacDonalds and then back to Camerons again. And then as the cheers were still echoing, the MacDonalds of Keppoch arrived with 300 more men with Bishop MacDonald in tow. Finally, the Stewarts of Ardshiel were heard in the distance. The Rising had commenced!

The Marquis of Tullibardine, hobbling on his cane, bowed to the Prince and then with a grand gesture, unfurled and held aloft the silken Bratach Bhan-the Crimson and White banner. Its motto, Tandem Triumphans (Triumphant at Last!), brought cheers to the assembled mass. The Marquis attached the banner to a pole and raised it over the highest part of the knoll.

Spontaneously, Bishop MacDonald stepped forward, raised his arms, and blessed the banner, the gathering, the Prince, and the Holy Uprising, as he called it. First, he proclaimed the blessing in Latin, then repeated it in Gaelic, English, and finally, in French. This too was met by wild cheers, even though the vast majority of the assembly where Protestant (for all the Camerons where Presbyterian). The Uprising had begun! To a man, it was begun in the eyes of God as a Holy Cause.

But Glenfinnan also revealed a dark truth. First, although the Camerons had come, they had come short of weapons, as had the other clans. Second, and far worse by far, was the fact that not all of the great Clans were rallying to the banner of Prince Charles. One in particular, the Campbells, saw in the Rising the grand opportunity for which they had waited for perhaps centuries. Having been loyal to the English king at Glencoe, they remained loyal now. This was their chance to avenge all the wrongs ever done by the MacLeans, the Stewarts of Appin, and the Camerons. Now, with all the might of England behind them, they might finally devastate and destroy their rivals once and for all. The Campbells, knowing that they looked much like their rebel counter-parts, as they wore kilts, dirks, plaids, muskets, and broadswords, wore a sprig of myrtle in their bonnets, as well as red or yellow saltire, as opposed to the white ribbon or cockade of the rebels.

Part VI: First Blood at High Bridge

> The tree of liberty must be refreshed from time to time with the blood of patriots and tyrants.-**Thomas Jefferson**

The MacDonalds of Keppoch brought more than just men to the gathering at Glenfinnan; they also brought news of the action at High Bridge.

"Just three days ago, as the clan gathered to meet the Prince here at Glenfinnan, Donald MacDonell of Tirnadris with but 11 men and a piper were at High Bridge when two companies of the 1st Royal Regiment of Foot wanted to cross the River Spean. Although they were outnumbered 7 to 1, they concealed themselves in the trees surrounding the bridge and kept up a brisk fire. They moved themselves from position to position making their numbers seem greater and greater!" MacDonald of Keppoch declared excitedly, "By their bluff, they outfoxed the 85 men of the 1st Royal Regiment of Foot. They held them at bay! They stopped them! The 1st Royal Regiment of Foot had been sent from Fort Augustus to reinforce the garrison at Fort William, but they never made it." MacDonald of Keppoch cheered and all the men of his clan roared their approval too.

Although it was small, it was the first of the victories of the Rising of '45. The Prince, surveying the men who had come from the Highlands to support him at Glenfinnan and hearing of their prowess in fighting the English, could only smile and cheer also. He waved his hands and tipped his hat to his men to encourage their cheering, knowing that no words were needed now, because the deed at High Bridge spoke more eloquently than any speech could ever have. He basked in the glow of victory and in his heart he hoped for many, many, many more.

Chapter 15

"Those Heady Early Days"

Success-keeping your mind awake and your desire asleep.-**Sir Walter Scott**

Part I: The MacDonalds of Morar

Bishop Hugh MacDonald had spent most of his life in the lands of the MacDonalds of Morar. He was born in Glen Meoble through which wended the river of the same name. Later, he lived in the village of Morar, at the end of the road to the Isles, just south of Mallig, the ferry point to the Isle of Skye. There, the people are simple in their faith, but fierce in their faith. They are Catholic and will not waver, will not bend, and will not give in. Hugh drank in this fierce faith as a boy.

Still later, it was on the island of Eilean Ban in the far western end of Loch of Morar in the seminary named Gaotal, where he trained to become a priest. It was with pride, which he knew in his heart was a sin, but was still there anyway, that he rose to teach others to become priests at the selfsame seminary.

When he became a bishop, the furthest extent of his authority ranged throughout the lands of Morar and across the whole Loch of Morar and beyond the Golden Estuary and over the water to the Isle of Uist. The Isle of Uist is but ragged peaks of purple just peaking over the horizon, when viewed from the far western end of the Loch of Morar.

There had been many times when he had traveled throughout Scotland in disguise, for often the English put a price upon his head. He was the only Catholic Bishop in Scotland and his death would be the end, or so the English thought, of Catholic insurrection in the Highlands.

Now, at age 46, although he did not know it then, he was on the road to an adventure which would take him beyond the lands of the Clan MacDonald of Morar throughout Scotland and with an army at his back, very nearly to the gates of London. This army he conceived would be a Catholic Army vanquishing the evil English Protestants who had so long plagued his country and had driven him to conceal his faith and hide in the glens, moors, and meadows of the Highlands for these many years.

His tale had been indeed a strange one. Scotland had been a land of famine and poverty throughout his lifetime. The supposed economic benefits of the Act of Union had not filtered down to the most men in society. The average Scot was, in fact, worse off, actually far worse off under the Act of Union. Food riots were common. The government seemingly did nothing to alleviate the situation. Their only response was to raise taxes, which only compounded the situation. Then after that, England stationed more and more troops in Scotland, which it expected the starving Scots to provision. Thus, the Scots were forced to support their own oppressors. Clearly, the English portion of the United Kingdom favored England over Scotland and viewed Scotland as a piggy bank to be raided as the situation demanded.

Normally, this would have been a situation ripe for rebellion. Still, this did not have the effect of rallying these disenfranchised Scots to the Jacobite Cause, because too many Protestant Scots feared the return of the Catholic Stuarts due to their propensity to destroy the Protestant Kirk of Scotland.

As a Catholic Bishop, in fact, the only Catholic Bishop in Scotland, Hugh MacDonald had spent much of his life and his ministry in disguise fleeing from the government. It was hard, extremely hard to build a flock under these circumstances. So the numbers of Catholics in Scotland had not grown in the last few decades. But not all was well with the government either. The Act of Union was designed to end the Stuart threat to Hanoverian rule, as such it had failed miserably.

Part II: Truth and Consequences

> Honesty is the first chapter in the
> book of wisdom.-**Thomas Jefferson**

"Is it true?" The Prince looked at the Bishop with his steely gray eyes.

"Yes, Your Grace, my half-brother is a devout Catholic."

Prince Charles turned away and fidgeted with the wooden markers upon his map. Although each one represented the position of a Regiment of Scots or Regiment of the English, he did not care that he disturbed their placement. "That was not an answer to my question. I asked 'Is it true?'" He tapped his fingers against the map emphasizing each word. "Was your brother a Protestant?" The Prince changed the tapping upon the map to punching with his fist in the air with the last word being emphasized by a fist pounding his other hand.

"Your Grace, what he was is not as important as what he is. And he is, without a doubt, a devout Catholic." The Bishop now too was emphasizing each word.

The Prince cast his gaze at the Bishop and squinted his eyes. He was now clearly angry. The vein in his neck popped large.

"I have given you and your brother my utmost confidence. You are my spiritual guide and an officer. Although you are Chaplain to the Regiment of the Clanranald, I offered to make you a Lieutenant Colonel, third in command, which you declined in favor of your brother, Allan, who accepted the commission and is now serving as such. I need to know if he will be a problem."

"Your Grace, Allan Ruadh, was the first of the Highland Chiefs to join you, to follow you, and to swear his allegiance to you, to kneel before you, and to proclaim you Regent. Does this not count for anything?" The Bishop placed his hands, as if in prayer, before his face. His gesture spoke the words that his tongue had not said: "I beg you not to make me tell."

The Prince looked at the Bishop. "Do you think this not pains me? Do you think I am not grateful to him? And to you? You are the one who brought the first men at arms to my side. Still, I must know, if I am to command! Obey your Monarch's chosen Regent. Knee now and tell me!"

Hugh MacDonald, as if whipped, fell to his knees, tears streaming down his face. The Bishop, looking like a cornered animal, looked both ways to his sides for escape, but seeing none, sighed.

"Yes, my Lord, Allan was a Protestant. His mother was a Protestant and because she was the daughter of MacDonald of Sleat, the chief of the Clan Donald, her wish, her opinion, her request, and her decision carried great weight in all family matters. Her husband, though a man of Meoble, Alexander, by name, was not as strong as she and although a Catholic, he acquiesced in her demand. It later served Allen to say he was a Protestant to inherit his estate, for under the 1700 act, this would've safeguarded his right to his inheritance. But later, he married his second wife, Mary, of the staunchly Catholic Kinlochmodiart family. It was by her hand that he came to the one true faith. He is now, as I said, a devout Catholic. He will not be a problem. The members of Clanranald have welcomed him into their midst as they have always welcomed the MacDonalds of Morar."

"Rise, Bishop. If I had 10 men as loyal to me as you and your brother, the Uprising would not fail. I will reward the MacDonalds of Morar. I will name Allan's sons, John and Ranald, as lieutenants. I will promote your brother, John of Guidale, who is presently teaching students at Gaotal, to be a captain. So too, I will name your mother's brothers, the MacDonalds of Kinlochmodiart as officers-Donald as a Colonel, Allan as a Captain, and John as a Captain."

Part III: The Scent of Victory is in the Air!

> Liberty's in every blow! Let us do
> or die.- **Robert Burns**

But I have gotten ahead of myself. After Bonnie Prince Charles rallied the clans at Glenfinnan, there was much to do. But what a day it was at Glenfinnan. I was there when Prince Charles raised the standard and told us he was the Regent for our King James VIII. There were about 1,200 of us then. I stood next to Young Ranald of Clanranald, but we were the only ones of Clanranald. Chief Ranald had forbidden the clan from turning out for the Prince. Young Ranald was defying him, but would not tell me why. Clan MacDonald of Keppoch was there, as was Clan Cameron, and Clan MacDonell of Glengarry. We cheered and cheered until our voices were hoarse and spent.

I did not know then that Alexander MacDonald of Sleat and Norman MacLoed of MacLoed had refused to support Prince Charles. I also did not know that King George had paced a bounty upon Prince Charles' head of £30,000-a vast sum in a country where two or three pounds a month was a man's income. I do not know what I would have done had I known, but I didn't know and perhaps it is better that I did not know. What I did know was not encouraging either: I knew that Old Ranald, the chief of our Clan, had not blessed his son in this endeavor and had not sent him with the 200 or so of our Clan who had come. I stood by Young Ranald, knowing that I was defying my Chief.

In the days that followed, men from the Highlands joined us. We grew to some 1,800 or so. None of us knew, however, that two clan chieftains had bargained for compensation before coming out for Prince Charles. The Prince though took it in stride: 'A man on my side, however he came to be on my side, is still a man on my side,' the Prince believed. He expected that every man would do his duty when the time came. He was looking at the future and saw that the men would be swept along, once the rock began rolling.

Next, we were marching to engage General John Cope's forces of some 4,000 men who had marched into the Highlands. We set a trap for him at the Pass of Corrairack, but General Cope sensed it and withdrew to Inverness. We then captured our first Scots city-Perth. We routed two troops of English dragoons at Coatbridge. The smell of victory was in the air. The smell of sweet, intoxicating, exhilarating, mesmerizing, laurel-wreathed victory filled our minds and hearts. We were going to win!

Part IV: A Lord Goes A-Calling

"Here's tae us. Wha's like us? Damn few, and they're a'deid."-**A traditional toast.**

Edinburgh was enjoying a beautiful late summer day. The sky was punctuated by a few wooly clouds that grazed blissfully over the blue meadows. It was a perfect day to go calling and Lord Lovat had determined that today he would make what he thought would be the most momentous visit of his life.

The Court of Session held its proceedings along the Royal Mile which stretched from Holyrood Palace at one end of Canongate Street to Edinburgh Castle at the other end. Canongate Street successively becomes named High Street, then Lawnmarket, and finally, Castle Hill, but all known collectively as the Royal Mile. His carriage ascended the steep hill from the Grassmarket, the horses grunting with the strain. In his heart, he knew that his massive girth was adding to their troubles.

Lord Lovat got out of his carriage. His gouty big toe of his right foot was swollen and painful. He shifted his cane to give himself better leverage to descend the iron steps the footman had extended. Although he was making a herculean effort to go out, still, he knew that he had to see Duncan Forbes, the Lord President of the Court of Session.

Lord Lovat mulled over what he would ask the Lord President, who was one of the most influential men in all of Scotland. Duncan Forbes hailed from the moors of Culloden and had risen above his low birth to become not only one of the most powerful, but also one of the highest men of the government. Duncan Forbes could sway many men to or away from the Cause. Lord Lovat knew that it was a forlorn hope that he could bring Forbes to the Jacobite Cause, but he had to try. Lord Lovat had dressed for the occasion in his finest clothes, but had left off any hint of tartan, plaid, or kilt, lest he offend the Lord President.

He slowly ascended the steps to the Court. This was agony for him, but he betrayed not a hint of the pain he was experiencing upon his face. 'Never let ye opponents see ye weaknesses,' he thought to himself.

A clerk ushered him into the chambers of the Lord President, for even though he was not expected, Lord Lovat was a man of such repute (whether you thought good or ill of him-everyone had an opinion of Lord Lovat, for he was the most despised and the most loved of the Scottish lords) that the clerk knew the Lord President would want to see him. The clerk officiously offered Lord Lovat a cup of freshly brewed tea and gave him the choice of lemon or milk. "How many teaspoons of sugar will ye take?" The clerk inquired. "Four," came Lord Lovat's the reply. The clerk offered him the newspaper and departed to find the Lord President.

Duncan Forbes appeared in his judicial splendor. With his black robes flowing, his snow white periwig, tied with a black ribbon in the back, briefs under his right arm, and a thick legal volume under his left, he was the picture of a biblical prophet.

"Well, Simon, what brings you here to Edinburg?" Forbes motioned to a large leather wing-back chair for Lord Lovat to sit in.

"Duncan, it is good to see you," said Lord Lovat, while he thought, 'Damned if it is good to see you, you old conniving rat.' "Thought I'd come to town and see what the government is going to do about these rebels."

"Ah, the rabble, rift-raft, flotsam and jetsam of the Highlands have come to rally round the Young Pretender. General Cope'll make short work of that, I think. The whole thing will take a few weeks, may be a month or so." Forbes bent down and placed his legal briefs upon his desk. He carefully settled the thick volume of law upon the top of a mountain of other books with the same binding, which mountain appeared that it might topple with a sudden breeze.

"So you don't think there's a thing to worry about." Lord Lovat settled deeper into the comfy chair. He tenderly rested his right foot upon the cushy ottoman. He sipped his tea as if he did not have a care in the world.

"No man, I don't." Forbes gaveled his right hand down as if he were rendering a verdict.

"There's no chance the government might negotiate with the Prince? It's war only? This will mean the ruin of the clans? Is that what you want?" Lord Lovat stirred his tea, pretending that this was all idle talk and nothing more.

"Yes, if I have my way. And given my recent correspondence with the King, I just might!" Duncan Forbes opened his robes and sat down. He smiled widely. "Those Jacobites deserve the gallows; they deserve to be drawn and quartered; they deserve the worst death imaginable." His face was twinkling with the prospects of bodies swinging from ropes and bodies torn asunder.

Lord Lovat knew there was no hope that his old friend might be swayed.

Part V: Edinburgh, the Capital lies at our feet!

We marched on Edinburgh. In the panic, the forces defending the city melted away in the night, leaving it virtually undefended and ripe for the taking, but for its walls.

The Camerons lay outside the city gate, Netherbow Port, which was shut tight. We had not the siege equipment, nor the men to besiege the city. Netherbow Port opens upon the Royal Mile and is not far from the Palace of Holyrood. Netherbow Port is an immensely impressive building. Its central tower is more than one hundred feet high and is flanked by four miniature towers. On either side of the central tower is a turret raising some 60 feet in the air. Upon the central tower is a gigantic clock. The depth of the building's brick is easily 75 feet. There was nothing that we could do to gain entrance there.

The civic leaders, led by the Lord Provost Archibald Stewart, called upon the Prince for a parlay. They went to see the Prince in their finest coach, hoping to make an impressive show.

"As is their wont, our merchants want to protect their goods and wares from the pillage, looting and burning that always seems to accompany an army taking a city," Lord Archibald deigned to say to the Prince. The Lord Provost was smug in the belief, that even though General Cope had marched away, the walls of Edinburgh would withstand the Jacobite Army, which had no siege equipment.

"My fellow citizens of the city of Edinburgh have seen your army of Highlanders, arrayed in their scruffy rags, shod in bare feet, and looking thoroughly mangy. We know that your men are awfully hungry, so my charges are naturally worried about what would happen to them, if we were to surrender our city to you. I am sure you can see." Archibald Stewart said haughtily and condescendingly. Tellingly, the Lord Provost did not acknowledge Prince Charles' rank as a Prince or as a Regent.

"My Lord Provost, I cannot pretend that I am able to assure you that there will be no incidents. I will deliver orders not to loot, pillage, cause rapine, or otherwise molest the city and its inhabitants." The Prince simply said to the Lord Provost, not returning the insult of denying his rank and title. The Prince was wise enough to know that the Highlanders could not restrain themselves after centuries of cattle raids and the like. So, therefore, he could not give the City Elders any assurances.

Out of earshot of the Prince, Lord Provost Archibald Stewart conferred with the other leaders of the city. He had long been urging calm. "It seems to me that our walls are strong. We have plenty of food and water. They have none. I think we can wait them out, not the other way around," the Lord Provost pontificated in his slow and deliberate manner. His voice was sonorous and deep. As he spoke, the heads of the merchants began to nod in agreement.

"Without iron-clad assurances, it is simply impossible for me to accede to your request to surrender my city." Without waiting for a reply, the Lord Provost Archibald Stewart turned on his heels and walked away from Prince Charles, deliberating showing his rear to the Regent, as an insult.

So the city worthies drove back to the city in their fine coach, right past the Camerons who were lying there in wait.

Now to the Camerons, it was, as if a sign from God had been given. The coach carrying the civic leaders of Edinburgh approached Netherbow Port. Almost miraculously, the gate opened to let the coach in. Without prompting or upon order, the Camerons swarmed through the gate. The few sentries were quickly overcome. The city, under the control of the Lord Provost Archibald Stewart, quickly surrendered and so the city fell into Jacobite hands.

The next day was, again, one of those heady days. I remember it, but as if it came from a dream. Prince Charles, with as much flourish, pomp, and circumstance as was possible, entered the city and made his way to the Palace of Holyrood. At Mercat Cross, outside of the Parliament Building next to St. Giles Kirk along the Royal Mile, King James the VIII was proclaimed King of Scotland and Prince Charles proclaimed his Regent.

CHAPTER 16

PRESTONPANS-A TASTE OF HELL

Part I: Duco (I Lead)

> "Hey Johnnie Cope are ye sleeping
> yet?"-**Scottish Pipe Tune**

We came up out of the mist that swirled deep and grey as the dusky twilight before dawn broke. We had marched all night and then just when we were within a hundred yards or less of the English lines, we huddled down in the dew laden grass of the moor to catch a snatch of sleep before the attack. The marsh, where we were, was dank, the night was dark, and the weather was drek. The men were expectant, exhilarant, and exuberant, but quiet. Not a whisper was heard as each man bedded down. We had tied our swords such that neither a clink nor a clank was heard as we moved.

Our foe, General Sir Joh Cope, had placed his men in what he thought was a grand and perfect defensive position. He had written earlier the evening before to the Prime Minister, Henry Pelham:

"To The Right Honorable Henry Pelham,

Prime Minister, we have assumed a strong, nay, unassailable defensive position, astride the Firth of Forth. Our right is anchored upon two stone walls, while our left is behind an impassable bog. Thus, our flanks are secure as our intelligence is that our foe has no cavalry with which to turn or threaten our flanks. Finally, we have dug a ditch across our front. My force is somewhat less than 4,000 men. Again, our intelligence is that Prince Charles has no more than 2,500 men. Neither side has had much training, so it is my belief that our numbers, our position, and our horse will carry the day, if the Prince is so bold and so foolish as to attack our position. God save the King.

General Sir John Cope, Commander in Chief of All Scottish Forces of the King"

How do I know this? I read the letter, just after we had captured it. This piece of luck paled beside the better and bigger piece of luck in the form of a farmer we encountered just as we started our march.

He had been out in the night and at first I thought him an English spy. Because who else would be out in the night, such a drek night? Only an English spy trying to gain information about our force, our arms, and our leaders would be out!

The more I talked with him, the more I believed his story that he was looking for us, such that he could lead us, that is guide us along a wee path, narrow and rocky that led through the bog.

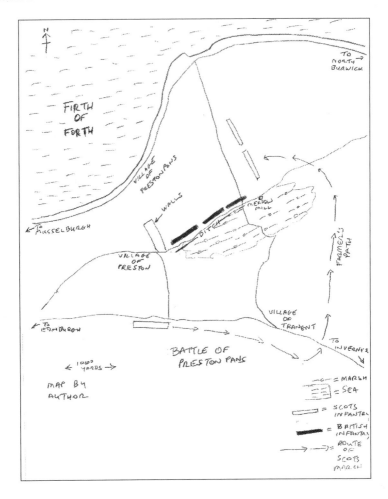

"I kin a'git ye behind Cope an' h's line!" He smiled a tooth-gapped smile that bespoke the innocence of a man who had lived a hard life in a hard place.

"Are you sure?" I asked, still not wholly convinced.

"May the Lord take me now if I lie." He crossed himself in the Roman fashion.

"This path is but a man or two wide. My coos take it and I's follow them. It'll come up near their line just on their left."

I reported back to Colonel Ranald. He went on to General Lord George Murray. The time ticked by slowly. Then the order came.

I was to lead the attack at Prestonpans. General Lord George Murray had honored tradition by giving the MacDonalds of Clanranald the lead of the column in the attack. Colonel Ranald had honored me by choosing my company to lead our regiment.

I trekked the night behind my farmer, my hand on my claymore to behead him if he proved false.

We moved by two's and three's-sometimes one at a time-winding our way through the bog along the narrow path. My feet squished in the muddy mixture of grass, water, heather, and earth. Churned by slogging feet into a goo that sucked my boots off as I pulled my feet out of the gelatinous morass to continue the march, the mud began to win the war of man versus the elements. The minutes turned to hours, but still we trudged on, emboldened by our mission, secure in the knowledge of our Almighty God, the rightness of our cause, and the blessing of finding a knowledgeable and willing guide.

We saw in the mist the faint orange glow of the bonfires Cope's men had set to assist them in seeing our men sneaking up on them. Somehow, our luck held and the posted sentries saw us not, heard us not, and sensed us not.

Around 5:00 am, I whispered orders to be repeated in whispers down the line. My orders were that the men should attack, when there was just enough light to see the form of men of the enemy. It was then our luck failed.

"Who goes there?" came the counter from the English.

I hushed the men. Again it came, "Who goes there?"

We made no response hoping that silence would lead to reassurance and reassurance would quiet the inquiry.

"Who goes there?"

This was followed almost immediately by, "Sound the alarm!"

General Sir John Cope then seemed to be everywhere at once. "Wheel men, now! Make the left, the front! Wheel now!" Cope's voice could be heard above the muffling effect of the misty fog that had till now swallowed our noise into the night.

Then I heard him clearer. "Dragoons cover each flank. Artillery to the right! Foot to the center! Now! Double quick! Now!"

His orders were echoed by Colonel, Majors, Captains, and Lieutenants, and men scurried here and there as rapidly a battle line appeared where one did not exist a moment ago.

Part II: Battle is Joined!

> "Stand Fast, Stand Firm, Stand Sure, Stand True." **– Harrison Gray Otis**

Dawn was breaking. I ordered my men up. I waved my claymore in the air. Clanranald's guttural, Gaelic battle cry rent the air, as the pipers' bagpipes were skerling, drums were beaten, men fired their muskets-I had hoped they would fire two volleys, but after just one-they charged, lochabar axes cutting the sky, dirks raised, and swords swinging. As they charged, our clan began its special pibroch, which, when added to the booming bursts of the carnivorous cannon of our foes, blasted our ears with such a clamorous cacophony of crashing, clanging, and clattering sounds as men met men in battle and flesh rent flesh asunder.

The blades of swords struck one another, sparks flew, muskets fired and misfired, the acrid smell of burnt gun power and smoke hung over obscuring the field. The caustic smoke caused my eyes to burn, while my tears flowed distorted my vision. Sweat poured out from every pore and the salty liquid creased the corners of my mouth and further stung my eyes. My hands controlled by nothing other than something otherworldly spun, sliced, smashed, thrust, cut, hacked on and on again. My claymore was doing the work for which I had trained for years. The din crescendoed. The racket was intense.

Parts of bodies were everywhere. A hand here. An arm there. A groan emanated from a body next to me. There was blood on my sleeve. A headless body was in front of me.

As our surge hit the English line, they broke and ran for the rear. The walls which they had thought would be their protection and safety quickly proved themselves to be their bottleneck and trap. All the gunners, save two, fled and left their cannon and mortars. Two men were left to fire six cannon and six mortars. They bravely loaded each gun and pulled the lanyards in the face of their attackers.

General Cope tried to stem the rout. He pulled his gun and yelled, "I will shoot the man who leaves his post! Stand with me men!"

Seeing General Cope standing against the flood, Colonel James Gardiner, the commander of the Dragoons, tried to help rally the foot soldiers, his own horsemen having ingloriously fled the field. He was atop his white charger, when three Highlanders attacked him. One using a musket with bayonet, obviously, an English gun, stabbed the horse causing it to rear, while another swung his sword missing the brave Colonel's head. The third one raised his pistol and shot the Colonel who fell from his horse mortally wounded.

With this Cope's army dissolved, disintegrated, and degenerated into clumps of men fleeing in all directions, throwing down their muskets, pistols, swords, and daggers. It was as if the starter of a race had yelled "Go!" In less than 15 or so minutes, an entire army had been wiped off the face of the earth.

General Sir John Coe rallied about 170 men, who retreated in somewhat good ordered from the field. The rest were scattered to the wind.

I was exhausted. The life just drained from my body and I was never more tired. I started to sit down when I saw across the field what I thought was Major James MacGregor, the son of Rob Roy. He was struggling to rise up from the ground which was wet with red blood all around him. I ran over to him and cradled his head.

"Major, is there anything I can do for ye?" I screamed.

He looked up into my eyes. "Mother, is that ye?" He asked. His eyes were dull and almost lifeless.

Not knowing what to do, I answered, "Yes, Jamie, my son."

"Did I do my duty?" His breathing was shallow, faint, and near final.

"Yes, my son."

"Bless me mother." A tear streamed from his eye.

"I give you my blessing. You are in God's care now." I bit my lip. I hurt inside for lying to him, but I counted it a great kindness to ease his last moments.

My heart sank as I saw him die. He was a brave man and true to the legacy of his father.

I came to my senses. There was much to do. There were many, many men around me crying out from their wounds. As my mind focused, I could see that most of the wounded were wearing Red Coats and not plaid. The dead, too, were mostly English. Then our men began to cheer. They were cheering for victory; they were cheering for life. They had lived through a hurricane of death and destruction and now it was good to be alive and to be unwounded.

We had captured their wagon train with more muskets, ammunition, and supplies than there were men in our army. Besides, there was gold, some £5,000 of it. This was in addition to their six cannon and six mortars, bringing our total artillery now to 8 guns and 6 mortars. Fortunately, too, we now had shot and powders for them to blaze away at the English.

I ordered my men to begin the task of burying the dead: ours and theirs. "We must tend to the wounded-all of the wounded." I ordered. We would care for them, even though I knew in my heart that they would never return the favor.

After all was said and done, it appeared that we had lost 30 Highlanders killed-it pained me that we had lost any man, but still our losses were so slight compared to theirs. We buried over 500 of them. Their wounded amounted to some 300 or so which dwarfed our 70 or so. Our problem, however, were the men we captured: some 1,500 or over half our number. General Sir John Cope was right: his army had dissolved, disintegrated, and degenerated.

Chapter 17

The Campaign of '45

Lay the proud usurpers low!
Tyrants fall in every foe!
Liberty's in every blow!
Let us do - or die!
Robert Burns

Part I: Why We Fight

"Oats. A grain, which in England is generally given to horses, but in Scotland supports the people."
– Samuel Johnson

I fought in the campaign of '45 for Bonnie Prince Charles and I would fight for him again, if only given the chance. Some have said that the outcome was foreordained from the beginning. Were the Clans fighting the tide of inevitability? Was the Jacobite cause just a romantic vision of gossamer?

Why did I fight? Yes, I fought to restore my King, but it was more than that. I was a Catholic and Bonnie Prince Charles would restore my King, the House of Stuart, and more than this, as a Catholic King, he would stop the English from persecuting my religion. But it was more than that. The

Act of Union stuck in my craw. Scotland was tethered to and subservient to England. Yes, we were supposed to be equals in this Union, but, of course, we were not. We were the junior partners, the younger brothers, oh, let's call it what it was, we were the enslaved. We owed more to London than we could ever pay. They knew it and relished in the inequality of the arrangement.

The Clan chiefs could see the future. If England had its way, then the Clan system was dead. The Clan chiefs would lose their feudal rights, privileges, and the way of the life of the Highlands would be changed forever.

Let me explain how life was in the Highlands. The chief was lord. He dispensed justice; he kept peace; he led us in war. Depending upon whether you were a Clansman or tacksman, determined what duties and rents you owed to the Lord. The tacksman owed rent to the Lord. He may or may not have been a member of the Clan. Usually, he was not. Still, the lord could ask him to join with the Clan, when the Clan went to war. He might bring his lochabar axe, a weapon much like a medieval pike, but with an axe blade. Nary would a tacksman have a broadsword. He would not carry a targe, or a pistol.

Now, to be fair, many a Clansmen might not carry a broadsword. Certainly, he would carry a dirk and a targe. Those who did carry a broadsword or a claymore would join the front line, when the Clan's regiment would face the enemy in battle. He had his musket and maybe a pistol or two with his powder and musket balls. Each ball of lead weighed an ounce or so, and then with the powder, and all else, we might be carrying over 50 or 60 pounds of weight.

A Highlander is proud of his sheep and his wool. Sheep are life in the Highlands. The sheep are your meat. Wool is life in the Highlands. It keeps you warm in the winter and protects you from rain all the year. Sheep abound throughout Scotland, thank the good Lord. They dot every hill and mountain. Thank the good Lord that sheep are stupid. There is no way to be polite about it. They will graze on the grass never looking where they are going up and up till the edge of a cliff and sometimes right to it and over it. That's one of the reasons you have to watch them. They would get themselves into the worst predicaments, if left untended. It is a wonder that they survive at all, even being watched.

But sheep are hardy creatures which endure the wind-swept, thumping cold rain, which beats upon one's eyes and face wind-driven as it is parallel to the ground, even in August across the green of the Isle of Skye. It does not matter what breed of sheep you have. All of them have their good points, and all have their bad point: they're sheep. Some say the small brown Hebridean sheep, which sprinkle the Isles, have been in Scotland forever and certainly are one of the first breeds of domesticated sheep. Their horns can fully spiral around themselves and make quite a show. Of course, the Shetland sheep, which, too, are small, but are always white and lacking the impressive horns of the Hebridean sheep, are a creature of the isles, but they are much better eating. I have never seen a North Ronaldsay sheep, which, I am told, is brown, but lighter in color than the Hebridean sheep, and with a much more narrow face. Their claim to fame is the fact that they eat seaweed on the rocky coasts of the Orkney Isles.

I mostly herded the Scottish Blackface sheep. But for their distinctive faces, these sheep are white, have small curved horns that curve towards their backs, and are generally pleasant to deal with, as much as one can say it is pleasant to deal with a sheep.

I have handled all the tasks one can imagine with a sheep. My favorite was to throw a sheep on its back whilst it is in my lap and shear them of their wool. You take your shears which are like large scissors. Then you cut the wool in such a way that it comes off almost in one large blanket. We then can make all that we need from this wonderful material. Woolen bonnets, scarves, shawls, jackets, coats, kilts, pants, blankets, tunics, and shirts are just some of the things the Highland women can knit out of the Highland wool.

It is tending the sheep that makes the Highlander tough and resilient. You have to be just to take the weather. It can be intolerably cold and snow and then be a summer's day within but a half hour or so in the Highlands. Tending sheep makes fine warriors. It makes men who are independent and confident. It makes men who are resourceful and practical. It makes men who can think for themselves, because you are alone and there is no one else to help you, your dog, or your sheep out of a jam. Tending sheep makes men and tending sheep in the Highlands makes Highlanders.

A Highlander is always topped with a bonnet. Your head needs the warmth that it brings and your outfit in not complete without one. They are invariably knitted from wool. You can take some ribbon and sew it to the rim to make a tie around the chin, but mostly they are just pulled on the head. My bonnet had a little button gathering in the top center. Most men place a sprig of heather or some other plant o'er the left ear. Because wool is white, brown, or black, depending upon the breed of sheep from whence it came, you don't have to dye it, less you want to, and still can have some color upon ye. Upon my bonnet, I bore the white cockade of the Jacobite.

I went to war with a wool jacket pulled over my wool waistcoat. Both of these came over the top of my wool plaid, which I wrapped around me first and placed o'er my left shoulder and wore in a kilt around my waist. This I did, because as a Captain, I was a gentleman. Now, many gentlemen wore breeches. Perhaps, as many wore breeches as wore the plaid, but I felt that the plaid was more versatile, what with it being a blanket and a raincoat. That was my choice, but I didn't think less of any who chose the breeches.

Now, in contrast, most of men wore neither a coat nor a plaid nor breeches, and went about with only their shirts out. Many men complained that the plaid was just too bulky to do any type of work in and that they could go into battle with their shirts tails tied between their legs. Obviously, a sense of decency was lacking in many of our men.

Across my chest slung from my right shoulder was my baldric to carry my claymore. It was black, shiny leather with shiny silver accouterments. I did not carry a firelock, or powder flask, or a ball bag. I figured that I would fire one round and then lead my men in a charge that would break the back of the enemy line.

Upon my legs, I wore trews (you might call them knee socks) trussed up with ribbons behind my knees. I did this because most of the time we were fighting in the winter and this was much warmer than mere stockings. Trews, or truibhs in my language, are always cross cut for greater flexibility of the cloth at the knee. This also gave it its distinctive diagonal check pattern. While some wore them like the Irish, that is one bland color, most were adorned in plaid, like their kilts.

My plaid was not the roy roy red and black check that later became so popular among the Lowlanders. I wore a true Highland plaid that my mother had woven for me. It was a plaid which had the dull blues, browns, and greens of most Highlanders, but with a stripe of red, as was becoming more and more popular.

A plaid is a complex garment. First, it is six double ells of tartan material. For those not from the Highlands, an ell is about 37 inches, so a plaid is quite long. A double ell is not twice as long, but twice as wide. The usual width of a plaid is about 27 inches. So to obtain double ell, one would have to sew two lengths together. As most gentlemen, I would fold over the six or so ells of my plaid to make it a double thickness, which was quite sufficient against the wintery cold of '45.

The wearing of a kilt is also complex. Once folded double thick, you wind it around your waist, so the bottom just touches the knees, the excess is draped o'er your shoulder. The plaid is belted to your waist to keep it in place. Many will secure the plaid o'er the shoulder with a clan brooch, as I did.

The kilt is pleated. How one pleats a kilt is a tedious business using any flat surface, but on campaign, it is impossible. I know that most of us let the pleating go and most times our kilts hung wrinkled and unpleated. Anyway, the pleat is worn in the back.

Now what did we eat on our march? Oatmeal. Any good Scotsman can make at least nine good meals out of oatmeal. I can tell you there were times when we had not time or ability to make a fire and we found out there was a tenth way to eat oatmeal: raw. It was carried in a linen bag hidden beneath the plaid, if one was wearing plaid, or slung over the shoulder, if one was wearing breeches. This was true even though Lord George Murray was said to have tried to obtain haversacks for all of us. We had to carry our griddle pans to make our oatmeal pancakes or cast-iron porridge pots.

I had no money for armor and knew few who did. A couple of men had chain mail. I had a padded akheton made of cotton, but that was as close as I came to armor. Ranald had given it to me and also told me its name, which he said came from the Arabic word for cotton. Most had nothing but their plaid or their linen shirt to protect them. We relied upon our targes, our Highland shields. These would shield us from blows of the sword, but could these protect us from cannon shot or firelock ball? No one knew. We all said that armor would have slowed us down as we charged. I don't know if that was more the way to pretend that we were all right without armor or whether it was the truth. It didn't matter anyway, because we had none and had no prospects of getting any.

We were armed. Some had the full accoutrement: a musket, a broad sword or a claymore, a targe, a pistol or two, a dirk or a dagger, with a powder horn, and a pouch for ammunition. There were those armed only with a bow, there were those armed only with a sword and a buckler, or an ordinary sgian, a long dagger similar to a dirk. And there were those who carried a pitchfork or a scythe or a lochabar. They hoped that they would find strewn upon the field something more suitable with which to fight.

The muskets we carried were a varied lot. Fowling pieces, obsolete matchlocks, and broken unserviceable weapons were carried, for we were in the age when every man thought he should carry a musket and, thus, every man tried to carry some sort of fire-arm. This view was reinforced by the stand of the MacDonalds at Falkirk Muir on January 28, 1746. Three times, the English Lieutenant General Henry Hawley, nicknamed Hangman Hawley, because he treated his own men so harshly, had ordered his cavalry to attack. Three times, the MacDonalds stood and leveled volleys which turned back and cracked the cavalry charges. After that, no one doubted that everyone needed a musket. We gathered all we could find from the Muir, confident now that our army could face whatever the English set upon us.

We were rag-tag at the beginning, maybe only an armed rabble. But as the campaign wore on, we received some arms from France, which helped, and we gathered the weapons of our foe, who left us bounty upon bounty upon the fields of battle, when they turned and ran.

The early days were ones of heady-stuff. We marched and came upon our foe and had a battle and we were victorious. We were undefeated. With each successive and successful battle we gained weapons, uniforms, cannon, food stuffs, haversacks, powder horns, ammunition pouches, wagons, horses, and most important of all: experience. We became veterans by doing. Yes, Lord George Murray did a wonderful job of training us. He drilled us and taught us how to do the complex maneuvers of those upon the continent. Our morale grew and our confidence grew in ourselves and in our leaders. It was not 1690; it was not 1715; it was 1745. This was our time and this was our destiny. The Jacobite Cause would not fail this time. Truly, the third time was the charm.

I was armed with my claymore at Prestonpans, Falkirk, and Culloden. A claymore is a fearsome weapon. Mine, like every one ever made, was forged just for me. It was forged by my uncle, my father died years before I could carry such a weapon. A claymore is made for the man. I loved my claymore and I dare to think my claymore loved me. And even if it did not, I liked to believe that it did. My weapon was made such that the point of the blade when the hilt was placed on the ground should just tickle the hair on the bottom of my chin. Its heft must be just right for me wield. The hilt must have just the right feel for the owner's two hands to grasp it comfortably and swing it o'er head in the air.

But it is the yell, the throat wrenching, guttural, scream from the bowels of hell, emitting from a maniac, who brandishes a glinting sheen of five feet of polished steel, slashing the air, held by two hairy arms above a sea of plaid, who is in the best form of a middle ages berserker rushing forward as an unstoppable tidal wave of death and destruction, which scares all but the best trained of men from the field and causes them to rout in panic.

We were an army. We were men from all backgrounds and professions. Some of us were doctors, chaplains, lawyers, poets, and philosophers, having attended some of the most prestigious universities throughout the United Kingdom and Europe. Of course, some of us were farmers, shepherds, brewers, bakers, and cowherds. Some had no education.

Part II: Divided Commands; Divided Loyalties

> It is the privilege of posterity to set matters right between those antagonists who, by their rivalry for greatness, divided a whole age.-**Joseph Addison**

As I believe I have said, Scotland is always a land of divisions and contradictions. Our army was a perfect example of that.

I have spoken of William Murray, the Marquis of Tullibardine, a fine gentleman, of whom I had become quite fond. Although he was an elder statesman and had a fine military record, he begged the Prince to put his brother, Lord George Murray, in command of the army. "I am simply your Majesty, too ill to lead. I cannot mount a horse. And if I get a bad attack of the gout, I will be useless to you and to the men." The Marquis pleaded.

Now, Lord George Murray appeared to be a good choice. Just prior to the Rising, he had been General Sir John Cope's second in command and, thus, he knew the mind of his opponent and the disposition of his opponent's forces. When he had defected to the Prince, he brought with him a contingent of trained fighters. He had fought for the Old Pretender in 1715. He had been wounded in battle at Glenshiel in 1719. Although he had been pardoned for his previous rebellions, when the Prince raised the banner at Glenfinnan, he immediately defected to the Jacobite Cause. His personality had one defect; however, he was an eternal pessimist. He also had one political defect: he opposed the Prince's intention to abolish the Act of Union.

He was a diminutive man, whose hair had greyed. He did not wear a periwig. His eyebrows were stark black in contrast to his crown and many men wondered whether he applied boot-black or dye to his eyebrows. This led to the speculation of why he would dye his eyebrows and not his hair, although no consensus was ever reached. His nose, although nicely portioned and shaped, was way too large for his small face. His eyes were dark and piercing. He was opinionated and ever confident that his decisions were completely correct and not subject to dispute.

Unbeknownst to William Murray, the Marquis of Tullibardine, Colonel John O'Sullivan, the Prince's main military advisor had advanced his own name to be the army's ccommander. Colonel John O'Sullivan despised Lord George. "He is a pompous buffoon without one wit of military sense," he told the Prince. "Can ye trust him? He's been a government man."

It was then that the Duke of Perth, John Drummond and I entered the Prince's war tent. "What say you to the selection of Lord George as commander of the army?" asked the Prince. Colonel John O'Sullivan's mouth hung agape at the directness of the question as well as its import. Drummond, who was known for his tact and diplomacy, hesitated to answer the Prince, I could see. The Prince looked at him, his eyes imploring him to answer. "Well, your Majesty, he is a fine candidate, he has experience, he brought men with him, he knows General Cope and his ways, but your Majesty has several fine candidates and you must weigh their credentials also."

"Such as whom?" The Prince leaned upon both of his hands atop his maps of Scotland and his troop disposition map with its wooden markers.

"Well, William Murray, the Marquis of Tullibardine would be a good choice and he is the elder brother. Then there's the MacDonalds who have held the place of honor on the right since the days of Robert the Bruce. Surely, one would consider one of them. Is there no one among your military advisers who might fit the bill?" The Duke's voice trailed off. "Maybe I shouldn't mention this, but the Romans used to rotate the command between their two consuls-that it would be a way of sharing the burden and the honor." He secretly signalled to me. We bowed and excused ourselves from the campaign tent.

"Yes, like the Romans. They had a way of winning. I could balance Lord George with the Duke of Perth," muttered the Prince as we left.

So we had two commanding generals, two men who viewed the world very differently and did things very differently. And each day, it seemed that the one undid what the other had done the day before.

Part III: On to London!

> It is your attitude, and the suspicion that you are maturing the boldest designs against him, that imposes on your enemy.-**Frederick the Great**

After we captured Edinburgh, the Seven Men of Moidart wanted to clear all of Scotland of the small garrisons of King George's men. Prince Charles wanted to invade England.

"If we invade England now, those Englishmen, who favor our Jacobite Cause, will rally to our support and join our army. Our numbers will swell. There is no armed force our equal between the Lowlands and London. If we capture London, England will sue for peace. We will have won." The Prince stood hands outspread before the Seven imploring them to follow his vision.

Lord George Murray bowed before the Prince, but was not bowed in his arguments. "Regent, Your Majesty, we must consider it essential to secure our base. We must needs drive those Clans who do not stand for you out of their secure holes; we must besiege those encampments of the English. We must secure our supply lines."

Colonel John William O'Sullivan, the Irishman who had served in the French army, echoed Lord Murray's point of view. It was a rare moment of agreement between these two military advisors. You could see that it pained him to agree with Lord Murray. "It is one of the first principles of war that you secure your base of operations and your supply lines, before going on the offensive. We violate this principle at our peril."

"What of time being of the essence?" the Prince queried. "If we do not act now, do we give them time to assemble a new army to oppose us in England? Do we give them time to recall the Duke of Cumberland and his force from the Netherlands? I say strike while the iron is hot!"

In those early, heady days, the Prince had been proven right time and time again. He had gone against the counsel of the Seven and had rallied the Clans at Glenfinnan. He had been right to move upon Edinburgh. Each time he had been right, more and more men joined the Rising. And in truth, I thought he might be right. I admit that I was young and headstrong, but as I stood next to the edge of the tent watching the proceedings, as I able to do as a Captain of Young Ranald and his aide, I was moved. I thought the time right. We seemed invincible then. Who could argue that now was not the time? We had over 6,000 men-our second largest army ever, although we did not know it at the time.

Both of the Royal tutors, Francis Strickland and Sir Thomas Sheridan felt out of their element and did not contribute to the debate, as also did Aeneas MMacDonald. Hugh MacDonald, as Bishop never voiced an opinion, except as to religious matters. The debate continued between the Prince and his military advisors.

Sir John MacDonald, who also was a veteran cavalry officer for the French, finally spoke up. "I am an old cavalry man. I see everything from the perspective of being on top of a horse. In cavalry actions, it is the speed, daring, and élan that allow the mounted arm to overwhelm the infantry. Normally, this should not be, because the heavier weapons of the infantry with their longer range should prevent the horse from ever getting near.

But it is the edge of speed, guts, and daring-do that allows the horse to cut up the infantry with but a sword. I say we go now and try to conquer England. If not now, then when?"

It was then that I fell in love, so to speak, with Sir John MacDonald. It was not because he was a clansman, although that certainly helped. It was not because I shared his view, although I did. It was because he spoke for action and action appealed to my young man's blood.

"We are but 6,000 men, Sire," protested Lord Murray. "6,000 men are not enough to conquer England. This is foolhardy. We were 8,000 at Falkirk, but now we're less!"

Prince Charles scowled. He glared directly at Lord Murray. "We were but a handful at Glenfinnan. And the Clans came. We were but 2,500 at Prestonpans, but we won. When we invade England, our Jacobite supporters will turn out. Of this, I am certain."

And so we invaded England.

Part IV: Sic Gloria Transit Mundi!

> An adversary is more hurt by desertion than by slaughter.-**Publius Flavius Vegetius Renatus**

We marched south. Our men were at first eager and willing. But as the miles were marched and home became further behind us, the grumbling began. Still, things held together.

We reached Carlisle, surrounded it, and it fell. This was another victory. It seemed as if the Prince would be proved right.

Then we marched on. The countryside was physically beautiful. As we marched, the grumbling began again. Feet became sore. Clothing began to wear out. Something was wrong, we sensed it. Numbers did not rally to our side. In fact, the populace became surly, resentful, and outright hostile to us. Although towns fell to us, although we were gaining ground, we were not winning hearts.

As we marched south farther and farther, men started to desert. "I am going home to my farm." "I didn't join up to conquer England, but to win Scotland." "My family needs me." "My harvest will be ruined." "My feet hurt." "My leg is lame." "My back hurts." All the excuses, that men are prone to, began to be spoken aloud. The Prince and his lieutenants could not but hear the complaints from the men. Each morning, the army was smaller. Men had melted away in the night.

Mary and I had begun writing to one another. At first, it was harmless. I would write Mary about camp life, what it was like to be on a march, the dreariness of our food, our shelter, the military life, and so forth. She would write of home, which sheep had birthed a lamb, sewing a tear in a dress, and the like. I do not know how it began, but it did. Each letter became progressively more intimate and more personal. The tinder had gotten a spark and now the fire was raging. I was full blown in love with her and she was in love with me. If I lived to see her again, if the war ever ended, I would marry her and live a life of happiness and joy.

Except, there was but one problem in all of this: Young Ranald. Mary had been betrothed to him since childhood. I knew that he loved her, but wasn't it the love of a brother? Surely, he would bow out once he knew how I felt about her. He would not see this as losing or that I was winning, because we were so close. He would want my happiness as I wanted his.

And the fact that I did in truth wish his happiness, made me hide her letters, hide my feelings, and hide the truth from him. For I knew in my heart of hearts that he would not understand. He would, as any true and good Scot, see this as a betrayal, the worst kind of betrayal that there could ever be. A best friend stealing his best friend's wife! Feuds, vendettas, and grudges were based upon less. Lasting generations style of vendettas. Feuds that Clans went to war about for generation after generation. And he was to be my Clan Chef!

Letters! I was not going to involve myself in the intrigue that seemed to be the watchword for the Isle of Skye. I remember my uncle telling me the tale of Donald Gorm Mor who was a clan chief in the 1500's. He plotted to kill his uncle to gain his inheritance early. He carefully planned the murder, thinking out each and every detail so he would not be caught. He would send a letter to invite his uncle to a dinner. During dinner, he would poison him. His accomplice had suggested that Donald Gorm Mor write everything down and to send it to him in a letter. Donald Gorm Mor sent his uncle the letter of invitation and he sent his accomplice the letter of instructions, as had been requested. Only he made one mistake. He sent his uncle his accomplice's letter and vice versa.

When he was caught, he was imprisoned. His uncle fed him only salt dried fish and salt dried meat. He gave him no water to drink. So, Donald Gorm Mor died an agonizing death.

Did I want to share his fate?

We reached Derbyshire. The Seven called upon the Prince to hold a council of war. Lord Murray began with his old song. "We are too few to take London. We must turn around and go back to Scotland, rebuild our numbers, re-outfit, and secure our base of operations."

To his voice, now was joined that of Colonel John William O'Sullivan. "Sire, there is no reason to go on. We have not siege equipment. We have not the men. We have not secured new recruits."

The Prince looked around. "What say you Ranald?" Young Ranald hung back and did not want to say anything. I nudged him in the ribs. "You must answer the Regent," I said.

"Your Majesty, I am but a Colonel of the Clanranald Regiment. It is not my place to advise you and your council." Ranald bowed, thinking that this reply would get him off the hook.

"I have asked you this question, because I believe you are closer to the men than any of my other advisors." The Prince's tone was insistent.

"Then your Majesty, the men do not believe in this mission. They fight for their homes, their fields, and their loved ones. They fight for Scotland. They do not fight to conquer England. If we continue, the army will melt away and all chance of the Rising be successful will have been lost. The men want to return to Scotland." Ranald bowed again, sure this time that he would not be asked to speak further.

The Prince was crestfallen. You could see it on his visage. The dreams of years in exile were being scattered by the dawn's breaking light. King of Scotland and England was not to be. The Prince covered his face with his hands and rubbed his eyes, as if he were massaging away a headache.

"Is this the opinion of all of you?" The Prince looked around the silent tent directly in the eyes of each man there, who in turn cast their heads sullenly downwards in agreement.

Lord Murray prompted the Prince, "Shall I order the preparations to be made to retreat?"

The Prince merely waved his hand in resignation.

We returned to Scotland.

Part V: Reversal

> As flies to wanton boys are we
> to the gods They kill us for their
> sport.-**Shakespeare**

As we marched north, a dejected, sorry lot of men, I could only think of Mary. How could I tell Young Ranald? Should I tell Young Ranald? How could this ever be resolved and all of us be happy?

Still, each and every day, I looked forward to her letters, as I knew that he did.

Then one day, we were called to receive mail. I eagerly rushed up to grab the letter from the hands of young solider dispensing the mail. I did not note that he had two letters in his hand. I grabbed one and rushed off to read it.

I ran across camp, my precious cargo in my hand. I could see her beautiful feminine handwriting. I could smell the perfume. It was ambrosia from the Gods! I was going to be with my love at least in spirit, when Lord Murray saw me.

"What ho! Young Captain Jamie! Come here." He called to me.

"Yes, Lord General Murray." I answered politely, as would any officer to a higher ranking officer.

"I was wondering if your Regiment would like the honor of leading the army tomorrow in its march?" The General smiled at me, knowing, that leading the army was a singular honor, as well as being the best place in a march. Being first meant you had no dust thrown into your face or engulfing your lungs as you marched, whereas everyone else behind coughed their way through the 20 or so miles we would cover.

"Why yes, I am sure we would." I eagerly replied.

"Well, then go and tell your Colonel." He waved his hand dismissively.

I immediately went to Young Ranald's tent to tell him the good news.

When I got there, I saw that his face was twisted with the most painful grimace I had ever seen.

"What's the matter, Ranald?" I queried.

"This!" He waved a letter in the air. Mary's letter.

"What's it say?" I blundered into it.

"That she loves you, you horse thieving, cattle reaving bastard!" The vehemence of his fury hit me harder than a blow from his fist across my cheek would have. The veins in his neck were growing in height and were pulsating with blood.

"She loves …me…" I weakly uttered as if I were mesmerized.

"Yes, you! You goddam-bastard! How could you?" He slammed his fist against his campaign table such that the table was thrown to the ground, the papers, books, and cups, upon it scattered.

"I…I…wanted…wanted to…tell yes tell …you." I was positively pathetic.

"Get out! I don't ever want to see you again. Get out! Before…I challenge you. Get!" He snarled.

I retreated, cowered, ashamed, distraught, and confused. It dawned on me slowly. Mary's letter to me and her letter to Young Ranald had been switched. I did it. I had grabbed the wrong one.

Chapter 18

The Battle of Culloden

"Had Prince Charles slept during the whole of the expedition, and allowed Lord George Murray to act for him according to his own judgment, he would have found the crown of Great Britain on his head when he awoke."

James de Johnstone, *aide-de-camp* to Commander Lord George Murray, 1745

Part I-A Night March

"Where is the coward that would not dare to fight for such a land as Scotland?"-**Sir Walter Scott**

I stood in line with the MacDonalds of Clanranald. Our position was on all but the very end of the left flank of the line. Only further to our left was Clan MacDonell of Glengarry. My men were grumbling that we were not in the position of honor, the point of valor, the place of bravery. Had not Robert the Bruce conferred that very honor on us forever?

The rain and sleet stung my eyes as the cold wind whipped the elements parallel to the ground. I closed my eyes to stop the pain of the pelting missiles, as well as to rest them. I was tired, bone weary, brain numbing tired. The night had been long, hard, demanding, exhausting, and utterly disappointing. We had not caught the English unawares as we had done in Prestonpans. We had not been victorious. We were simply tired having spent the night wandering around and getting nowhere, except right back where we started. But now back where we had started, we were excruciatingly tired.

The wind. I remember the wind. It whipped us. It twirled our kilts. It was blustery, brutal, knife-sharping cold cutting through clothes, wrapped woolens, furs, leggings, coats, jackets, and pants. It was relentless. And with the wind, came the sleet, sometimes wrapped in flurries of snow, sometimes wet with rain, and all of the time from the north, bringing with it more and more cold. The wind was biting; it was bitter; it was blistering. The wind was merciless; it was heartless; it was inhuman.

Dante had imagined that hell was a frozen wasteland of bitterness. This was Culloden, one of Scotland's moors on a cold, blustery, sleet-filled day, but we could see but little difference between what Dante had envisioned and what lay before us.

Throughout this morning as we stood in the cold, the wind, the sleet, the snow, the rain, the British were breaking camp where they had lain snug in their beds, their warm, cozy beds last night, while we prowled the moors in the dark. Now we stood in the sleet and rain. They cooked their breakfast and still we stood. Slowly, they made their battle line and still we stood.

For reasons unknown to us all, except maybe the traitor, Lord George Murray, we had turned away, when we were but a stone's throw from their camps as they lay sleeping, after drinking their fill of ale to celebrate the butcher's (William, the Duke of Cumberland's) birthday. Now, I faced the English Army across the moor. Around my feet, the mist swirled. And I, barely half awake, still lived in the ghost of the night before. I could see it all, as if it still wrapped around me as the mist hugged my feet.

Last night, I had not a morsel for dinner. The oats, which were in the baggage train some 4 or 5 miles behind our lines, were not distributed.

Some other battalions received biscuits, but nary had a bite reached the MacDonalds. We were hungry.

This added insult to our injury, because we were stationed on the left of our line. We groused that we should have the post of honor, the right of our line. Then no food. No honor and no food. The evening had begun badly and from there we descended further down the Cornices of Dante's Hell.

Around 8 or 9 that evening, we were ordered up. It was the first that we had heard of a night march. We had not prepared to march at night. No food had we in our haversacks, no water, nothing. We waited in line to march away into the inky dark night. That is the hardest thing a soldier can do: wait for an order that seems to never come. I fell into line and did as I was told. We all did as we were told. The Prince had seen to that. We were not the mottled armed group of raw volunteers and pressed men we had been just a few months ago. We had trained. We had drilled. We had learned our trade and now we were really and truly soldiers. We were as trained as any army on the Continent. The French regulars we had with us complimented us on how much we had learned and how well we had learned it.

We began. We could not see our feet, nor could we see the way to step. No moon lighted our way. Some of the men turned their ankles in rabbit holes. Others tripped on the tall heaps of grass or where peat had been removed. Each time this happened, the man behind fell over the man in front of him, leaving both cursing and both rubbing shins, ankles, or calves. I touched the shoulder of the man in front of me to keep pace and keep my place. I promised myself that I would not stumble. Or if I did, I would not call out. I would take my pain as a man.

All night, we tripped, stumbled, lost footing, and hunted for purchase of our feet. The wind blew a gale and was wet with mist. The boggy land was so wet that most of us were covered with mud and wetness up to our knees or the bottom of our thighs. With the wetness, came the cold, as the wind sliced through the night chilling with its icicle sharp blade cutting muscle to the bone. I could only think of something hot to drink or some whiskey, both of which were in short supply. Much as a man could rub his hands together, it brought no comfort to fingers that were beyond feeling anything but the stabbing of millions of pointed metal dirks. Our plaids were wrapped around us leaving only but a slit of eyes peering above the squares of color, but even the wool of Highland sheep worked little magic of bringing warmth to men frigid beyond thawing.

Eyelids began to close with a weariness that can't be imagined. The boys amongst us called out for mother or sister to end their suffering. The haze of a dream descended upon the men and rendered them immune to the terrors of the night. We trudged on and on, not knowing where we were going, or even why we were going. Some asked if we were retreating. Some claimed we were going to the wagon train and would be eating shortly. I knew we were not. I could sense the battle spread before us. "No talking in the line," whispered a form of grey shadow which I took to be an officer. I hushed the boy behind me.

Time marched on in her own way, as if the seconds were a long ode told long ago when Odin walked the earth. The minutes became years and I saw my bread grow and become grey and flow down to my knees. The hours became eons, with the oceans cutting rock cliffs to dust before our eyes. Someone whispered that we were flanking the English like we had done at Prestonpans months before. That thought, and that thought alone, inspired us for a while, but soon the gloom of the night, the dank of the dark, the drek o'erwhelmed us and the spirit left us.

As we marched, men, completely exhausted, left our ranks and sat by the wayside. When they did, they fell asleep, such that our numbers ever dwindled. We struggled with each step. The interminable night stretched before us and there was no respite. We knew not where we were going and in not knowing, we had no reason to go on.

The dream wrapped us tighter now. We slept on our feet. Then we halted. Man upon man tumbled upon the man in front of him, till there was nothing but a jumble of men on the ground sorting themselves out. All the while, we tried to keep our powder dry. The bog laughed at us and threatened to engulf us in waves of peaty-muddle-grass. Then we stood for a long while. Then the column, such as it was, started again, then halted again and the whole process of stumbling, sorting out, standing and waiting, and beginning again, cycled again and again.

Thus, the night was consumed and with it the heartiness of men was consumed, those brave Highland men, upon whom all our hopes rested. Our robustness was being consumed by the darkness of a never ending night, until there was nothing left but the bitter exhaustion of men going on solely because there was nothing else to do. Many more fell by the wayside. The boys first, then the older men, and then nearly everyone tumbled to the ground in the darkness to sip a taste of the wine of Hypnos, who seductively washes herself in ambrosia and anoints herself with oil and then donning her most beautiful and wondrous dress, uses her charm to cast gods and men asleep. We did not take rest breaks for if we did no one would rise again to heed the call to go on. The officers hit the men with the flat of their swords to encourage further herculean effort. When would this night of damnation end? When would we be free of the drudgery? When could we rest our feet and legs that begged to be put up before a fire to drive out the wet, the cold, the bitter tiredness, and the pain of spent muscles from them?

Just when we could do no more, we stopped. Those few, who were left, dropped to the ground and dropped instantly into sleep in the cold.

Then the officers went forward. Lord George Murray was very angry and had raised his voice. His words carried over the stillness of the night to where we lay upon the frost covered bog's strands of grass. He argued to turn around, that the time to daylight was not enough for the men to get to the enemy's rear and flank. He complained that gaps had opened leaving one of the regiments a half mile or so from the next. "Before our lines could be formed, the English will see us framed in the sunlight of the breaking day and our surprise will be gone," Lord George shouted at John O'Sullivan. A courier rode by searching for the Prince. "Is he here?" "No, he must be further back," was the whispered reply. The horse turned and his mane flared in the wind, twin geysers of breath-smoke tunneled from his nostrils, and horse and rider were gone.

We went back to sleep. Bits and pieces of an argument amongst the officers carried on the breeze. Then was issued the order to reverse our march. We were going back where we had come from. But at least this time, we would take the road. Men's hopes and spirits were dashed. Prestonpans was not to be repeated. The night's march had been in vain.

Part II-Morning Breaks

> [Unless   Highlanders]…could
> attack the enemy at very considerable

advantage, either by surprise or by some strong situation of ground, or a narrow pass, they could not expect any great success, especially if their numbers were no ways equal,....-**Lord George Murray, after Falkirk**

The morning came with sleet slamming into our eyes as we made our way into our battle line. Few of us remained from the ordeal of the night. Hunger growled in our bellies. The thirst was great. Men did what they could to keep their precious powder dry. The gale swept around the men carrying wet mist into those awkward places where you want to touch but dare not for civilities' sake. A couple of men who had claymores began grinding the blades to hone them to a sharpness such that but one great swing of the mighty weapon could lope off a limb or a head. But only a few possessed that mighty weapon. The French had brought hundreds of them forged in Germany with inscriptions cut upon them that butchered the English language, for example, "Hack Header."

I glanced around. All I saw were shivering men, readying themselves as best they could for the day's work. We were on the extreme left of the line.

"That's the rump of the devil," said one man out loud. Others groused aloud as to why the MacDonalds had been slighted. "It's not the Princes' doing", said Ian MacDonald.

Daniel Giles replied, "Well, it's still the asshole of hell we're in!"

"I think we're here because the MacDonalds of Skye joined the Loyalists in Edinburgh." We turned around to glare at Donald MacKinnon.

"Why wouldst ye say such a thing?" I countered.

"'Cause it's true!" He blurted in reply.

"The Prince knows it was but a few poor misguided fools. The MacDonalds of Clanranald, the MacDonalds of Glengarry, and the MacDonalds of Keppoch would give their lives for the Prince!" I defended.

"Lord knows they will! But will it be enough?" Donald queried. That and that alone was the question on every man's mind. "But will it be enough?"

I could have left it there, because Giles and MacKinnon were farmers, and my rank demanded that I stay above the men, but I was in the midst of farmers. Angus MacCormack, Angus MacGarrie, John MacQuarry, Donald MacQuilly, and Ross Alexander had circled around us and they awaited their Captain's reply. Farmers are true to the earth and expect that the earth and all upon it be true to them. Farmers were the backbone of our army. They were really what we were fighting for. I would not let them down.

"Yes, our numbers are few, but our courage, your courage is great. Our Cause is good and true. Our God stands with us. So what if men do not give us what our honor demands? We shall do our duty and we shall be victorious or we shall die." I did not know then that I was talking to a

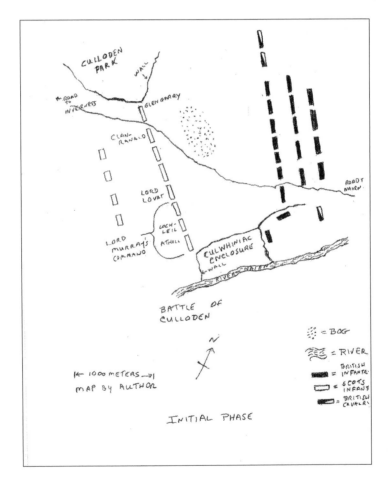

band of dead men. But still they cheered. MacCormack said, "Huzzah for our Captain!" Even Giles and MacKinnon joined in. We threw our arms around one another. And we cheered our deaths.

Our numbers were few. Yes, as the morning wore on men, alone, in couples, and small groups of three or four, appeared on the field, slowly finding their regiments after the night march. Nonetheless, it was clear that every regiment was but a shadow of its former self. Most of our men had been lost during the night and none knew whether they would appear before English would come.

By noon, the English army had drawn up on the field. Our left, where I stood, was anchored on the walls of Culloden Enclosures-a walled off pasture. We wanted to make sure that none of the enemy's horse would flank us and cut into our rear. These walls would prevent them-for hours, certainly-from doing just that. We placed our faith, our hope in those walls such that their horse could not get behind us and cut us down.

Our line slanted away from the English line. Thus, by our flank, we were nearly twice as far away from the English as was the right flank of our army. This meant that, when we charged, we would have to go twice as far as would the troops under Lord Murray.

But strange things were abrew that day. It would be a day for confusion, for lost orders, for men not being where they ought when they ought. It was a day of questioning whether the men, we were fighting with, were betraying us as Scots since time immemorial have betrayed their brother and fellow Scots. Did Lord Murray lead us astray? Did the Prince's nerve give out?

The artillery of the English was booming away. First they fired cannon balls at us. Their fire was slow and deliberate. The secret to firing a cannon ball was to fire it in such a way that it skipped just in front of the enemy line and then hopped up such that it would hit men about waist high. In this fashion it could take out men in the front line and then men in the back line, too.

It is the hardest thing in the world to stand and receive fire. You cannot do anything about it. We were too far away to fire with our muskets; we had no cannons of our own to return their fire. When you see a man get wounded, it tears your heart out. When you see your friends get wounded, you want revenge, bloody, intense, immediate revenge. "Let me kill them," every fiber of your body says. "Let me rip their heads off," cries your heart, but your brain says, "Stand and take it. There is nothing you can do now." You must do your duty; you must obey your orders; you may only advance when the time is right. You cry out to your commander, "Can we go in? Please God, can we go in? Oh, God, let me go in now!"

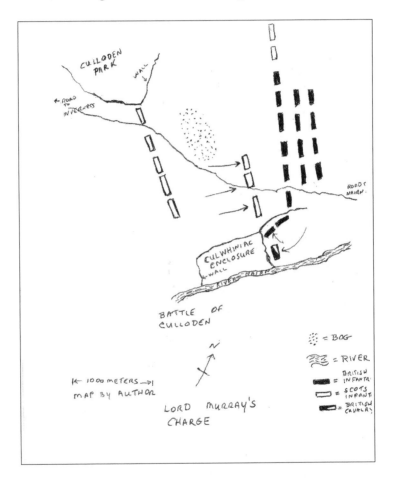

We stood there for what seemed to be an eternity. No orders came. We saw the right flank advance and attack the English left flank. Still, no orders came. Atholl's brigade was engaged. So too, it appeared, were Lochiel's men. Why were we not advancing?

Lord Murray's men were charging their English counterparts. The battle was joined hand to hand. Claymores waved high. Muskets continued to be fired. The surge seemed to break the English line or at least the line started to give and sway back. Highlanders yelled their unearthly guttural scream. Then the Highlanders broke through the first line only to meet English reserves thrown in to stem the tide. Lord Murray's men appeared to be slowly being surrounded.

I was mesmerized by the sight far over on our right flank. "Jamie, go and find out what's happening?" Ranald ordered me.

"Yes, Colonel." I started off.

We were on the far left of the line, only the MacDonalds of Keppoch were beyond us. Our line was not parallel to the English line, but slanted away from it, so that our flank was the furthest away and the right flank, the flank lead by Lord George Murray was the closest. As I ran along our line, the ferocity of the fight intensified. The artillery of the English continued booming away.

I got to the center of the line. Lord Lovat was struggling to get on the back of his horse. His bulk was preventing him from gaining purchase upon the back of the beast, which clearly did not want to carry the mass of the heaviest man in Scotland yet once again. It was a beautiful horse and I knew in my heart that I would love to own such a fine horse someday. Lord Lovat was suffering from a bad case of the gout, but still was determined to lead his men forward.

I cried out, "Lord Lovat, Colonel MacDonald of Clanranald's regards. We've received no orders to advance. What should we do?"

He was atop his horse. Had it been a different time and place, I might have laughed, because here was one of the most obese men I had ever seen astride a beast and the horse seemed to be wobbling from side to side trying to gain its balance due to vast weight upon its back. "I don't have any orders from Lord Murray. I think he has advanced with his men, but I think it's time to have a go at them. If I was Colonel MacDonald, I'd have a go at 'em now too!"

I was out of breath, but I raced back to my regiment.

At first I did not see Ranald. I found Duncan Cameron, his servant. "Where is the Colonel?" I pleaded.

"He went down the line towards the MacDonalds of Keppoch. Think he's going to confer to see if they should move forward on their own." Duncan was an older gentleman. He had been Ranald's servant and valet since Ranald and I were boys. I remember him reading stories to us when we were boys, with each of us perched upon a knee. Now, he was stooped over, but still he would not leave Ranald for the world. His head was bandaged; the white bandage was bright red with fresh blood. Still, he stayed when others would have left due to the wound. His loyalty was a thing of wonder.

I went to our left. There I found Ranald conferring with Colonel Alexander MacDonald of Keppoch.

I bowed to each of them and then I addressed my Colonel. "Colonel MacDonald, Lord Lovat's regards and he says he hasn't orders from Lord George Murray, but that he thinks it's time."

"Why that miserable, scurvy dog! Is Lord Murray trying to lose this battle? Was this his plan all along?" Alexander MacDonald spat upon the ground. "Can't trust that rogue!" Young Ranald had long harbored the belief that Lord Murray was a traitor, as most of us thought. He seemed too cozy with General Cope. His continual arguing with the Duke of Perth and with John Drummond coupled with his actions at Prestonpans had convinced many that he just wanted to betray the Highlands. Ranald had said this to me in confidence, but here was Alexander MacDonald, the Chief of the MacDonalds of Keppoch saying it out loud. This was the man who was the first chief to side with Bonnie Prince Charles. I was stunned.

Alexander MacDonald of Keppoch continued his abuse of Lord George. "First, he orders a night march-the most dangerous thing an army can do! Next, in mid-course, when the troops are near to the spot from whence they could rush the English lines, he orders us to turn around and march back. Damn him! This only made the men excruciatingly tired. We lost men along the way who have not returned to fight today! I say he's a traitor. This was his plan to betray us all!"

Ranald completely exasperated yelled at Alexander MacDonald, "What say you? Go it alone?"

"Aye, Young Ranald. Your father would be proud of ye." Keppoch turned to his men. "We're to give them Hell and cold steel!"

Ranald turned to me. He had a flinty look in his eye. "Captain, get your men ready to charge. Pass the word to our left flank and I'll pass it on the right flank of our regiment. Wait for my signal-I'll raise my claymore and slash it downwards towards the English lines. Remember, wait for my signal." Young Ranald cautioned me. Then he hugged me. "May God go with you, my brother. I love you." He smiled at me for an instant. In my heart I knew that I was forgiven.

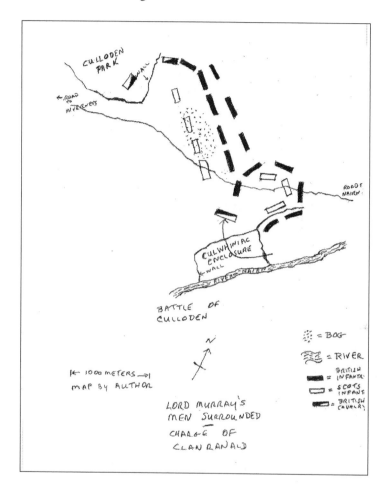

CULLODEN PARK

ROAD TO INVERNESS

ROAD T NAIRN

CULWHINIAC ENCLOSURE

WALL

RIVER NAIRN

BATTLE OF CULLODEN

N

|← 1000 METERS →|
MAP BY AUTHOR

LORD MURRAY'S MEN SURROUNDED
CHARGE OF CLAN RANALD

= BOG
= RIVER
= BRITISH INFANTA
= SCOTS INFANT
= BRITISH CAVALRY

Though he started to walk away from me, he thought a moment and then he circled back. "Hell and Cold Steel! Tell them!"

"I will. Hell and Cold Steel! I love you too!" I yelled back at him. He nodded. Maybe in that instant everything that had passed between us about Mary was over. I loved him and I knew that I loved him. Mary was his and I knew that also.

I returned to my company all the while passing the word to each company's captain as I strode down our line. "We're going to go forward men. Do this for Scotland, your wives, your mothers, and your sisters! Give them Hell and Cold Steel is our watch word!"

I called to Captain Ranald MacDonald of Belfinay to my right and gave him the Colonel's order. I did not know then that this would be the last time I would ever see him.

Then we waited. The cannons still boomed and every once in a while another man fell. The wait was excruciating, intolerable, insufferable. I kept my eyes on Ranald. More time passed.

Then he raised his claymore and pointed it towards the enemy.

I gave the order and started off. I saw Ranald out in front, his claymore slicing the air above his head, urging his men onward.

At that, I yelled to my piper, "Play loud man!" The pipes blared out "Lady Louden's Strathspey." I turned to my men, "Forward!" As we were 250 yards or so away, I ordered, "Quick Step!" I didn't want them to charge yet for as the ancient Greeks were wont to say, "A breathless man cannot fight."

The men responded with a controlled quick step. The English artillery fire grew more intense. The first row of the 21st Royal Regiment, kneeling, opened fired. At this range, it had little effect upon us. The second rank lowered their muskets. When we closed within about 150 yards I ordered the men to "Double Quick Step." They responded and our paced quickened.

The second rank of the 21st volley fired. Several of my men fell wounded or dead. The sound of the musket fire of the 21st Royal Regiment greatly increased as we came nearer. We were now about 80 yards away. Their third line then fired. My men stopped as if they had hit a brick wall. Part of the trouble was that we were now in a bog and our feet stuck in the mud with each step. Our charge had slowed to a crawl. We were screaming and yelling, the volume of our howl was as great as any piece of artillery. But we could see the 3rd Foot, Howard's Buffs, join the firing line of the 21st. The English musketry was a continuous roar. My men were dropping left and right. It was a holocaust

Captain Ranald MacDonald of Belfinay stumbled and a red flame bled across his chest. He turned back towards his men as he fell.

Then their cannon began firing canister at us. Canister is the most merciless weapon one man can fire at another. A tin can is filled with rocks, nails, bullets, and anything else small and weighty and then the filled tin can is rammed home in the cannon atop a double load of gun powder. When the touch hole is lighted, the cannon sprays a vast barrage of flying projectiles of death and destruction which slice, cut, pummel, mash, tear, bite, kill, and maim men leaving their bodies a gelatinous, liquefied-jelly mass of mess of what were once bones, muscles, blood, arteries, veins, brains, and assorted and a sundry organs. So that now men were dropping around me and being converted into goo.

"Forward! Hell and ..." Young Ranald fell. I saw him hit. It looked like a musket ball to the head. Maybe it was canister. Duncan Cameron came up, his head covered in red now, and threw himself across Ranald as a shield. It was then that he too was hit. I was too far away to get to them and I had my men to lead.

With the greatest of efforts, we surged forward. We fired off our muskets in a ragged volley fashion. Actually, there was no volley, no order, and no control. And as Highlanders are wont to do, many cast off their muskets after a shot or two and drew their broadswords or their claymore, begging for the order to charge.

I urged my men forward and some started to follow me. I raised my claymore and shouted: "Hell and Cold Steel!" Then my feet went out from under me. My shoulder was hit and I spun around from being hit with the shot. I hit my head or my head was hit and the black surrounded me.

I was not awake to see Lord Murray's men get surrounded and cut off. I did not see the Dragoons of the English break around on both of our flanks. I did not hear the order to retreat or withdraw. I did not hear the Prince in despair shout, "All is lost. Well, they won't take me alive." I knew not the Prince and his entourage had spurred their horses and had fled the scene of the battle once Lord Murray's men-the regiments of the Atholl's-broke in rout, casting off their muskets, swords, dirks, claymores, and lochabars. It was a long while later when I woke up, only to hear the Duke of Cumberland's men beginning the bayoneting of the Scots forms lying on the ground. I got up and I ran off.

Chapter 19

The Isle of Skye Lies O'er the Sea

The aftermath of Culloden exacted penalties which were to leave a permanent scar on the Highlands of Scotland in the deliberate extinction of the Celtic way of life - by killing, destruction, confiscation and deportation. A tragic time, unequalled by any other in Scottish history.
- **Iain Campbell**

Part I: Flora MacDonald

"Her name will be mentioned in history, and if courage and fidelity be virtues, mentioned with honour."-**Dr. Samuel Johnson**

The tale of Flora MacDonald is a tale of a bed and who slept in it and when.

Of course, Flora slept in this bed, for it was her bed. But I get ahead of my story.

Bonnie Prince Charles had lost the Battle of Culloden, or rather the Battle had been lost for him. Whether it was his fault or no, is rather something which did not really matter then, for no matter how the battle was lost, he was now a fugitive in his own land. The Duke of Cumberland wanted to end these incessant Jacobite uprisings once and for all. He was next in line to the throne and really did not want to be annoyed about the matter anymore. The Highlanders had rebelled once too often for his liking and he was determined to end this forever. Thus, he knew that he had to capture Bonnie Prince Charlie or, if it so happened, that Bonnie Prince Charles was killed in the taking, so be it. It might even be better to be rid of the rallying point, the cause célèbre, the personage sine qua non, now and for good.

So even as the mist began to settle upon the moors of Culloden, the Duke of Cumberland ordered his men to go after the Highlanders, hunt them down, slay them, one by one, and be done with it. The men understood this to be a license to do as they willed when they willed. It began on the moors. If a Highlander writhed in pain, then they bayonetted him. As they caught up to those that fled, few, very few, for some reason, became prisoners. The farmers and the farmers' wives that harbored the fugitives faced the same threat. Any village found with a man or even a wounded man, who had fought upon the fields of Culloden, was sentenced to the punishment of being burned to the ground, the men being shot, the women being raped, and the children being carted away to who knows where.

The Duke kept up the relentless pressure. His one mission remained: Find the Prince. His troops leapt on and on, the blood lust fully feeding their hungry depraved souls. Goods and riches filled their haversacks. Revenge was the watchword. The cavalry swept the countryside, up the hills, and down to the dales, across the chilly lochs, through the tangled heather, across the glens, scampering upon the rocks, the hooves scraping their iron footings till sparks of fire caused by iron upon granite flared and flamed. The infantry needed no incentives to spur them on: their hearts filled with rage were enough. The officers, freed from having to restrain the baser elements of the souls of their men, concentrated upon one thing: Find the prince. A rumor here, led the troops to dash there. A whisper of a sighting here and the horse sprang to clatter their hooves in the night.

A tell-tale sign prompted the officers to mark their maps and issue orders for the taking of their quarry. The cause was all the same: Find the Prince.

A week passed. Still the trail of the Prince took them westwards. Then a second week passed. Somehow, against all odds, he was still ahead of them, always just ahead of them, while what was behind them was a wasteland of burnt villages and towns, farms despoiled, women raped, and bodies of men left to rot in the sun. A third, and then a fourth week passed. No matter what evil the Duke visited upon the Scots, they did not yield up the Prince. The Duke's anger spilled over and his men knew it and took their cue from it. Even the £30,000 reward produced no results. Not a single Scot came forward with information. Not a one turned the Prince in.

Rapine, looting, plunder, butchery, hecatomb, and havoc were practiced as if the four horsemen had been released with the breaking of a seal to hasten the coming of Christ anew. The fifth week lapsed into the sixth and then finally the seventh. The Duke ordered that the Prince could not be allowed to make it to the west coast of the Isle of Skye, where a French ship was reported to be waiting.

With the dead still unburied and laying on the moor of Culloden, William, the Duke of Cumberland, began his pogrom against the Highlanders. He appealed to his father, King George II, for Letters of Intercommuning, which would forbid anyone to commune with the MacDonalds of Clanranald, amongst others. Those Letters were duly issued by the Privy Council and the Court of Sessions and authorized, "… Whatever slaughter, mutilation, bloodshed, fire-raising or other violence, shall happen to be acted…" by anyone assisting the forces of the law in "… Seizing, reducing, and bringing them in dead or alive shall be held as laudable, good, and warrantable service to his Majesty." Armed now with writ of law, Cumberland sought to eradicate the Highland clans that rebelled time and time against their lawful King, his father.

Cumberland was still not satisfied. He sought a Commission of Fire and Sword from the Privy Council. This Commission, if secured, would have had empowered him to eliminate down to the last man, the members of the Clans he had singled out. Cooler heads prevailed in the Council, fearing that such a commission would only unite the now scattered and defeated clans in a last stand-a do or die situation-for they would have no reason not to resist. Cumberland, insulted but not discouraged, carried out his plan without this order, knowing his men, if placed on the long leash, would read the freedom of license and do what had to be done without recourse to order or right.

The Clans melted into the hill country, hiding in the glens and moving time and time again. They knew they were outlaws and fugitives "frae the laws" and, if caught, would be executed. The reality set in that they were extinct, they were to be driven from the earth. Their former lives were lost. The Highlands' life was gone forever. Dispirited, depleted, destroyed, doomed, despairing, dreading, they roamed the earth as lost souls or as flotsam and jetsam from the shipwreck of their lives in rebellion. So too, their women, their children, and their babes, were to be put to the sword, were to be burned out, were to be uprooted, and cast upon the perilous sea of banishment or death. Cumberland would not allow a flicker of flame or a ray of light to remain in the Highlands to rekindle the conflagration of rebellion to the Crown. He vowed a sacred oath to ne'er to leave a single heather alive and standing to remind the Scots of what they had once been.

Part II: A Chance Meeting

Give me Scotland or I die.-**John Knox**

I had fled from the field of the Battle, just as had so many other Highlanders. I saw no shame in fleeing for my life. At first, I thought that we would re-group and, thus, fight again another day. But the relentless pursuit of the Duke chastened me and hastened that idea from my brain. I knew within a day that I had to flee to home. But then, I thought, "If I go home, I only bring death, destruction, and devastation to those I love. I must seek shelter somewhere else."

I had a kinsman, Angus Maceachain. We were distantly related as the differing spelling of our name relayed. I knew that he was the son-in-law of Angus MacDonald of Borrodale on the Island of South Uist. Angus lived on the Isle of Eriska. The Isle of Eriska was east of the Isle of Mull and its small companion of Iona. I thought if I could get there to Eriska, I might be safe. I could maybe get a ship to France or the continent. I knew that going to my home was now an impossibility. They would hunt me down there and kill my family.

I stole a horse. Well, rather, there was a horse complete with a fine saddle and bridle wandering the battlefield. Now, if I were trying to be particular about it, I might have thought that this horse, this specific certain horse, belonged to Lord Lovat. It had the same beautiful chestnut color; its saddle seemed to have a similar family crest. It was certainly an extremely beautiful animal. It seemed to be in no great hurry to find the vast bulk of Lord Lovat, said to be the most rotund and heavy man in all of Scotland. I looked around in a full circle and I did not see him. If I left the horse, the English might get him. If I borrowed the horse and took good care of him, I could return him later. It seemed to be a shame to leave this beautiful horse out on the moors of this battlefield, particularly when I was in such great need of a horse.

The McEacherns were the Lords of the Horse for the MacDonalds so I had been riding since shortly after I learned to walk. I had the talent to whisper sweet nothings in the ear of an equine and have them do whatever I wanted. I stroked her mane and neck and then I rubbed her muzzle. I had a bit of oats on me and filled my hand and let her eat. All the while, I stroked her and told her how beautiful she was. Without her even realizing it, I was on her back and we were riding westward. I was fleeing to Angus Maceachain.

The Isle of Eriska is north of Oban. Now, I could tell you of how the distillery of Oban is on a small street that runs perpendicular to the main street fronting the water. I could also tell you of how sweet the whiskey is, for I drank a wee dram of it once, but Oban is not the center of my story. Oban is along the Great Glen, which would require me to pass by Ft. William and Ft. Augustus. I could have fled into Inverness, but I thought too many of army of the Prince would congregate there, meaning that Duke of Cumberland would move most of his army there to exact retribution.

I would skirt the east side of Inverness and then go south and cut over to Ft. Augustus after a while. With luck, I would make the hundred miles or so in two or three or four days. A horse can walk about 5 miles an hour and can go for about 3 or so hours at that pace before needing rest. So 15 miles and then rest, then another 15 miles, and then a rest, and then maybe another 10 miles or so, before needing a night's rest and food, and water, meaning about 40 miles in a day. I headed south.

The wind, sleet, and rain had begun again. I was heartbroken now, for my estimates of how far I could go were too optimistic. I wrapped my plaid around me and headed the horse into the squall. Night fell and the dark gloom surrounded me, as drek as it was, I kept on going. The horse seemed to not mind the constant movement. At least it kept the horse warm. If I made two or three miles an hour and just kept going, maybe my estimate wouldn't be so bad.

Later that night, I was falling asleep, and nearly fell off the horse, who I suspected was asleep on her hooves also. I leapt to the ground and began leading the horse, thinking I might find a barn or a building somewhere ahead.

The wind howled and the night was as bleak as was my heart. We had failed. The Prince was in danger. I had lost Ranald in the battle. Last I saw he was wounded, but Duncan Cameron had carried him away as I continued to fight on. Was that head wound a mortal wound? How would I tell Chief Ranald of the death of his only son? If he was dead, then what of Mary? I banished the thought of her from my mind. I would not hope for the death of my friend to win the woman I loved.

Through the night, my mind mused on so many things. I recalled the look of the moors when I was a boy as we travelled to John O'Groats at the far end of Scotland where one could almost touch the Orkneys.

There amongst the fuchsia purple heather with its thorns unbarred grew the loveliest yellow flowers.

Strewn boulders, grey and dappled, were set along the wayside as if some giants had thrown them after a game of knots. The sky was grey and swirling white with but bits of blue flaming through the wispy tendrils of the clouds. The green of grass waving in the wind as if a sea, with turns of browns and yellows, where the waves have yet to crest, swept me along. Raging torrents of water everywhere, some with enough vertical drop to call a waterfall, but some just the burbling and gurgling of rain collected as a stream with all froth and anger of the inclement weather stored within. Piles of peat were fashioned in some tent-like sculpture to dry in the air, which is always heavy with dew and moisture. The darkly loamy soil mightily contrasted against the green of the grass. But without that special fuel that heats the winter hearths, we Scots would not be able to live. Every mountain was capped with a cloud that settles flat against the mountain top as if the heavens were pressing downwards squashing the clouds and spreading their watery world like an oat pancake. Here and there a trail-a person width-if that, splits the moor leading who knows where. The streams become wider but are sprinkled with rocks that V the water in white surges and dark blue reflections. Of course, the sheep wander the green munching their way across the moors, fattening and becoming more bulbous in their ever-expanding wool cocoons, reversing the march of the silk worm which struggles to escape its silken prison, while sheep become ever more embraced in theirs. They stand white against the grey of the rocks, white against the grey of the skies, white against the green of the moors, and white against the dark steel blue of the streams, always looking as if they are clouds ready to take flight for the heavens and hide a mountain top or two. Once in a while a rock and stone fence appears marking off some ancient line of land. Now is forgotten who built it and when.

For some reason I began to think of a bandit. I seemed to be able to recall that Balnakeil Church was founded in the 8th century by St. Maelrubha and became an important Celtic religious center. The Bay of Balnakeil stretches around to the south like a lazy letter "s" and finally becomes the Kyle of Durness. The Loch of Borraine bounds the church. Nearby is Cape Wraith which I am told in the most northwesterly point in Great Britain-of course, we all say Scotland, for the Act of Union is the Act of Treason to us. I looked upon the grave of Domhnuall MacMhurchadh who is reputed to have killed 18 people while in the employ of the Chief of the MacKay Clan. He put his victim's bodies down a local waterfall at the bottom of which was believed to be the home of the Devil. Apparently Domhnuall believed that his crimes would not be found out, because the Devil would keep them secret. Obviously, there must have been a falling out among thieves, for he was caught, sentenced, and executed by the authorities. This was not before though he had the chance to arrange his tomb to be in the walls of the church. He did this in hopes that his remains wouldn't be interfered with! Today, there are only ivy covered ruins where once the church stood. The stone wall of the church with its stepped top and window cut-out like a cross against the glooming sky is a sight I will not forget.

I came back to reality. It was now. The Battle of Culloden had been fought today. The pain in my shoulder had called me back to here and now.

My shoulder hurt a lot. I sat down to examine it. Had I taken a musket ball to my left shoulder? The thought frightened me and brought me to my senses. I needed shelter. Suddenly, my horse neighed. I slunk my body low to the ground and loosened my grip on the reins. I had my dirk out.

The air hung heavy with tendrils of mist meandering in the night air. The rain had stopped. The sky was starting to clear. As the clouds diminished, the temperature was dropping. My dirk felt icy cold in my hand. I placed my other hand over the muzzle of the horse to keep it quiet. Floating also on the air were nebulous sounds of whispering voices. Was it French I was hearing? Who would be speaking French? Certainly, it was not the English. I decided to take a chance and asked in Gaelic, "Who goes there?" I gave the sign-"Have you found any White Heather?"-hoping for the proper countersign. Several moments passed. Then it came: "No, but I have plenty of purple Heather."-the proper countersign.

I had happened upon the Prince.

Part III: A Home Coming of Sorts

> But pleasures are like poppies spread;
> You seize the flower, its bloom is shed.
> Or like the snow falls in the river,
> A moment white--then melts forever.-
> **Robert Burns**

I explained to the Prince that I was making my way to the home of Angus MacEachain. Although, the Prince was tired, I could see that he retained that energy that had characterized his actions to date. His mind was easy able to understand the current situation. He was still a man of charisma, even in adversity. I suggested, "Why don't ye go with me to the home of Angus MacEachain? Ye might remember that he is the son-in-law of Angus MacDonald of Borrodale, who had first greeted ye upon your arrival in Scotland." Although I might have been presumptuous, the Prince readily agreed that this would be a good place to go.

It was the evening of April 18, 1745, when we came to the Angus' home. Angus was only too glad to see the Prince safe and sound, as well as to see me, until...

"Is it true that there's a price upon ye head?" Angus asked the Prince.

"£30,000." The Prince looked Angus in the eye. "Is that a trouble to ye?" asked the Prince.

Angus realized that we were putting a price upon his head. His furtive glances and hesitant answers only confirmed in my mind that he was not as happy as he pretended that we had come. Still, he took good care of the Prince, giving us food and shelter that night.

But when morning came, the first thing Angus said was, "T'is a fine day for travelling. The dawn is clear and bright. I just fill up yer haversacks with food and top off yer water." He hurried himself in the kitchen pulling together a leg of lamb, some boiled oats, and a few onions.

I looked at the Prince. He was in a state that might be only described as shock. He kept shaking his head, as if he were trying to wake up from some bad dream. He lifted his cup of tea to his lips and muttered something inaudible.

"Well, thank you, Angus. Couldn't we stay here another night?" I asked him with, in my mind and to my credit, just the right amount of entreaty and supplication.

Angus shook his head no. "I don't think you are safe. There are many who know that I housed the Prince when first he landed." It had just enough ring of truth to save Angus from embarrassment.

"Are ye sure?" I implored.

"Yes."

We took to the woods nearby. Angus promised to bring us food, water, and news. We settled in to our arboreal home and passed the day in rest. The Prince did not talk, but appeared to be resigned, as if he were a martyr about to be chained to the post and burnt at the stake. There was none of the fiery nature, that charisma, and that confidence that had inspired us to achieve herculean feats against an implacable foe.

Eight days past. With each day, somehow someone or another found us and our crew grew. I was most glad to see Young Ranald come up. His wound was not as serious as I had thought. A ball had passed through his side, but had not hit anything vital. A second spent ball had hit his head and had knocked him out. It was this ball that I saw that caused him to slump on the field.

"Ranald, I am truly glad to see ye alive and this side of heaven." I could not but exclaim.

"I too am glad to see ye well, Jamie." Ranald was pale and had lost some blood, but still had a smile for me.

"How about Duncan?" I asked.

"Taken by the Duke of Cumberland's men," was the curt answer.

"Then, thank God, Cumberland didn't have him bayoneted on the spot." I truly felt for the old man. He was more like a father to me than anyone else, except for my uncle.

As the days passed, the Prince grew more animated. "We should re-group the army and continue on the fight." He looked around his circle which now included O'Sullivan, O'Neil, Rory MacDonald, Donald McLeod, and Young Ranald of Clanranald. Each of them averted his eyes. None would look the Prince in the eye. "Do you think the Cause is lost?"

Each slowly nodded their heads in agreement that it was.

The Prince looked away, stricken as if a dirk had rent his side. "Is there no hope?"

Seeing that no one else would do the deed, I spoke. "Your Grace, there is no hope. The hosts of our army are spread far and wide. The Duke of Cumberland slays each and every one of our men he finds. He is burning those villages that were loyal to ye. There is no hope. Ye must leave Scotland and return to France. Ye must save yourself."

Young Ranald, who had been staring at me in what I took to be awe, said, "Your Majesty, it is no longer safe for you to be here. We must get you to France."

It was later in the day. I was talking with Angus. "Ye must take my boat by force. Ye must allow me to say that it was stolen and that I did not help ye. I am an old man and I do not have the ability to resist torture." He bent his head down in shame that it had come to this. I must hit him and mark him so that when the English came, and they would come, he could lie convincingly. I really did not want to punch a clansman of mine and particularly one who had always been so kind to me. I remembered him fondly from my childhood taking me on his knee and playing horsey with me. Now, I was reduced to striking him and striking him hard.

"I am stealing your boat." I punched him in the face so hard he fell to the ground. I kicked him in the ribs hoping to leave a mark but not break a rib and puncture a lung. I hit him again in the face. "Ye tell them my name. I am James Augustus MacEachern and I am stealing your boat. You do not know why your clansmen would treat you so and why he would steal your boat."

It was later that evening about 6:00 pm when we launched the ten oar boat. As luck would have it, we were but out a short while on the water when a storm arose. The wind began to howl. The rain was icy cold as it beat our faces. As the wind rose, the rain turned to sleet and hail. The waves formed whitecaps and broke over the sides of our boat. As we rowed, each man became afraid that we were all going to perish. We sailed all night, but seemed to make little headway. It was all we could do to keep the bow of the boat facing towards the waves as they pummeled us. The darkness surrounded us and added to our fear, because all things in the night, especially one as black as this, are magnified. The night spawns horrors and terrors that haunt the mind, reducing even grown men to little quivering children. We fought the currents; we fought the waves; we fought the wind. I could tell that Ranald and I were both thinking only one thing: "Save the Prince." It seemed that the night would never end. The darkness was enveloping us more and more in black, as if the bowels of hell had opened and belched forth icy blasts of frozen terror.

The morning dawned, grey, and misty; it was but the barest amount of light. The rain and hail had slackened in the wind, which, although not as strong as before, was still fresh and powerful. Still, Rory MacDonald recognized the harbor of Benbecula on the Isle of South Uist. Although we were all weakened by our travails, we put our backs into it and pulled and pulled to make headway to land at the harbor. Still, the currents were against us and the wind was too fresh. It was much later that morning that we landed at the harbor of Roshiness. For Young Ranald, this was a fortuitous and joyous event. The harbor of Roshiness was but 5 miles from Clanranald.

Sometimes, it seems that the world is an extremely small place and that its parts fit together as if they are well meshed gears. We were near to Clanranald.

As I believe I have told you, my home was the Isle of Skye. Until then I had not realized how much I missed my home. Yes, I could tell you how much I missed Mary, but I was fully reconciled to the fact that she was another man's woman, my best friend's woman.

When we made our landing, we were all exhausted and unable to gather ourselves up to walk the five or so miles to Clanranald. It was then that luck smiled upon us. Our landing had been observed by a shepherd of Clanranald, who immediately sent his son to speak to Ranald, chief of Clanranald. The shepherd then helped us ashore and welcomed us. At his fire, he had a pot of tea, warm and waiting for us.

After a while, Neil Maceachain, but not Chief Ranald, came to meet the Prince. Neil warned the Prince that it was not safe to stay there, but promised provisions, water, and whiskey. The Prince and Neil discussed what the next steps should be for the Prince in his escape from the English. Neil offered the rumor that a French warship had been seen off of the Isle of Lewis.

With the next tide, although we were still exhausted, but less hungry and thirsty, we tried to make our way to the Isle of Lewis. The tides, currents, and winds conspired against us and we ended up at the Isle of South Uist. Although we tried, we were not able to get to the Isle of Lewis. After nearly a week, we gave up hope for the rumored French ship.

We made our way back to the harbor of Roshiness. I walked the 5 miles and begged my clan Chief Ranald for help.

"How of Young Ranald?" The old Chief begged.

"I saw him fight at Culloden, but he lives! He is with us now and is healing. I, too, was hit with a spent shell or ball and fell to the ground. The Battle had been lost, the MacDonalds were in rout."

"Why are ye here Jamie?" The Chief looked at me like I was a rotten piece of beef and the smell was so bad all he wanted to do was consign me to the trash heaps.

"I have come to beg for your help to shelter the Prince until the French can send a ship to rescue him." I blurted it all out. I might not have another chance to ask.

"You want me to put my neck on the chopping block after I forebade our clan to join the Rising?" He eyed me cautiously for the thought had crossed his mind that I might have been taken, turned, and sent to ferret it out whether Ranald, the Chief of Clanranald, was a traitor or no to King George.

It then came to me, how I do not know, but then I said it. "Father, I have never asked anything from you as a son, nor have I ever implored you to do anything on account of the sake of my mother. I am asking you now. I beg you. Father, help our Prince."

The old Chief's face wrinkled in surprise. He was clearly rattled. "How did ye know that lad? How long did ye know that?"

"I know it now and that is enough. I know also I upset your plans for Ranald to be chief after you as I am the older son. But I know that he is the better choice and that he wants it, too. If I leave, then you can blame me for joining the Rising. And hopefully that'll save Young Ranald."

"And what of Mary?" His question caught me off guard. Did he know?

"Mary is Ranald's wife to be. I give them my blessing and my love." I said it, but it hurt terribly, worse than any wound I had ever suffered. "Too, if I go, then Mary will marry Yung Ranald, and all will be as it should be."

"So that's your deal, eh?" The old Chief tugged on his red beard.

"Aye. That's it."

Chief Ranald promised that he would help the Prince and that he would conceal him from the English. He ordered Neil and all the Clan to provide the care and shelter for the Prince and his party.

It was then that I saw Mary hiding around a corner. She had been listening to all that had transpired.

"Mary …" I stammered. What do you say to the woman you love, but have just renounced?

"You needs say nothing, James." She looked into my eyes. I could see that the fire that had once burned so brightly flared for a moment and then was snuffed out. "Thank you for what you are doing for Ranald and… for…me." She simpered.

"Mary…" I was stuck upon that word and could utter nothing more. What could I say? I love you and will always love you, but I must let you marry another man, my best friend and brother. My duty lies elsewhere and I must do my duty for your benefit and for his benefit. Could I say all this and more? I looked into her eyes and saw that she understood. Words were not necessary. Her eyes were misted over. She was near to breaking down. I was near to breaking down.

"Mary..." That sole solitary word again.

Then I opened my mouth and said what needed to be said. "Good bye, Mary. May God always be with you." I bowed and turned away, although my heart was bursting. I wanted to sweep her up into my arms and kiss her face and her neck. I wanted this and so much more. But it was not to be.

I left the Castle. I did not look back, for if I had my will would have broken. I would have fallen at her knees and begged for her love, no matter what the consequences.

Part IV: Learning to Trust

Neil guided us to Bareness on May 6, 1746. After a few days, Neil moved us from there to his home, Corrodale on May 10th. We entrusted ourselves and our lives to Neil. He knew too, he was taking his life in his hands by taking care of the Prince. Still, he displayed no fear and went about his day as if there was nothing at all to worry about. The beautiful spring days of May melted into the first hints of summer in June. The Prince no longer showed any hints of the depression that had overcome him after the Battle of Culloden. Now, he was positively possessed by gaiety.

During these four weeks that we stayed at Corrodale, Neil would leave us for a day or two to gather intelligence about the movements of the English troops. During each of these adventures, we worried about him and feared he would not return. We also feared that he would be taken prisoner, tortured, and we would be given up and betrayed. Still, every time, he came back and brought the best information as to what was happening.

We daily kept a watch not only for the English, but also for a French ship. Why the English had not come to Corrodale was a mystery to us. We recovered our health and with it, we recovered our will to live and survive. The Prince used the time to learn more and more Gaelic. I used the time to recover from my wounds as did Young Ranald.

Although the Prince seemed to be recovering, Young Ranald, while recovering his health, was not recovering in spirit. He became more withdrawn and morose. Something had gone out of him on the Moors of Culloden. At night, although the whiskey flowed, the bawdy songs were sung, tales of bravery and deeds done were recited, Young Ranald did not smile and did not enter into the merriment.

I decided to see what I could do to help him. "My brother, what can I do to help you?"

He looked at me and did not answer. Again, I asked, "What ails you?"

Again, all he did was to look at me. His look had a tinge of anger in it, which I chose to ignore. "Can I help you?"

"What the hell makes you think you can help me?" With that, Young Ranald turned around and walked off.

Neil was a perfect host during all this time. Each morning, he made sure that there were eggs and ham cooking for us. The smell of the wonderful food wafted in the air and pleasantly tickled our nostrils. During the day, he appeared time and time again bringing a drink of water, a cup of milk, or even a shot of whiskey to make sure we were comfortable and happy. When the nights were cold, he shared out blankets to keep us warm. Anything the Prince asked, Neil did or if Neil could not do it, he made sure to find someone who could.

The summer days passed slowly. We did the chores that needed to be done. Because I had been a shepherd, I helped with the flocks of sheep. The Prince, of course, was exempt from these duties. We told him that it was because he might be recognized and thus lead to his capture. The truth, of course, was that the Prince had no experience in doing any of the things to run a farm. While he wanted to share in our deprivations and hardships, none of us could bring ourselves to make the Prince submit to ordinary everyday life.

Finally, after one of his reconnaissance trips, Neil came with the news, "It is not safe to stay here any longer." We quickly made preparations to leave for our destination was Benbecula, which we thought was such a deserted place, the English would never think to look there.

We hid at Benbecula for eight days. June became July and the Prince became restless.

"I worry that I tarry far too long here. I worry that I am subjecting Chief Ranald, the members of the Clan of Clanranald, and Neil Maceachain to grave danger. There is a price upon my head and a price upon the heads of everyone who helps me. I should leave and those of my entourage should leave. We need to go somewhere else where there might be harbors where

French ships can land and take me back to France." The Prince looked around at his make shift Council. His face made it clear that he would brook no opposition.

We convened a council of war which made several decisions. The first dealt with Ranald, for Ranald was now fit enough to go home.

I helped Ranald gather his things. "I have loved you as my brother and as my best friend since your birth." I hugged him and to my surprise, he hugged me back.

"T'is a brave thing you are doing, Jamie." He whispered. "I could not do it." He shook his head.

"I know that I hurt you. I never meant to. Take care of Mary. I hope to see you again sometime." Tears were running down my cheeks. I was totally unmanning myself.

"What will you do?" He wiped my face with his hand.

"I will sail to Europe. Maybe go to Amsterdam. From there, I don't know."

"Thank you for my life. Thank you for Mary. I truly love her." He said the last so tenderly so sincerely, I knew he loved her truly and well. If she could not be happy with me, then it was best that she be happy with him.

We hugged again and he was off.

It was later when Neil spoke up. "Your Grace, if I may be permitted to speak, I think there might be a way to get you to the Isle of Skye."

Part V: I Do for You What I'd Do for Others

I apologize that it has taken me so long to get to Flora. By the time I met Flora in June of 1746, she was a lass of 21 years. She was a slight woman. Her eyes were a dark, steel-grey, which set off her dark auburn hair. She had milk white skin. While she was not a beauty, she was a handsome woman who had a kind heart. She was a devout woman who worshiped as a Presbyterian.

Angus took me to her to see if she could help in some way to get the Prince to the Isle of Skye. She was a daughter of the Outer Hebrides and, therefore, knew the area well. She was born on the Isle of South Uist. She was also a relation-albeit distant-of mine. Her father was Ranald MacDonald of Milton. But far more important, was the fact that Flora, you see, was the step-daughter of a Hugh MacDonald. He had remained loyal to the English crown and so had retained his command of the local militia. This was a great shame to us, for he was of our clan. Now, however, the fact that he was of the Isle of Skye could work to our advantage.

"Is there anything ye ken do to h'lp the Prince?" Angus blurted out. I would at least have said hello first. Flora looked at me and I could see as she eyed me, I did not please her. Fortunately, we had brought the Irish Captain Conn O'Neill with us. He was a soldier's soldier. He stood ramrod straight. His slick black hair, his large side burns, and mustachio made him cut the figure of a fine man. Flora clearly liked what she saw and did little to hide it.

"What do ye think I can do?" She asked, blinking her large steel grey eyes. She tossed her hair with her right hand over her ear and tilted her head.

Captain O'Neill intervened just then. "Could you be so kind as to obtain a pass to the Isle of Skye from your father?"

"Step-father!" Both Angus and I corrected him.

"I mean, fine lady, your worthy step-father?" O'Neill was as polished and polite as an officer could be.

"There's a price upon his head. The Crown has threatened death or banishment for anyone who aids the Prince." She looked down at the floor, as if she were ashamed of her fear. "I am sorely afraid for my life. I think any endeavor to hide the Prince and then spirit him away is far too fantastical to be true."

Captain Conn then started to talk to Flora in a low voice, one that was both wooing and yet persuasive. I heard not the words, but I could gather the intent. Finally, he said louder, "Isn't there anything that can be done? For otherwise, surely the Prince will be taken, and he will be hung, drawn, and quartered."

Flora looked around as if searching for something. The thought of a man being so tortured to death clearly hurt her sensibilities. I should have mentioned that Flora was an intelligent woman, having been educated in Edinburgh. But she had that something special, that je ne sais pas, as the French say, she was clever too. After a few moments, she looked up, her face brightened. Flora had a twinkle in her eye.

"The Prince is bonnie fair, isn't he?"

"Yes, he is a man of fair features," answered O'Neill, who did not see where she was leading. "What of it?"

"I could say I need to go to Skye with my maid, my spinning maid, to help a relative deliver her baby." She laughed. "I'm doing this out of charity. I'd do the same thing for the Duke, if he were defeated and in distress."

Part VI: Do the Boatmen Cross the River Styx?

All was made ready in three days' time. Now, this is where Flora's bed comes back into the spotlight. For during this time, Flora was gracious enough to let the Prince sleep in her bed. Now, of course, she was not in it at the same time, but still the bed gained some luster by having been slept in by the Prince. Years, later, people came to Flora and asked her if they could sleep in her bed, the bed the Prince had slept in.

Our small party consisted of Flora, her spinning maid, Betty Burke (that is the Prince disguised as Flora's maid), a man servant, played by Captain O'Neill, and a boat crew of six men, including me.

After some struggle, we landed at Kilbride, Skye, near Monkstadt, the seat of Alexander MacDonald. This area was strewn with rocks and boulders. The 'maid' and 'man servant' were hidden here. Flora went off in search of her friends and relatives in the area. Bravely, she did this alone, so as not to draw attention to us. I stayed with the boat crew.

The moon slowly rose over the waving waters. It created a silver lattice ladder across the ripples. My mind turned to home. I grew melancholy and nostalgic. I thought of my mother. I kissed her goodbye in my reverie. I knew I would never see her again in this life. A tear seeped out of the corner of my eye. The light breeze of the night rose and the moon's lattice-ladder swayed with the current.

Then, I was thinking that I would never see Mary again. In my heart, I knew that I loved her. I also knew that if I stayed in Skye, I would be drawn to her like the moth to the flame. I could see the war that this would cause 'tween Ranald and me. I knew she loved me, but she had chosen Ranald, she had chosen duty; she had chosen to be the wife of a Lord and a chief. I had nothing to offer her. I had no future. I was an outlaw. I was a fugitive. What life could I offer her?

No matter how much I rationalized all of this to myself, I knew my emotions were greater than my rational thoughts. Distance from her was what I needed to save her and me from a life filled with the potential of stolen glances, furtive thoughts, purloined moments, and possible dishonor and disgrace. I could not inflict this upon her. Distance was what I needed and distance was what I would get.

I also thought of Ranald, my best friend and brother, whom I had deeply hurt. Could he ever completely forgive me for my betrayal? Can a friendship, even the best of friendships withstand the oldest curse known to man-the betrayal?

My mood was broken by the words of one of our boatmen. "Who da ye thin' w're abringing h're in the night?" The others grunted in response and tried to wave him off by flipping their hands. "T'is the Prince, aye thin'. That's warz I thin." The others murmured. "Ye think?" They asked one another. "Then's w're'um gonna needs mo' clink f'r this'um job." The sounds of dissent were rising.

I went over to the boat men. "Wait! You men! You have been paid a fair wage to bring over the Lady Flora, her maid, and manservant." I said in a firm voice, hoping it had enough command in it. The grumbling did not cease. "All right then, I will see to it, from my own pocket, if needs be, that you are paid more. But you must be still now and stop this infernal chatter about the Prince. Just the thought of the Prince might be enough for the local militia to take our heads, Prince or no Prince among us be!" I raised my voice and stamped my sword's sheath against the rocks.

I looked at the moon, but no amount of concentration could conjure up my dreams of home again. Flora came back a short while later.

Flora, her 'maid', 'manservant', and me, gathered in a circle away from the boatmen. Flora began in a loud voice, which hopefully carried to the other boatmen, "My cousin, Anne, has not yet delivered her baby. We must hasten to her home down the lane. I'll pay and dismiss the boatmen."

At that, I piped up, "I've promised them another pound each." To this, I could hear the boatmen utter sounds of sheer delight.

I walked over and paid them. We watched them row away into the night as a black shadow on the moon's silvery waterway.

When Flora knew they were clearly out of earshot, she said, "I have arranged passage to Portree, for your Majesty."

Part VII: Mussels Alive-o

We had dismissed the boatmen. Then we hid for several days on the moors of the Isle of Skye. One night was particularly memorable. Flora directed us to pick up the dried tufts of grass left by the sheep, as well as any dried sticks. She foraged for mussels.

There by the shore, we steamed mussels over a small fire. Flora also served us steamed seaweed, but after a few bites, even the ever polite and diplomatic Prince begged off of eating the kelp. The mussels, however, were most succulent.

I then thought of an old drink my uncle had taught me. You take bog myrtle and place it in hot water, as if you were brewing tea. This drink, my uncle assured me, was known to the Vikings, which he used as another occasion to remind me that we were descended from Vikings and, in particular, Lord Somerled.

We laughed as we ate around that wee fire. It was as if we were on a lark. We had not a care in the world. We raised a mussel shell to each, as we tasted a particularly delicious one, as if we were toasting with the finest of wines in the grandest of Castles with servants aplenty, a fireplace aroaring, like Knights of the Round Table after finding the Holy Grail. We laughed until our sides ached and then we laughed some more. The moon rose boasting its last quarter. Deep in the night, it shed a sliver tinge upon the dark of the moor. One by one we fell asleep and when the dawn came, we were in the finest spirits. Flora had worked her magic and we were all the beneficiaries of her magic spell.

Sometime after dawn, O'Neill whispered, "What was that?"

We all looked up with a start.

He hushed us and we listened to the freshening morn. At first, I heard nothing. Then faint upon the dawn's breeze, as soft as a far-oft loon cry, came the jangle of horse tackle.

We all made ourselves as flat as we could against the moor. Fortunately, our fire had died, none of us having rekindled it.

The jingling-jangling came closer. Faint voices split the night. "Straighten up you!" An officer's command. Redcoats!

Were we discovered?

We held our breath. The seconds ticked by, each an eternity. I grasped my sword. I could see that O'Neill had done the same also. It would be us, the two of us, against how many of them.

"Flora, get ready to run," I breathed at her. "Take the Prince."

The soldiers got closer. A horse stopped. "Get yer ass moving again," came the command. The horse stood still in the night, a framed silhouette of black against the starred-sky. "I'll not be telling yer again. Git moving!" Louder the voice came. The horse tossed its head, whinnied, and began moving again.

We huddled in the twilight against moor. I will never forget the loamy smell of peat as the grass and heather seemed to grow up my noise. Time passed. None of us moved. More time passed. Still, we did not move. The voices and the horse receded into the dank dark twilight.

Part VIII:

FLORA MACDONALD'S LAMENT

Far over yon hills of the heather so green
And down by the corrie that sings to the sea
The bonnie young Flora sat sighing her lane
The dew on her plaid and the tear in her e'e.
She looked at a boat with the breezes that swung
Away on the wave like a bird on the main
And aye as it lessened she sighed and she sung
Farewell to the lad I shall ne'er see again.

Farewell to my hero, the gallant and young
Farewell to the lad I shall ne'er see again.
The moorcock that craws on the brow of Ben Connal
He kens o' his bed in a sweet mossy hame
The eagle that soars on the cliffs of Clanronald
Unawed and unhunted, his eyrie can claim
The solan can sleep on his shelve of the shore
The cormorant roost on his rock of the sea
But oh! There is one whose hard fate I deplore
Nor house, manor hame, in this country has he
The conflict is past and our name is no more
There's nought left but sorrow for Scotland and me.

The target is torn from the arm of the just
The helmet is cleft on the brow of the brave
The claymore forever in darkness must rust
But red is the sword of the stranger and slave
The hoof of the horse and the foot of the proud
Have trod o'er the plumes on the bonnet of blue
Why slept the red bolt in the breast of the cloud
When tyranny revelled in blood of the true?
Farewell, my young hero! The gallant and good
The crown of thy fathers is torn from thy brow.
- Ettrick Shepherd

Days later we made it to the Island of Raasay. The rumor was true. A French warship awaited us there. The date was July 2, 1746.

The Prince bowed to Flora and gave her a locket with the Prince's picture inside. As he bestowed this little gift, he said, "I hope, madam, that we may meet in St James's yet."

With that, he was gone. With him, the hope of the Stuarts left Scotland forever.

Chapter 20

Departure from Scotland

"Did not strong connections draw me elsewhere, I believe Scotland would be the country I would choose to end my days in."
-Benjamin Franklin

O Scotia! my dear, my native soil! For whom my warmest wish to heaven is sent; Long may thy hardy sons of rustic toil Be blest with health, and peace, and sweet content.
-Robert Burns

"The birth-place of Valour, the country of Worth; Wherever I wander, wherever I rove, The hills of the Highlands for ever I love."
-Robert Burns

I hid in Scotland until late 1749. I had met a woman and had not wanted to leave her, especially since she was bearing my child. But for reasons not clear to me, the Duke of Cumberland still pursued me, even after the amnesty. His minions were coming for me and it was only a matter of time.

I made my way to a ship and set sail for Holland, for Amsterdam. From there, I do not know where I will go, but I will call for my child and for my woman and create a new life in a new land.

Epilogue

Tandem Triumphans?

> For that is the mark of the Scots
> of all classes: that he stands in an
> attitude towards the past unthinkable
> to Englishmen, and remembers and
> cherishes the memory of his forebears,
> good or bad; and there burns alive in
> him a sense of identity with the dead
> even to the twentieth generation.
> **-Robert Louis Stevenson**

Qui obiit in bello?

What happened after Culloden to the men, with whom I supped and talked, drank and cursed, bathed and deloused, smoked and gambled-the men with whom I had lived closer than all, except my wife?

So very many of us were taken captive at Culloden or just shortly thereafter. Fate or fortune spared not the high, for Colonel Donald MacDonald of Kinlochmodiart, the second in command of MacDonalds of Clanranald's was taken. William, Duke of Cumberland, the King's son, spared him not and he was executed on October 18, 1746. Neither fate nor fortune spared the low either. For Donald MacDonald, the farmer, a sergeant, he too was taken. His fate was to be transported to a far oft colony. So, Duncan Cameron, who was Young Ranald's servant, who carried his bag and laid out his clothes, was taken, but spared and earned a pardon.

Some were taken. And some who were taken, escaped. Ranald MacDonald, son of Borrodale, a Lieutenant, was taken at Culloden, but managed later to escape. His escape was first to the Highlands and then later to North Carolina, where I met him some years later, although he was then known as Ranald MacRanald, but this is a tale for my next book.

And some who were taken and escaped, later died, like poor John MacDonald, the nephew of Captain Alexander MacDonald and the cousin of Ranald MacDonald, the son of Morar. He made safe his escape only to flounder in some river and drown.

Wounded, there were many. I have already written on how Young Colonel Ranald MacDonald, my friend, fell at Culloden during our charge. He was able to overcome his wound and though taken, was able to escape. He returned to the Isle of Skye. I saw him before I left for North Carolina. I begged him to come with me. I had visions of us starting our new lives there together. We would farm and continue our antics, as if we had never left the Highlands. I saw it clearly that our Clan would flourish and grow anew in the hills and mountains of that new world. Having to leave him behind was one of the hardest things I have ever had to do. Leaving him to marry Mary was the hardest thing I have ever done. But I knew in my heart that it was the right thing to do. My departure for the New World gave them a chance at life in the Old World.

Captain Ranald MacDonald of Belfinay was wounded, captured, and then later pardoned.

But others, who were taken, did not fare as well. Daniel Giles, Murdoch Campbell the farmer from Clatil, Angus MacCormack, Angus MacGarrie, Donald MacKinnon, also a farmer, Dougal MacLoed, John MacQuarry, Donald MacQuilly, and Ross Alexander, all were captured and died in their captivity. All those farmers, who had crowded around me and begged for my inspiration before the Battle of Culloden, were dead.

Upon the field of Culloden, the artillery fire and the muskets took brave men to heaven. My friend, Lieutenant John MacDonald of Borrodale, died leading his men into the mouths of the cannon. Fortunately for his family, his brother escaped.

But there were men, who were not as brave and who were not as honorable. They were the men who threw their conscience to the winds and abandoned all hope of redemption by turning King's Evidence against their brothers in arms. Men like John Bane MacDonald, the servant to Benbecula, farmer Donald MacDonald of Guilin, and Bencula's other servant, Angus Smith, all of whom testified such that others might be banished, or transported, or executed. But even some of these who turned King's Evidence found that the wheel of justice grinds exceedingly fine, such as Alan MacMurich, a farmer from Galmistal, was transported after he gave his Judas' kiss.

Those who deserted in the hopes that they be spared found also that William, Duke of Cumberland, had little or no pity or mercy for them. Ranald MacDonald of Inverness-shire deserted and was captured on April 11, 1754, just before Culloden. He met his final fate and was executed on October 21, 1746.

Even poor Flora MacDonald did not escape the Duke's wrath. One of the boatmen went to the authorities with his suspicions. She was arrested and brought to London, where she was imprisoned in the Tower of London. After a while, she was allowed to live outside of the Tower, under the custody of a gaoler. Finally, in 1747, after the Act of Indemnity was passed, she was released. She married Allan Macdonald of Kingsburgh, a kinsman, in 1750. Thereafter, Flora MacDonald left Scotland for North Carolina. I'll leave the rest of her tale to my next book, *New Caledonia, the Song of Scotland in America*.

One more thing I should related about her bed. It was years later, the famed essayist, Samuel Johnson was making a tour of Scotland with his friend, James Boswell, when he met Flora. She welcomed him to her cottage and he spent the night, staying in the same bed in which the Prince had slept. Johnson said of Flora, "Her name will be mentioned in history, and if courage and fidelity be virtues, mentioned with honour."

And what of HMS Lion which had fought so valiantly against L'Elisabeth. The Captain and most of her officers were court marshalled. In a twist of fate, one of the Seven Men of Moidart, Aeneas MacDonald, testified, to no avail, at the court martial as to how bravely the Lion had fought and how impossible it was for the Lion to have captured and taken the L'Elisabeth.

Speaking of the Seven Men of Moidart, what happened to them? Their numbers too reflected the debacle that was Culloden. Two died: William Murray and Francis Strickland. Three escaped and fled to France and were forever exiled there: Sir Thomas Sheridan, John William O'Sullivan, and George Kelly. One surrendered to William, Duke of Cumberland. One was captured and was banished, never to see Scotland again: Aeneas MacDonald.

The Prince, who had been so charismatic, so bold, and so dynamic, fell into a life of dissolution and drink, lamenting forever his failed campaign. Perhaps he, too, like his father, spoke the pathetic words "if only" like an endless dirge.

So, the stories that could be told of the Battle are far more than one man can relate. Not all are heroes, not all are cowards, some died, some were wounded, some deserted, some were captured, but all, each and every one, was scarred, deformed, shaped, and mutilated by the events, whether their bodies exhibited the wounds or whether they were hidden in the minds of men, only to be revealed years later in tales in a bar over a tankard of ale or in tears in the night, when the storms raged and the lightning cracked. These were men who raised their hands against what they perceived as injustice. They raised their hands for their religion and the right to follow it no matter what. They raised their hands for their homeland, their farms, their children, and their wives. They raised their hands to preserve their way of life as it had been for hundreds of years in the glens, the lochs, the mountains, and the fields of Scotland.

They too raised cairns, but not to victory, not to restoration of the Stuart line, and not to proclaim a Catholic king come to preside over his people. Glenfinnan was celebrated. The Moors of Culloden are still and windswept today. Crude grave stones mark where the members of the various clans died with a dream in their hearts that was never fulfilled.

Appendix

The Complete Text of the Declaration of Arbroath 1320 Written by Hugh MacDonald, Bishop

To the most Holy Father and Lord in Christ, the Lord John, by divine providence Supreme Pontiff of the Holy Roman and Universal Church, his humble and devout sons Duncan, Earl of Fife, Thomas Randolph, Earl of Moray, Lord of Man and of Annandale, Patrick Dunbar, Earl of March, Malise, Earl of Strathearn, Malcolm, Earl of Lennox, William, Earl of Ross, Magnus, Earl of Caithness and Orkney, and William, Earl of Sutherland; Walter, Steward of Scotland, William Soules, Butler of Scotland, James, Lord of Douglas, Roger Mowbray, David, Lord of Brechin, David Graham, Ingram Umfraville, John Menteith, guardian of the earldom of Menteith, Alexander Fraser, Gilbert Hay, Constable of Scotland, Robert Keith, Marischal of Scotland, Henry St Clair, John Graham, David Lindsay, William Oliphant, Patrick Graham, John Fenton, William Abernethy, David Wemyss, William Mushet, Fergus of Ardrossan, Eustace Maxwell, William Ramsay, William Mowat, Alan Murray, Donald Campbell, John Cameron, Reginald Cheyne, Alexander Seton, Andrew Leslie, and Alexander Straiton, and the other barons and freeholders and the whole community of the realm of Scotland send all manner of filial reverence, with devout kisses of his blessed feet.

Most Holy Father and Lord, we know and from the chronicles and books of the ancients we find that among other famous nations our own, the Scots, has been graced with widespread renown. They journeyed from Greater Scythia by way of the Tyrrhenian Sea and the Pillars of Hercules, and dwelt for a long course of time in Spain among the most savage tribes, but nowhere could they be subdued by any race, however barbarous. Thence they came, twelve hundred years after the people of Israel crossed the Red Sea, to their home in the west where they still live today. The Britons they first drove out, the Picts they utterly destroyed, and, even though very often assailed by the Norwegians, the Danes and the English, they took possession of that home with many victories and untold efforts; and, as the historians of old time bear witness, they have held it free of all bondage ever since. In their kingdom there have reigned one hundred and thirteen kings of their own royal stock, the line unbroken a single foreigner. The high qualities and deserts of these people, were they not otherwise manifest, gain glory enough from this: that the King of kings and Lord of lords, our Lord Jesus Christ, after His Passion and Resurrection, called them, even though settled in the uttermost parts of the earth, almost the first to His most holy faith. Nor would He have them confirmed in that faith by merely anyone but by the first of His Apostles — by calling, though second or third in rank — the most gentle Saint Andrew, the Blessed Peter's brother, and desired him to keep them under his protection as their patron forever.

The Most Holy Fathers your predecessors gave careful heed to these things and bestowed many favours and numerous privileges on this same kingdom and people, as being the special charge of the Blessed Peter's brother. Thus our nation under their protection did indeed live in freedom and peace up to the time when that mighty prince the King of the English, Edward, the father of the one who reigns today, when our kingdom had no head and our people harboured no malice or treachery and were then unused to wars or invasions, came in the guise of a friend and ally to harass them as an enemy. The deeds of cruelty, massacre, violence, pillage, arson, imprisoning prelates, burning down monasteries, robbing and killing monks and nuns, and yet other outrages without number which he committed against our people, sparing neither age nor sex, religion nor rank, no one could describe nor fully imagine unless he had seen them with his own eyes.

But from these countless evils we have been set free, by the help of Him Who though He afflicts yet heals and restores, by our most tireless Prince, King and Lord, the Lord Robert. He, that his people and his heritage might be delivered out of the hands of our enemies, met toil and fatigue, hunger and peril, like another Macabaeus or Joshua and bore them cheerfully. Him, too, divine providence, his right of succession according to or laws and customs which we shall maintain to the death, and the due consent and assent of us all have made our Prince and King. To him, as to the man by whom salvation has been wrought unto our people, we are bound both by law and by his merits that our freedom may be still maintained, and by him, come what may, we mean to stand. Yet if he should give up what he has begun, and agree to make us or our kingdom subject to the King of England or the English, we should exert ourselves at once to drive him out as our enemy and a subverter of his own rights and ours, and make some other man who was well able to defend us our King; for, as long as but a hundred of us remain alive, never will we on any conditions be brought under English rule. It is in truth not for glory, nor riches, nor honours that we are fighting, but for freedom — for that alone, which no honest man gives up but with life itself.

Therefore it is, Reverend Father and Lord, that we beseech your Holiness with our most earnest prayers and suppliant hearts, inasmuch as you will in your sincerity and goodness consider all this, that, since with Him Whose vice-gerent on earth you are there is neither weighing nor distinction of Jew and Greek, Scotsman or Englishman, you will look with the eyes of a father on the troubles and privation brought by the English upon us and upon the Church of God. May it please you to admonish and exhort the King of the English, who ought to be satisfied with what belongs to him since England used once to be enough for seven kings or more, to leave us Scots in peace, who live in this poor little Scotland, beyond which there is no dwelling-place at all, and covet nothing but our own. We are sincerely willing to do anything for him, having regard to our condition, that we can, to win peace for ourselves. This truly concerns you, Holy Father, since you see the savagery of the heathen raging against the Christians, as the sins of Christians have indeed deserved, and the frontiers of Christendom being pressed inward every day; and how much it will tarnish your Holiness's memory if (which God forbid) the Church suffers eclipse or scandal in any branch of it during your time, you must perceive. Then rouse the Christian princes who for false reasons pretend that they cannot go to help of the Holy Land because of wars they have on hand with their neighbours. The real reason that prevents them is that in making war on their smaller neighbours they find quicker profit and weaker resistance. But how cheerfully our Lord the King and we too would go there if the King of the English would leave us in peace, He from Whom nothing is hidden well knows; and we profess and declare it to you as the Vicar of Christ and to all Christendom. But if your Holiness puts too much faith in the tales the English tell and will not give sincere belief to all this, nor refrain from favouring them to our prejudice, then the slaughter of bodies, the perdition of souls, and all the other misfortunes that will follow, inflicted by them on us and by us on them, will, we believe, be surely laid by the Most High to your charge.

To conclude, we are and shall ever be, as far as duty calls us, ready to do your will in all things, as obedient sons to you as His Vicar; and to Him as the Supreme King and Judge we commit the maintenance of our cause, casting our cares upon Him and firmly trusting that He will inspire us with courage and bring our enemies to nought. May the Most High preserve you to his Holy Church in holiness and health and grant you length of days.

Given at the monastery of Arbroath in Scotland on the sixth day of the month of April in the year of grace thirteen hundred and twenty and the fifteenth year of the reign of our King aforesaid.

Endorsed: Letter directed to our Lord the Supreme Pontiff by the community of Scotland.

Printed in the United States
By Bookmasters